WATTERS · LEYH · ROGERS · LAIHO

LUMBERJANE

BIRTHDAY SMART

D0405347

BOOM!
BOX

Ross Richie..CEO & Founder
Joy Huffman...CFO
Matt Gagnon...Editor-in-Chief
Filip Sablik...................President, Publishing & Marketing
Stephen Christy........................President, Development
Lance Kreiter.............Vice President, Licensing & Merchandising
Arune Singh.............................Vice President, Marketing
Bryce Carlson.............Vice President, Editorial & Creative Strategy
Kate Henning..................................Director, Operations
Spencer Simpson...................................Director, Sales
Scott Newman........................Manager, Production Design
Elyse Strandberg.............................Manager, Finance
Sierra Hahn.....................................Executive Editor
Jeanine Schaefer..............................Executive Editor
Dafna Pleban..Senior Editor
Shannon Watters....................................Senior Editor
Eric Harburn..Senior Editor
Matthew Levine..Editor
Sophie Philips-Roberts.........................Associate Editor
Amanda LaFranco.............................Associate Editor
Jonathan Manning...............................Associate Editor
Gavin Gronenthal.................................Assistant Editor
Gwen Waller...Assistant Editor
Allyson Gronowitz.................................Assistant Editor
Ramiro Portnoy.....................................Assistant Editor
Shelby Netschke......................................Editorial Assistant
Michelle Ankley.................................Design Coordinator
Marie Krupina....................................Production Designer
Grace Park.......................................Production Designer
Chelsea Roberts.................................Production Designer
Samantha Knapp.........................Production Design Assistant
José Meza...Live Events Lead
Stephanie Hocutt...............................Digital Marketing Lead
Esther Kim......................................Marketing Coordinator
Breanna Sarpy...............................Live Events Coordinator
Amanda Lawson................................Marketing Assistant
Holly Aitchison.............................Digital Sales Coordinator
Morgan Perry.................................Retail Sales Coordinator
Megan Christopher.............................Operations Coordinator
Rodrigo Hernandez.............................Operations Coordinator
Zipporah Smith...................................Operations Assistant
Jason Lee...Senior Accountant
Sabrina Lesin....................................Accounting Assistant

BOOM! BOX™

LUMBERJANES Volume Fifteen, August 2020. Published by BOOM! Box, a division of Boom Entertainment, Inc. Lumberjanes is ™ & © 2020 Shannon Watters, Grace Ellis, Noelle Stevenson & Brooklyn Allen. Originally published in single magazine form as LUMBERJANES No. 57-60. ™ & © 2018, 2019 Shannon Watters, Grace Ellis, Noelle Stevenson & Brooklyn Allen. All rights reserved. BOOM! Box™ and the BOOM! Box logo are trademarks of Boom Entertainment, Inc., registered in various countries and categories. All characters, events, and institutions depicted herein are fictional. Any similarity between any of the names, characters, persons, events, and/or institutions in this publication to actual names, characters, and persons, whether living or dead, events, and/or institutions is unintended and purely coincidental. BOOM! Box does not read or accept unsolicited submissions of ideas, stories, or artwork.

BOOM! Studios, 5670 Wilshire Boulevard, Suite 400, Los Angeles, CA 90036-5679. Printed in USA. First Printing.

ISBN: 978-1-68415-551-4, eISBN: 978-1-64144-717-1

THIS LUMBERJANES FIELD MANUAL BELONGS TO:

NAME:_____

TROOP:_____

DATE INVESTED:_____

FIELD MANUAL TABLE OF CONTENTS

A Message from the Lumberjanes High Council......................................**4**
The Lumberjanes Pledge..**4**
Counselor Credits...**5**

LUMBERJANES PROGRAM FIELDS
Chapter Fifty-Seven..**6**
Chapter Fifty-Eight...**30**
Chapter Fifty-Nine..**54**
Chapter Sixty..**78**
Cover Gallery: Life of the Party Badge..**102**

NEWPORT PUBLIC LIBRARY
NEWPORT, OREGON 97365

LUMBERJANES FIELD MANUAL

For the Advanced Program

Tenth Edition • March 1985

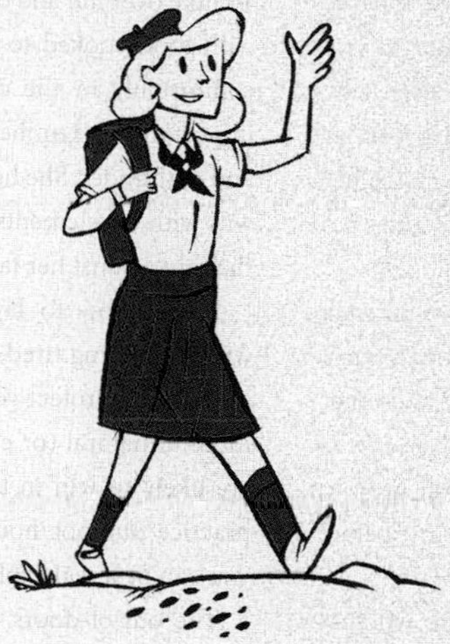

Prepared for the

Miss Qiunzella Thiskwin Penniquiqul Thistle Crumpet's

CAMP FOR [redacted] HARDCORE LADY-TYPES

"Friendship to the Max!"

A MESSAGE FROM THE LUMBERJANES HIGH COUNCIL

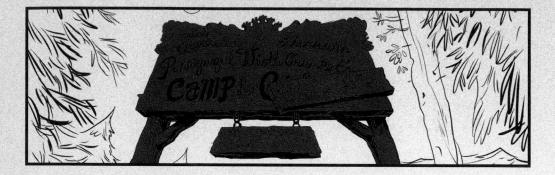

Wisdom is something we all must earn--slowly, and only with much time and effort. And as much as we members of the High Council and other adults might wish, it isn't precisely something that can be given. While the seeds of wisdom may be handed down from generation to generation, those seeds still need to germinate, to be cared for, and left to grow. Often, it can be easy to take this offered knowledge for granted. We may question the wisdom of our elders, or even scoff at their hard-earned experience. We learn from listening and watching, yes, but those lessons don't always feel real until we solidify them ourselves, through experience and doing. After all, oftentimes the best way to learn to navigate in a new place is to get lost. That knowledge is yours and yours alone, and all the sweeter for it.

At the same time, setting out on your own can be perilous when you don't know the area (or yourself) well. In hiking, there are always certain safety precautions: never hike alone, and always tell people back home where you are going, and when you expect to return. These guidelines help to keep you safe, while also keeping the adventure alive. They ensure you will find your way back home again, all in one piece, while still making sure that that you are the one doing the navigating: that you are deciding whether to turn left or right, to head up or downhill, to follow the path or turn away. You choose your path, and in doing so, all of the knowledge that has been handed down to you begins to mature into your very own newly-discovered wisdom, and your awareness of the world solidifies into familiarity.

THE LUMBERJANES PLEDGE

I solemnly swear to do my best
Every day, and in all that I do,
To be brave and strong,
To be truthful and compassionate,
To be interesting and interested,
To pay attention and question
The world around me,
To think of others first,
To always help and protect my friends,

~~To respectfully pray to myself in God~~

THEN THERE'S A LINE ABOUT GOD, OR WHATEVER

And to make the world a better place
For Lumberjane scouts
And for everyone else.

BIRTHDAY SMARTY

Written by
Shannon Watters
& Kat Leyh

Illustrated by
AnneMarie Rogers

Colors by
Maarta Laiho

Letters by
Aubrey Aiese

Cover by
Kat Leyh

Series Designer
Marie Krupina

Collection Designers
Chelsea Roberts & Grace Park

Series Editor
Dafna Pleban

Collection Editor
Sophie Philips-Roberts

Collection Executive Editor
Jeanine Schaefer

*Special thanks to **Kelsey Pate** for giving the Lumberjanes their name.*

Created by Shannon Watters, Grace Ellis, Noelle Stevenson & Brooklyn Allen

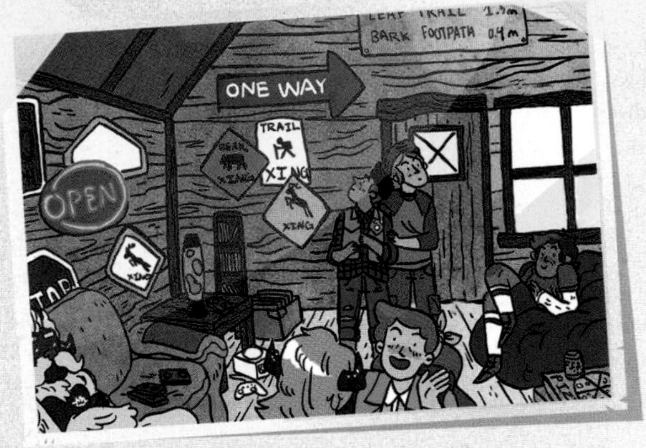
BARK FOOTPATH 0.4 m
ONE WAY
OPEN
TRAIL XING
XING

LUMBERJANES FIELD MANUAL

CHAPTER FIFTY-SEVEN

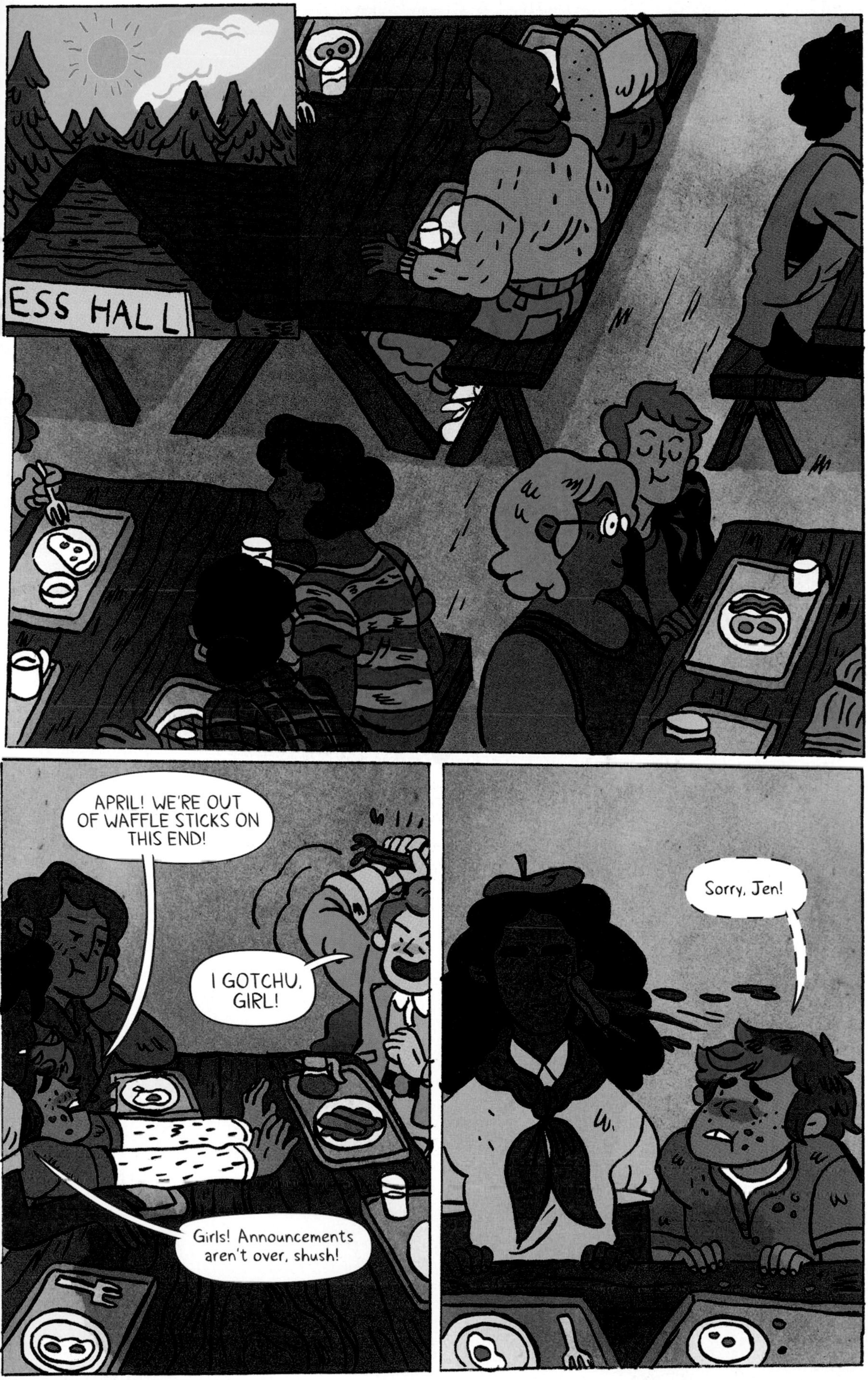
ESS HALL
APRIL! WE'RE OUT OF WAFFLE STICKS ON THIS END!
I GOTCHU, GIRL!
Girls! Announcements aren't over, shush!
Sorry, Jen!

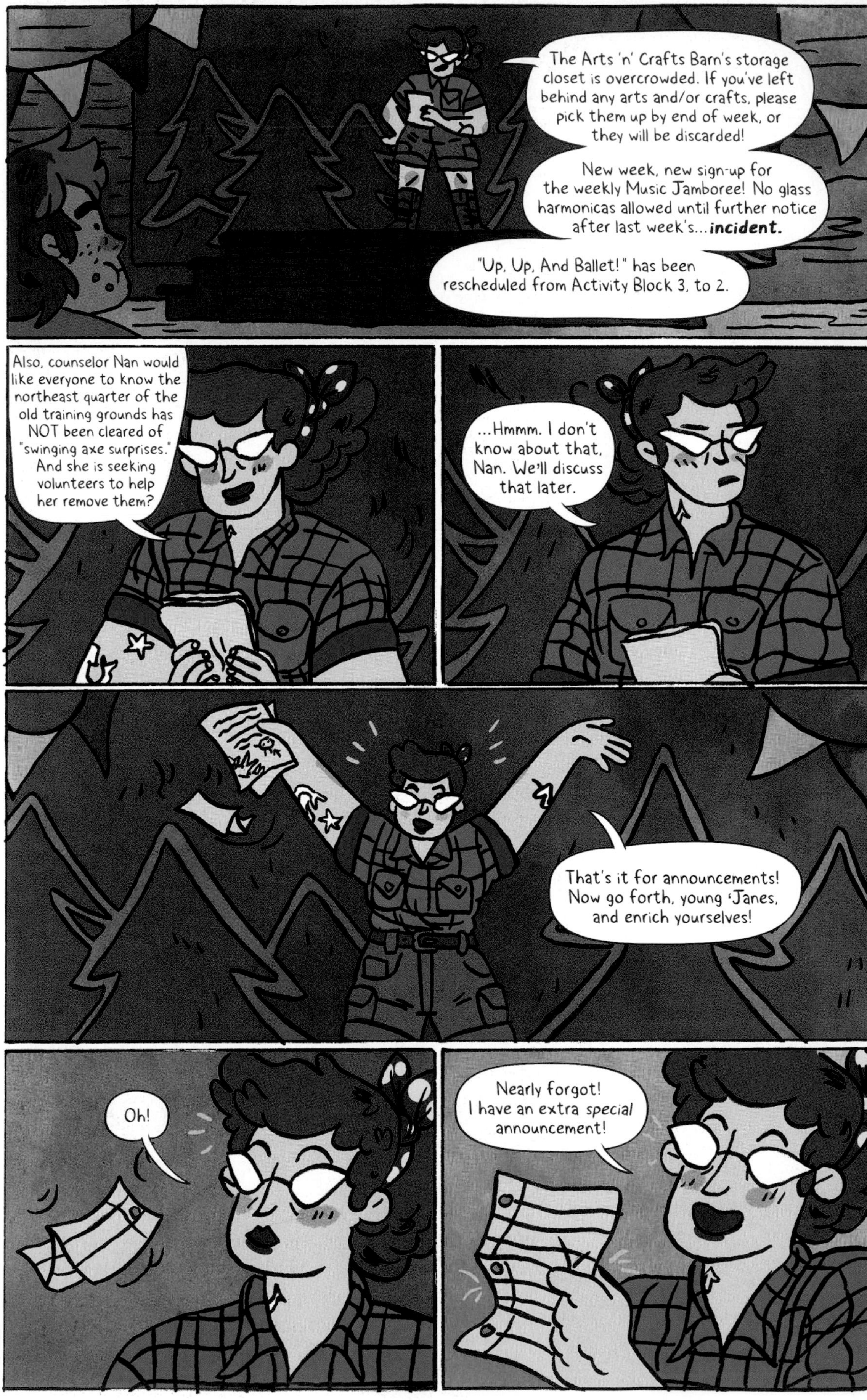
The Arts 'n' Crafts Barn's storage closet is overcrowded. If you've left behind any arts and/or crafts, please pick them up by end of week, or they will be discarded!
New week, new sign-up for the weekly Music Jamboree! No glass harmonicas allowed until further notice after last week's...**incident.**
"Up, Up, And Ballet!" has been rescheduled from Activity Block 3, to 2.
Also, counselor Nan would like everyone to know the northeast quarter of the old training grounds has NOT been cleared of "swinging axe surprises." And she is seeking volunteers to help her remove them?
...Hmmm. I don't know about that, Nan. We'll discuss that later.
That's it for announcements! Now go forth, young 'Janes, and enrich yourselves!
Oh!
Nearly forgot! I have an extra *special* announcement!

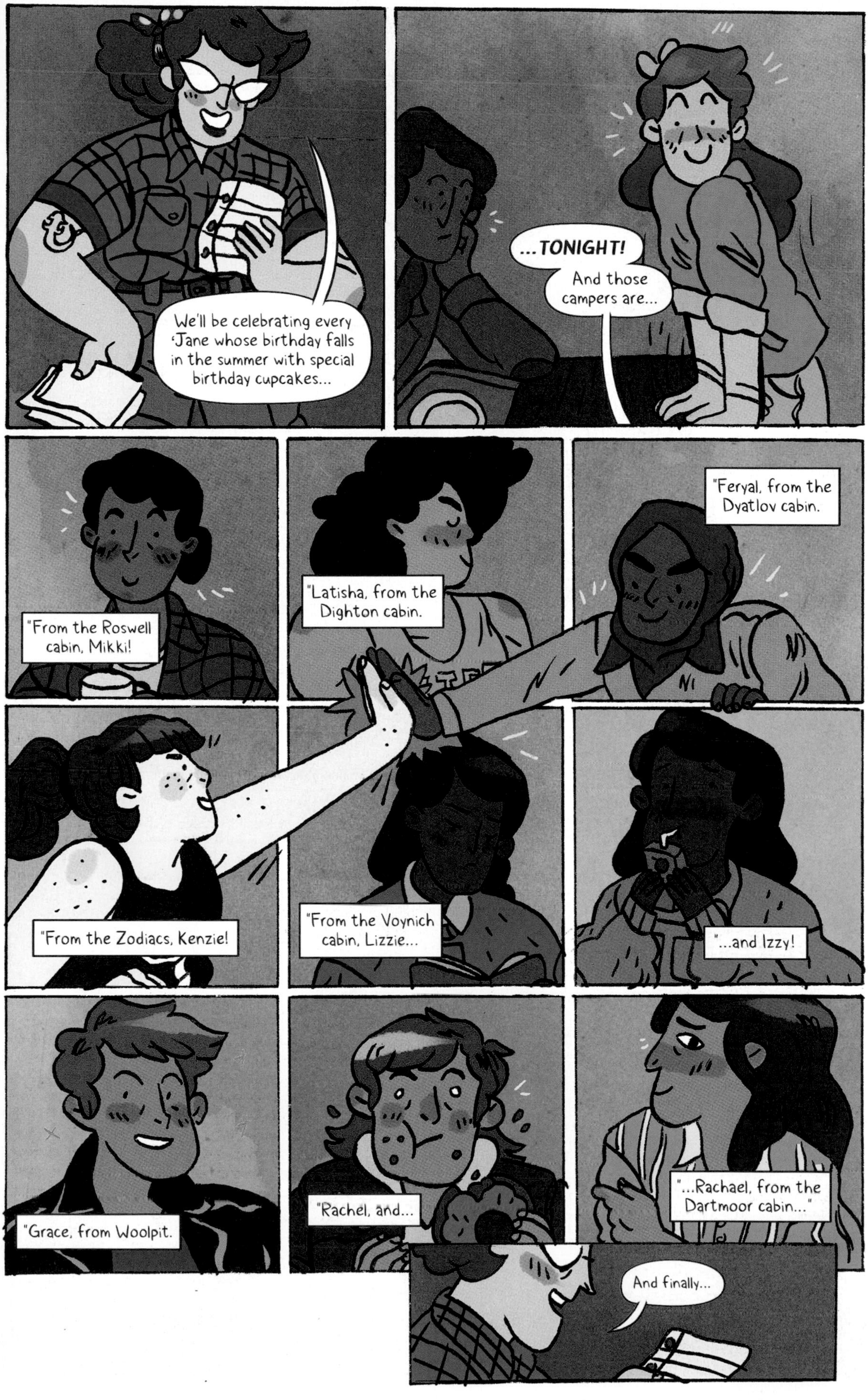

We'll be celebrating every 'Jane whose birthday falls in the summer with special birthday cupcakes...
...TONIGHT!
And those campers are...
"From the Roswell cabin, Mikki!
"Latisha, from the Dighton cabin.
"Feryal, from the Dyatlov cabin.
"From the Zodiacs, Kenzie!
"From the Voynich cabin, Lizzie...
"...and Izzy!
"Grace, from Woolpit.
"Rachel, and...
"...Rachael, from the Dartmoor cabin..."
And finally...

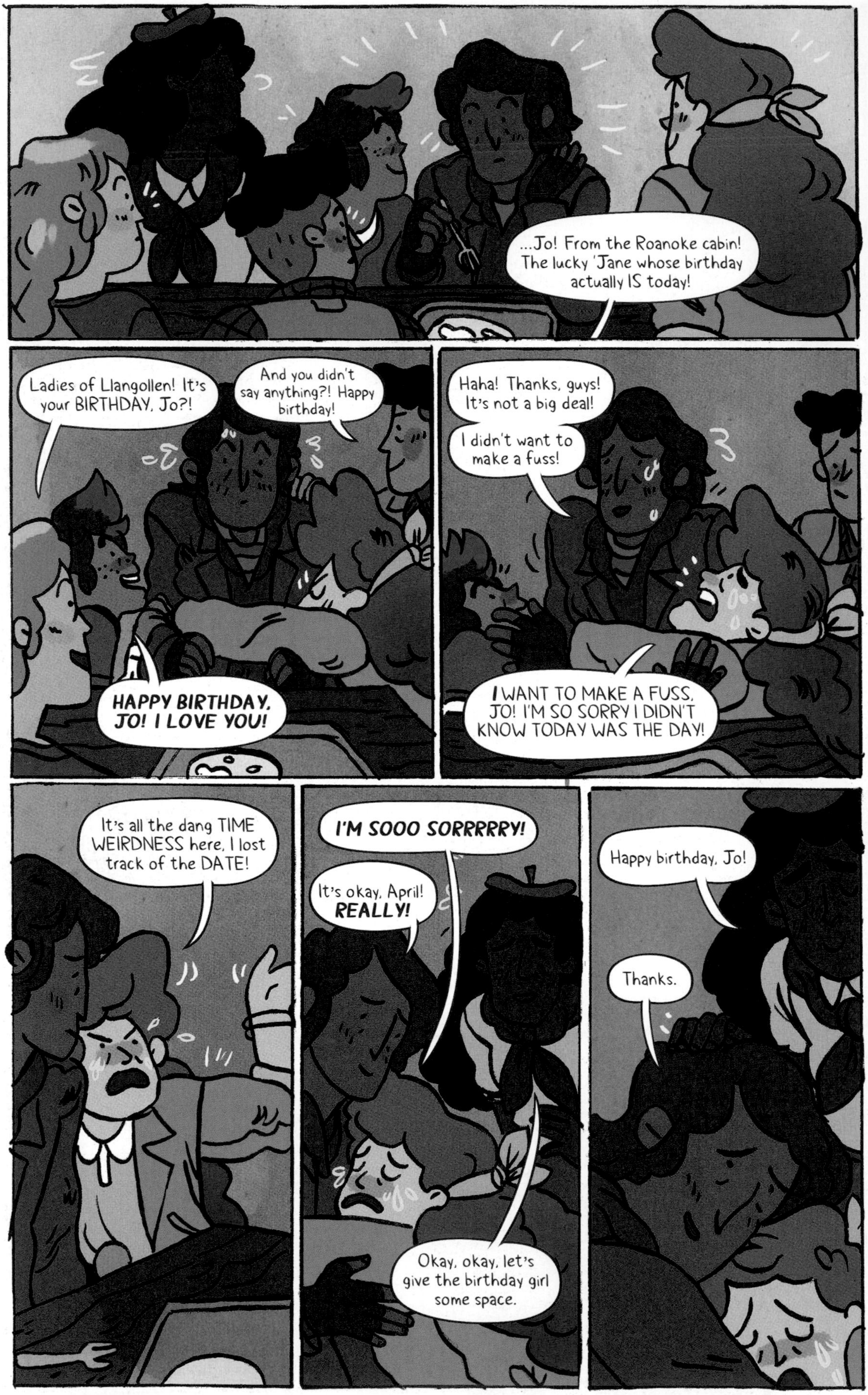
...Jo! From the Roanoke cabin! The lucky 'Jane whose birthday actually IS today!
Ladies of Llangollen! It's your BIRTHDAY, Jo?!
And you didn't say anything?! Happy birthday!
HAPPY BIRTHDAY, JO! I LOVE YOU!
Haha! Thanks, guys! It's not a big deal!
I didn't want to make a fuss!
I WANT TO MAKE A FUSS, JO! I'M SO SORRY I DIDN'T KNOW TODAY WAS THE DAY!
It's all the dang TIME WEIRDNESS here, I lost track of the DATE!
I'M SOOO SORRRRRY!
It's okay, April! REALLY!
Okay, okay, let's give the birthday girl some space.
Happy birthday, Jo!
Thanks.

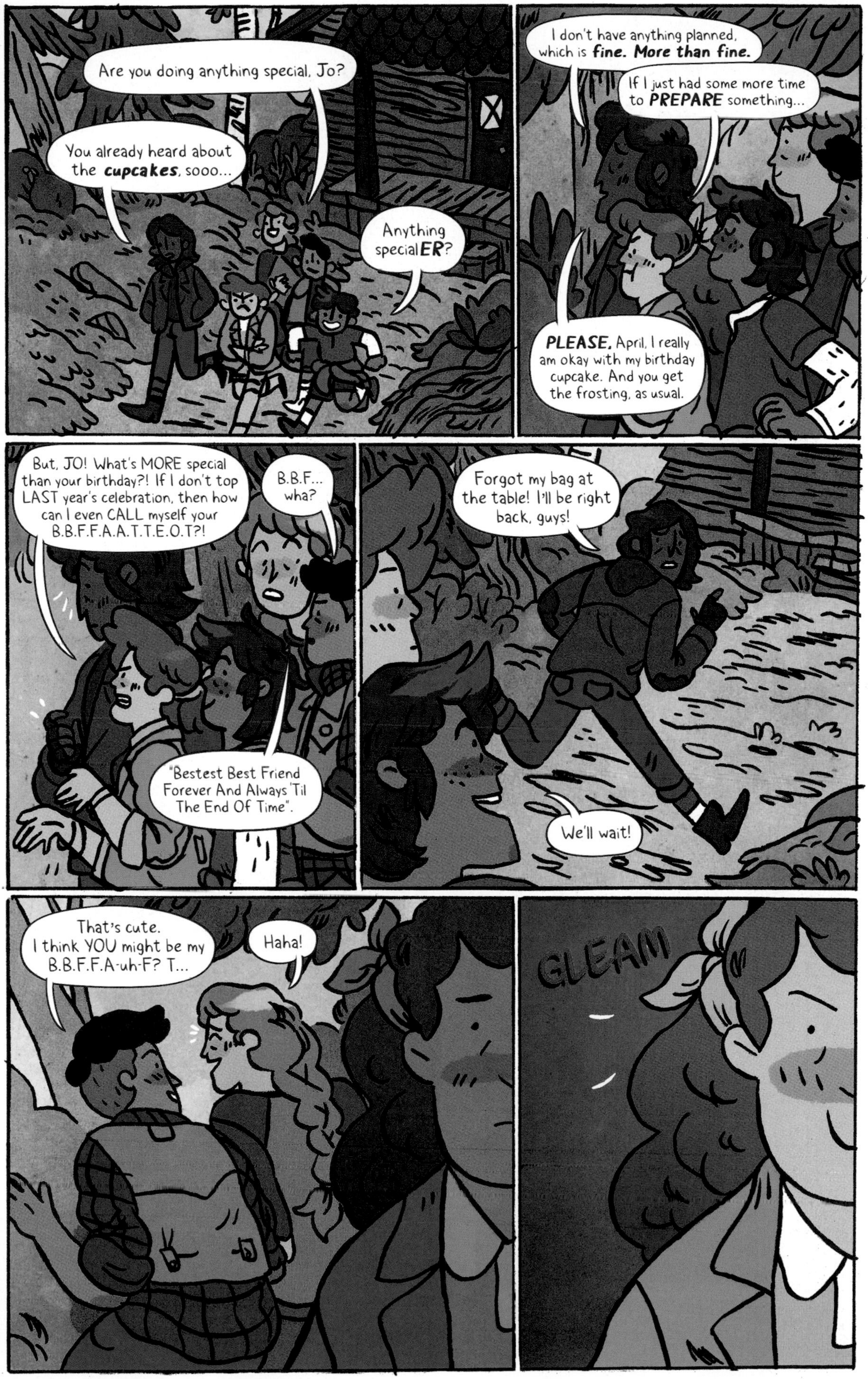
Are you doing anything special, Jo?
You already heard about the **cupcakes**, sooo...
Anything special**ER**?
I don't have anything planned, which is **fine. More than fine.**
If I just had some more time to **PREPARE** something...
PLEASE, April, I really am okay with my birthday cupcake. And you get the frosting, as usual.
But, JO! What's MORE special than your birthday?! If I don't top LAST year's celebration, then how can I even CALL myself your B.B.F.F.A.A.T.T.E.O.T?!
B.B.F... wha?
"Bestest Best Friend Forever And Always 'Til The End Of Time".
Forgot my bag at the table! I'll be right back, guys!
We'll wait!
That's cute. I think YOU might be my B.B.F.F.A-uh-F? T...
Haha!
GLEAM

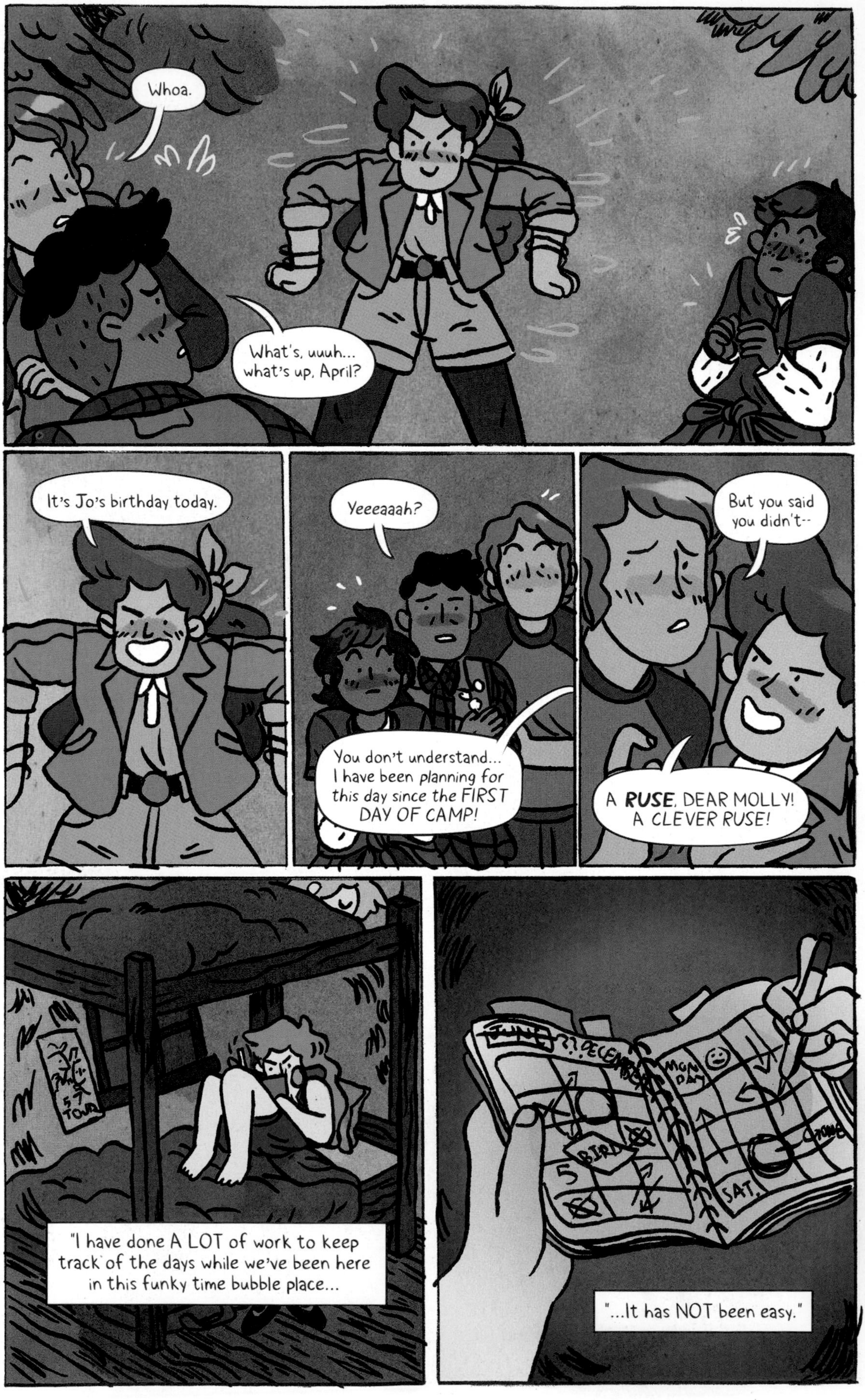
Whoa.
What's, uuuh... what's up, April?
It's Jo's birthday today.
Yeeeaaah?
You don't understand... I have been planning for this day since the FIRST DAY OF CAMP!
But you said you didn't--
A **RUSE**, DEAR MOLLY! A CLEVER RUSE!
"I have done A LOT of work to keep track of the days while we've been here in this funky time bubble place...
"...It has NOT been easy."

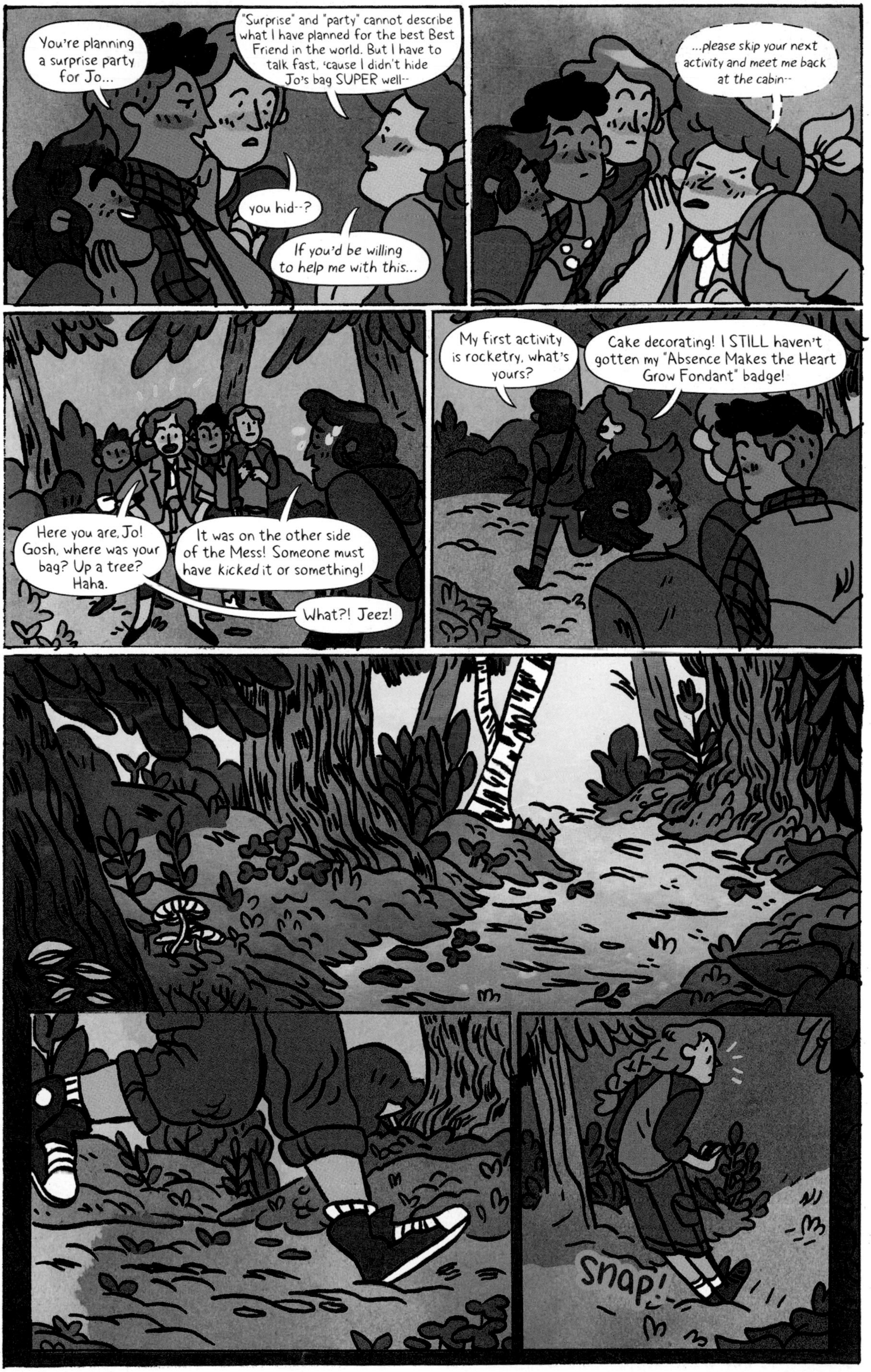
You're planning a surprise party for Jo...
"Surprise" and "party" cannot describe what I have planned for the best Best Friend in the world. But I have to talk fast, 'cause I didn't hide Jo's bag SUPER well--
you hid--?
If you'd be willing to help me with this...
...please skip your next activity and meet me back at the cabin--
Here you are, Jo! Gosh, where was your bag? Up a tree? Haha.
It was on the other side of the Mess! Someone must have *kicked* it or something!
What?! Jeez!
My first activity is rocketry, what's yours?
Cake decorating! I STILL haven't gotten my "Absence Makes the Heart Grow Fondant" badge!
snap!

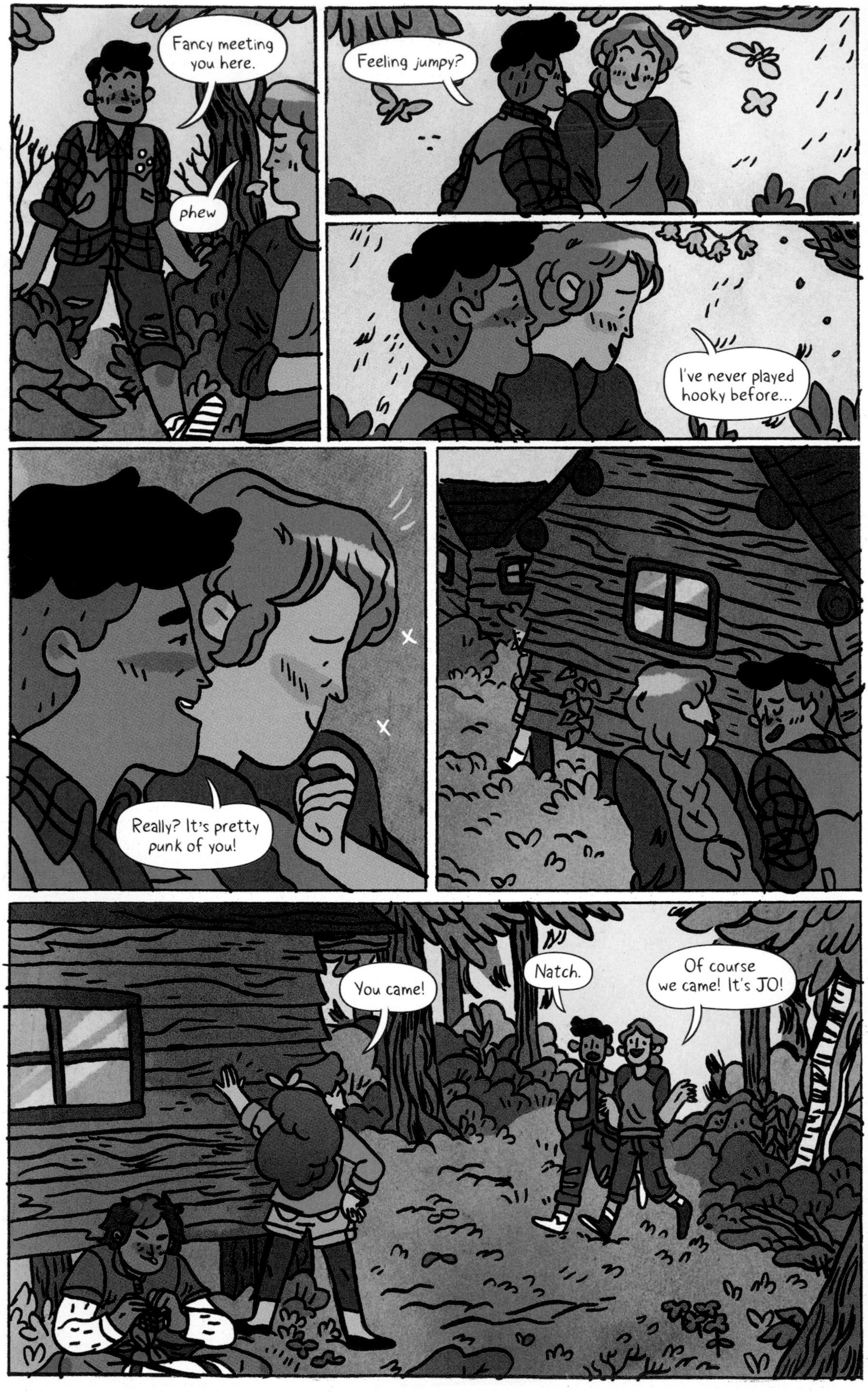
Fancy meeting you here.
phew
Feeling jumpy?
I've never played hooky before...
Really? It's pretty punk of you!
You came!
Natch.
Of course we came! It's JO!

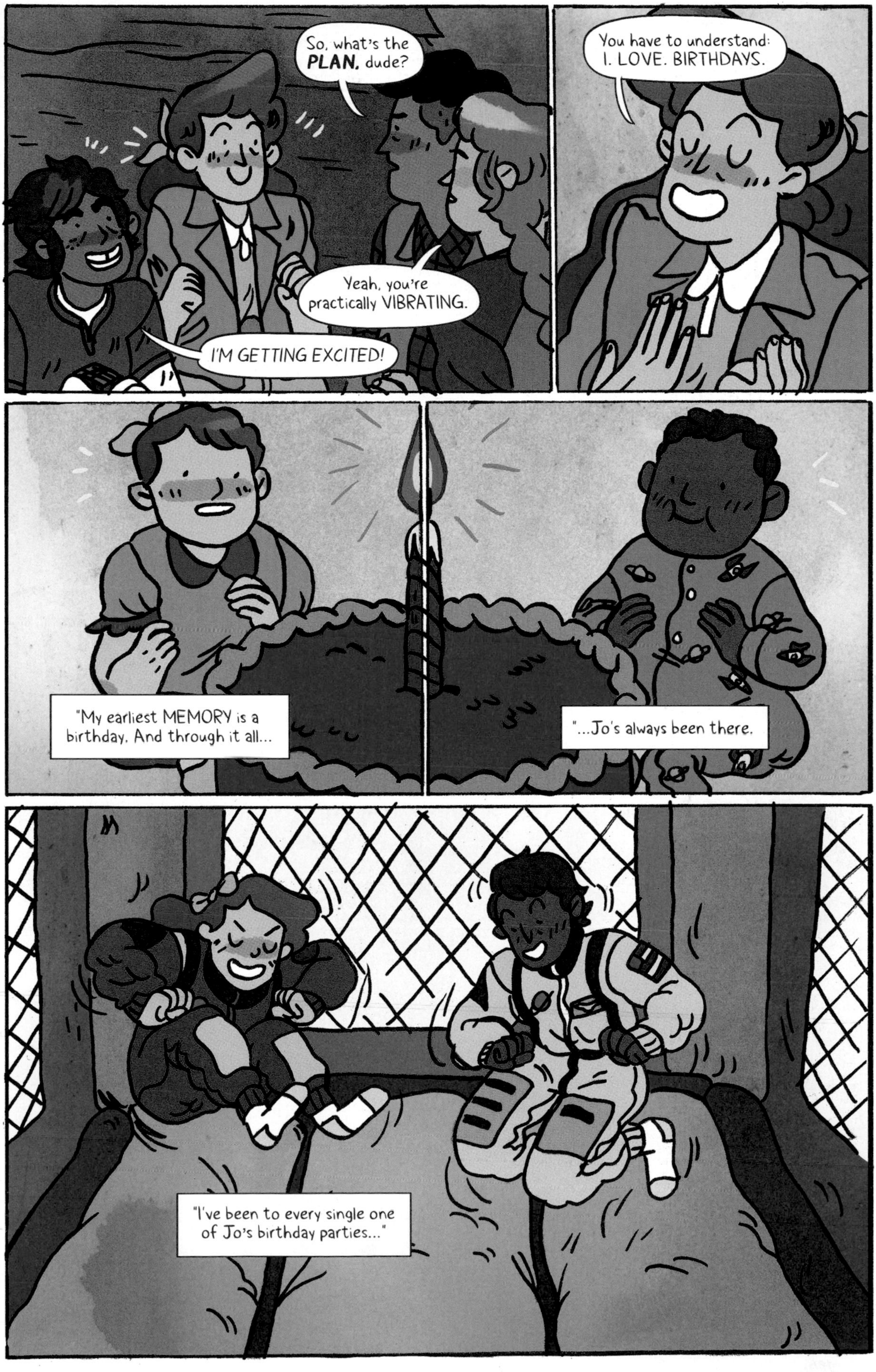
So, what's the **PLAN,** dude?
Yeah, you're practically VIBRATING.
I'M GETTING EXCITED!
You have to understand: I. LOVE. BIRTHDAYS.
"My earliest MEMORY is a birthday. And through it all...
"...Jo's always been there.
"I've been to every single one of Jo's birthday parties..."

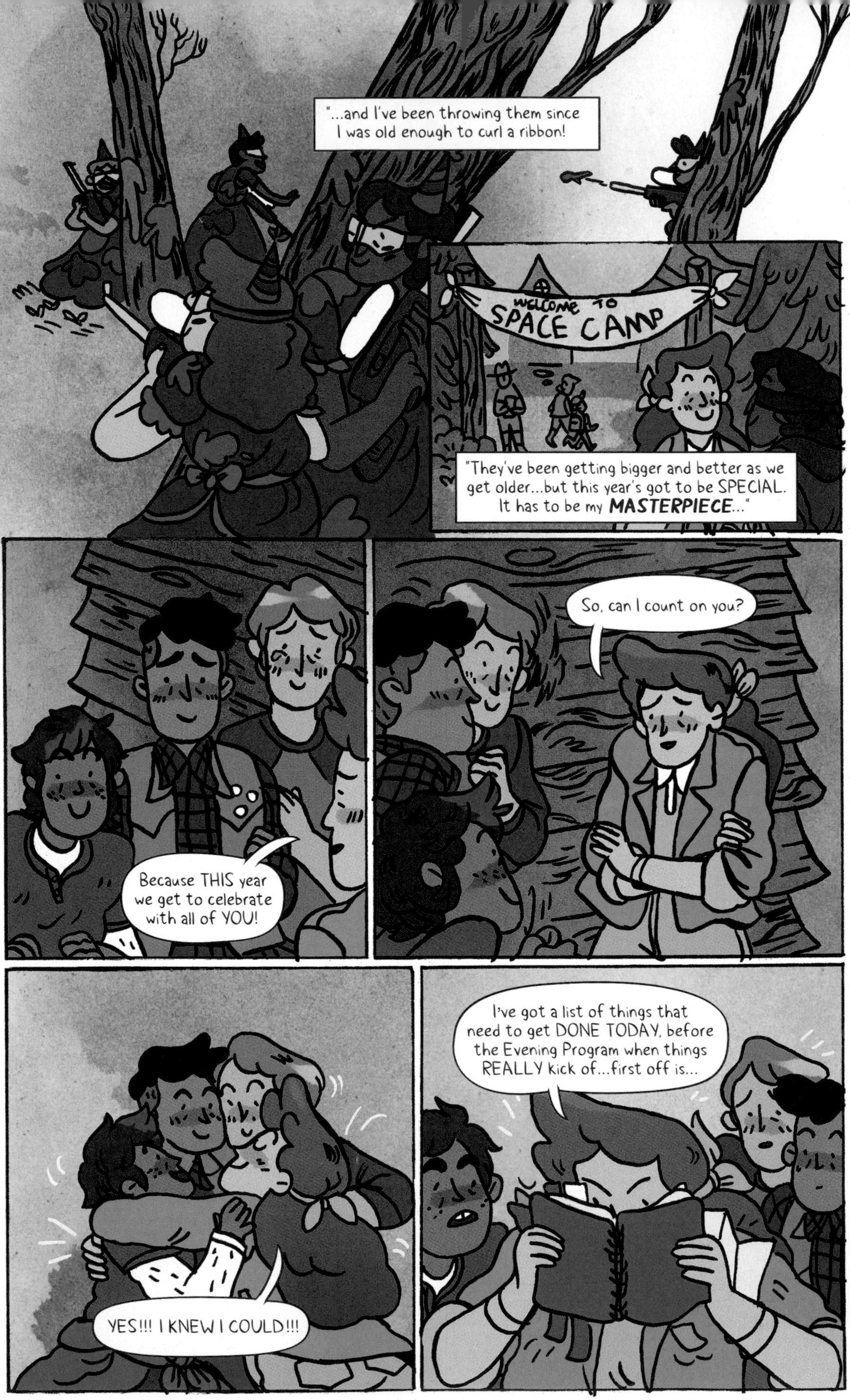
"...and I've been throwing them since I was old enough to curl a ribbon!
WELCOME TO SPACE CAMP
"They've been getting bigger and better as we get older...but this year's got to be SPECIAL. It has to be my **MASTERPIECE**..."
Because THIS year we get to celebrate with all of YOU!
So, can I count on you?
YES!!! I KNEW I COULD!!!
I've got a list of things that need to get DONE TODAY, before the Evening Program when things REALLY kick of...first off is...

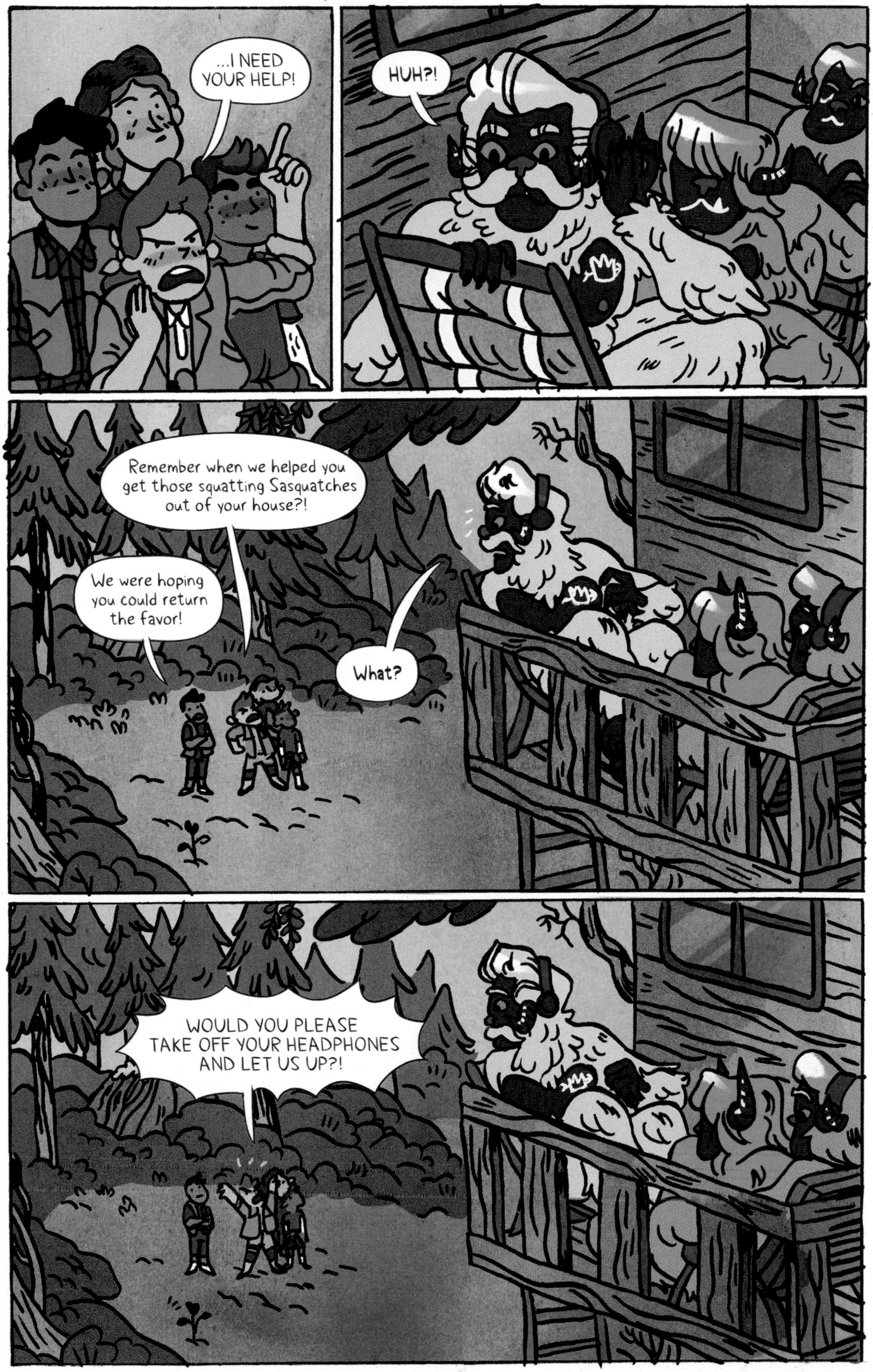
...I NEED YOUR HELP!
HUH?!
Remember when we helped you get those squatting Sasquatches out of your house?!
We were hoping you could return the favor!
What?
WOULD YOU PLEASE TAKE OFF YOUR HEADPHONES AND LET US UP?!

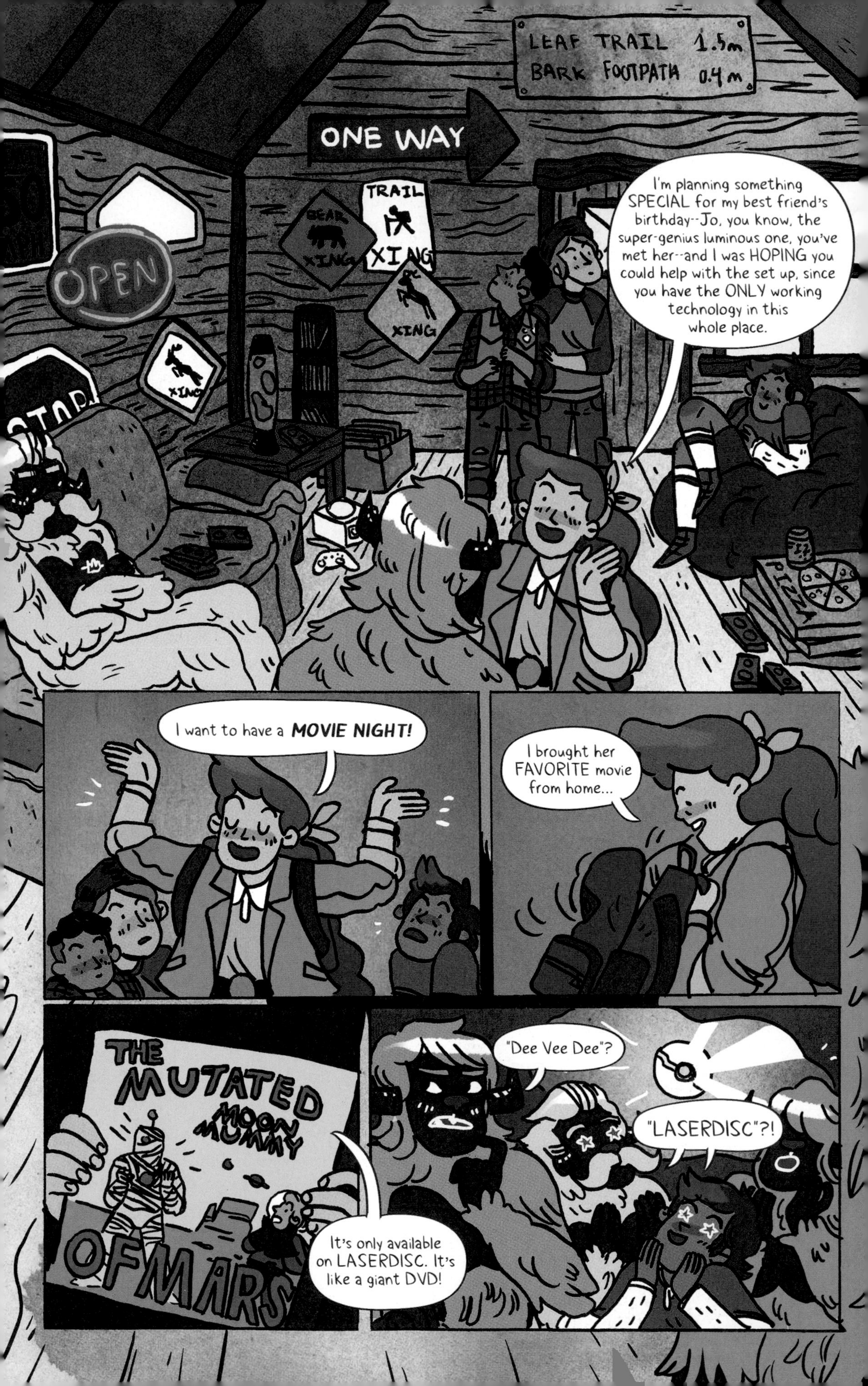
LEAF TRAIL 1.5m
BARK FOOTPATH 0.4m
ONE WAY
OPEN
TRAIL XING
BEAR XING
XING
XING
I'm planning something SPECIAL for my best friend's birthday--Jo, you know, the super-genius luminous one, you've met her--and I was HOPING you could help with the set up, since you have the ONLY working technology in this whole place.
PIZZA
I want to have a **MOVIE NIGHT!**
I brought her FAVORITE movie from home...
THE MUTATED MOON MUMMY OF MARS
It's only available on LASERDISC. It's like a giant DVD!
"Dee Vee Dee"?
"LASERDISC"?!

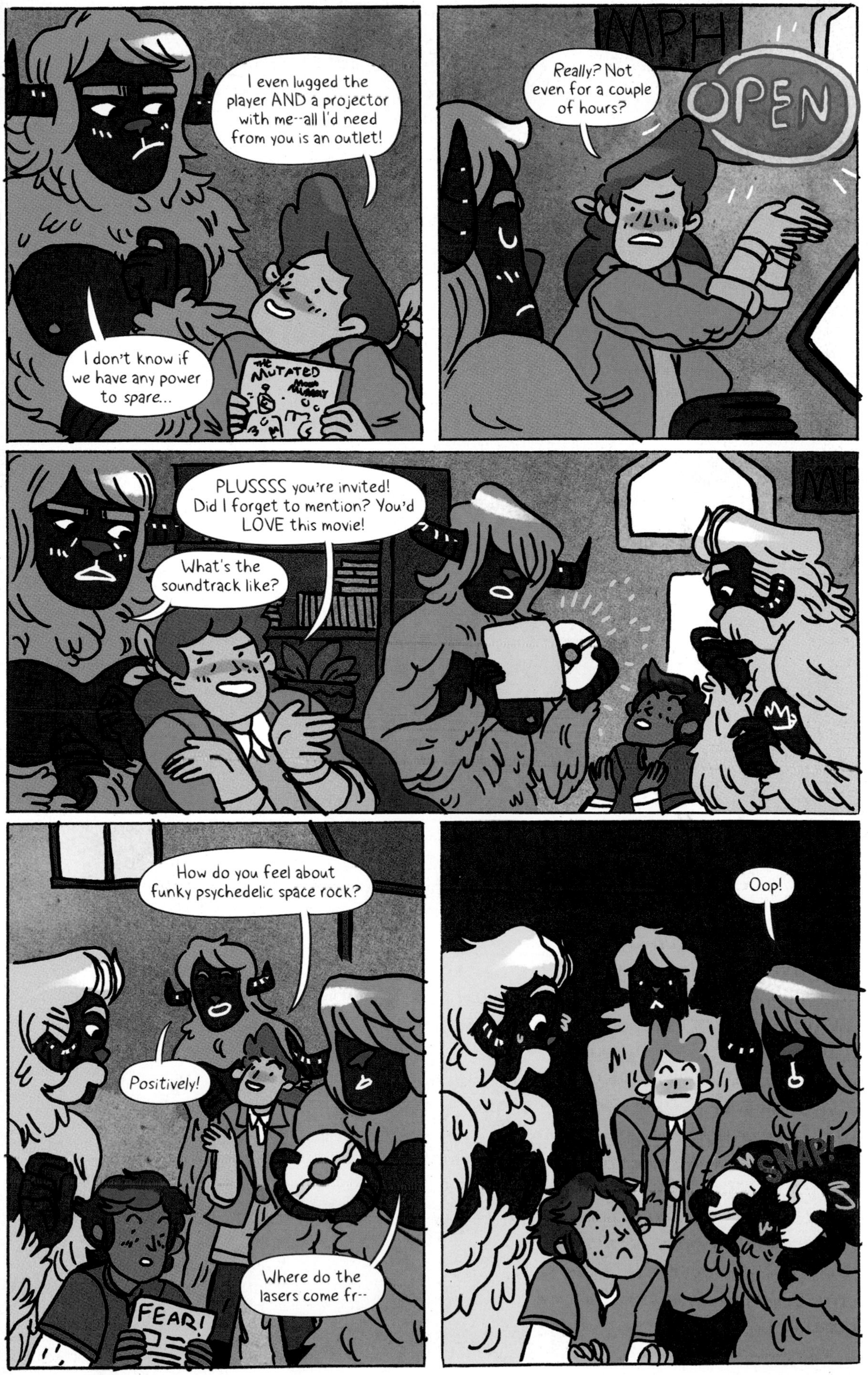
I even lugged the player AND a projector with me--all I'd need from you is an outlet!
I don't know if we have any power to spare...
THE MUTATED
Really? Not even for a couple of hours?
MPH
OPEN
PLUSSSS you're invited! Did I forget to mention? You'd LOVE this movie!
What's the soundtrack like?
How do you feel about funky psychedelic space rock?
Positively!
Where do the lasers come fr--
FEAR!
Oop!
SNAP!

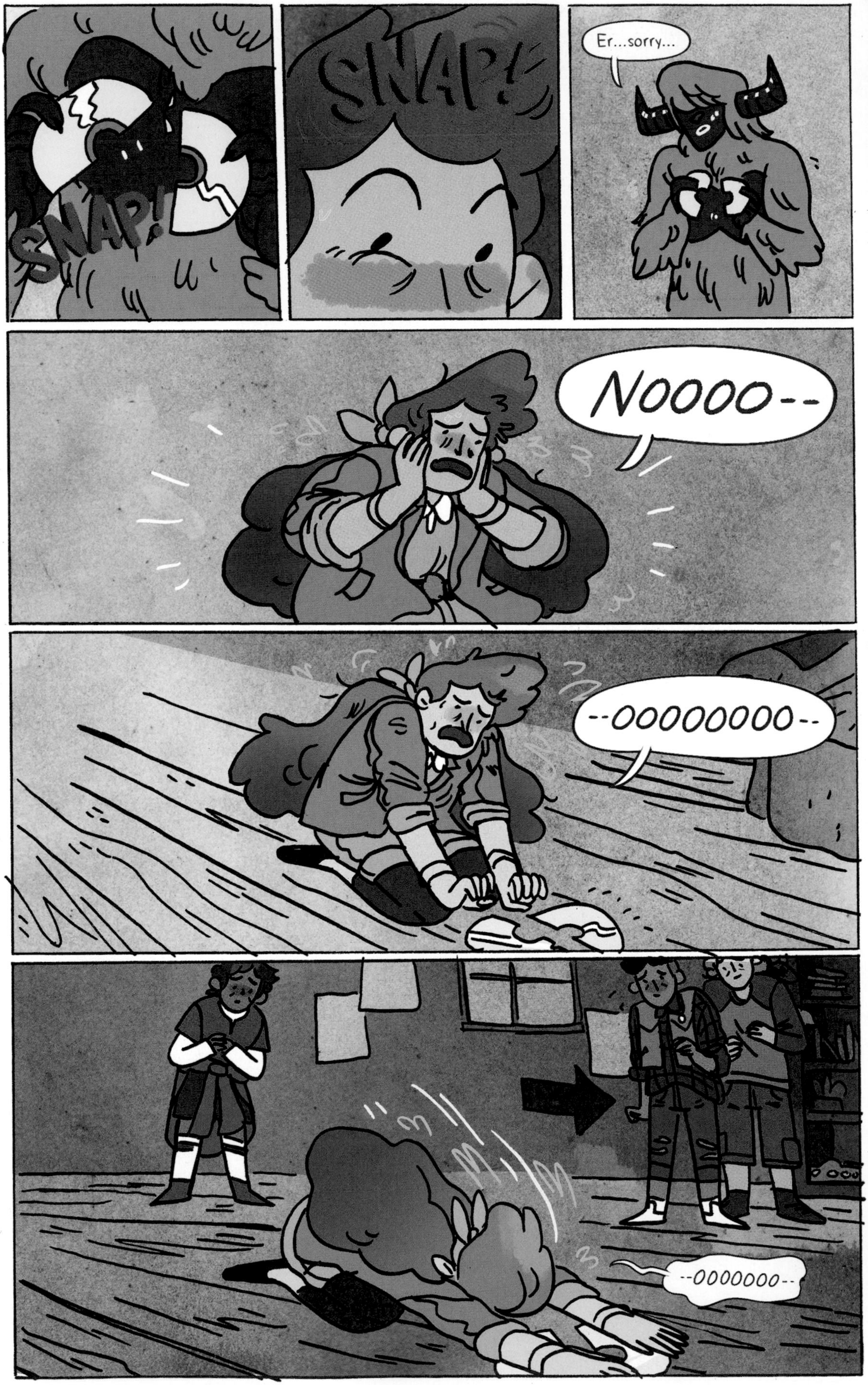
SNAP!
SNAP!
Er...sorry...
NOOOO--
--OOOOOOOO--
--OOOOOOO--

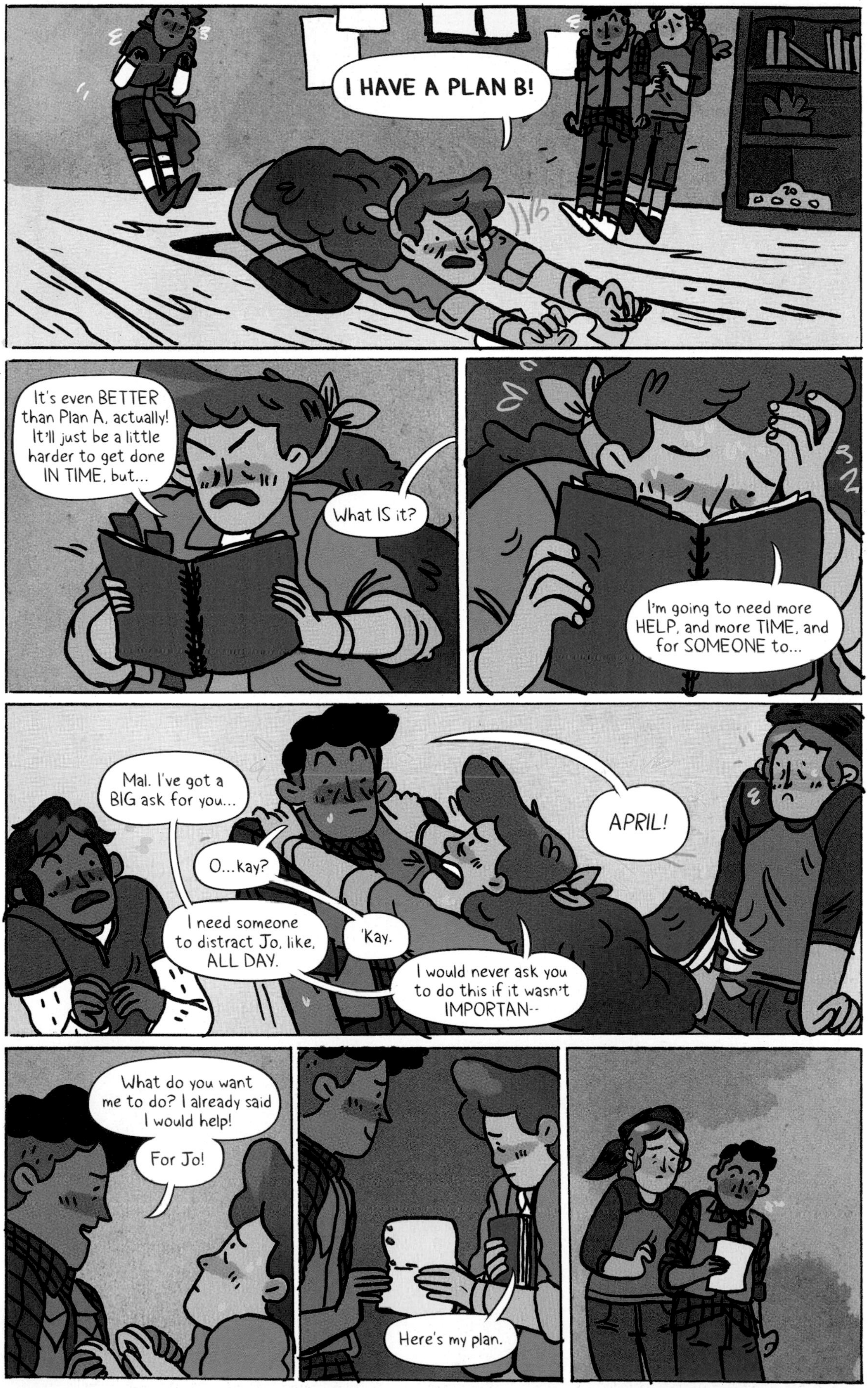

I HAVE A PLAN B!
It's even BETTER than Plan A, actually! It'll just be a little harder to get done IN TIME, but...
What IS it?
I'm going to need more HELP, and more TIME, and for SOMEONE to...
Mal. I've got a BIG ask for you...
APRIL!
O...kay?
'Kay.
I need someone to distract Jo, like, ALL DAY.
I would never ask you to do this if it wasn't IMPORTAN--
What do you want me to do? I already said I would help!
For Jo!
Here's my plan.

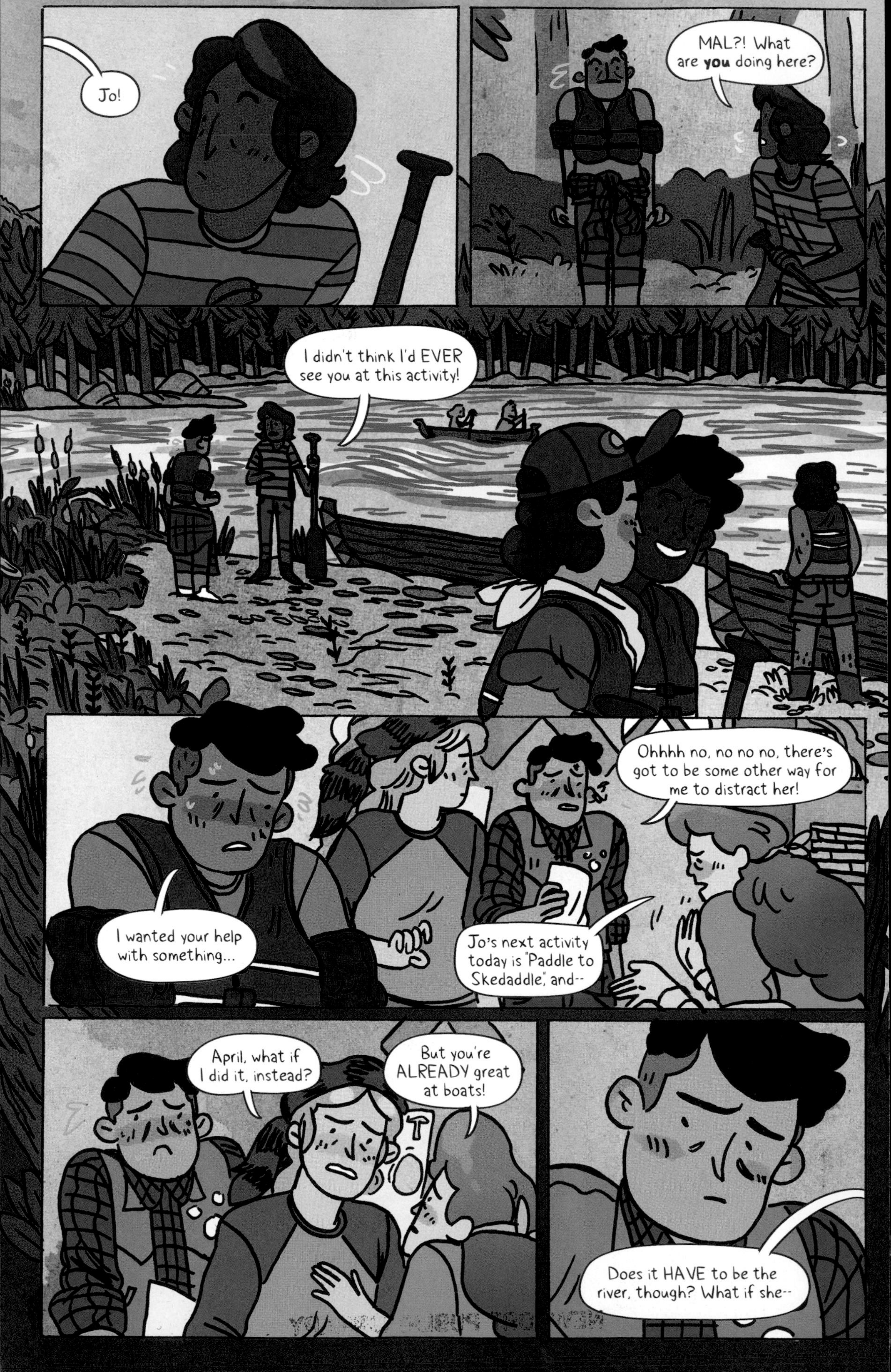
Jo!
MAL?! What are **you** doing here?
I didn't think I'd EVER see you at this activity!
I wanted your help with something...
Jo's next activity today is "Paddle to Skedaddle," and--
Ohhhh no, no no no, there's got to be some other way for me to distract her!
April, what if I did it, instead?
But you're ALREADY great at boats!
Does it HAVE to be the river, though? What if she--

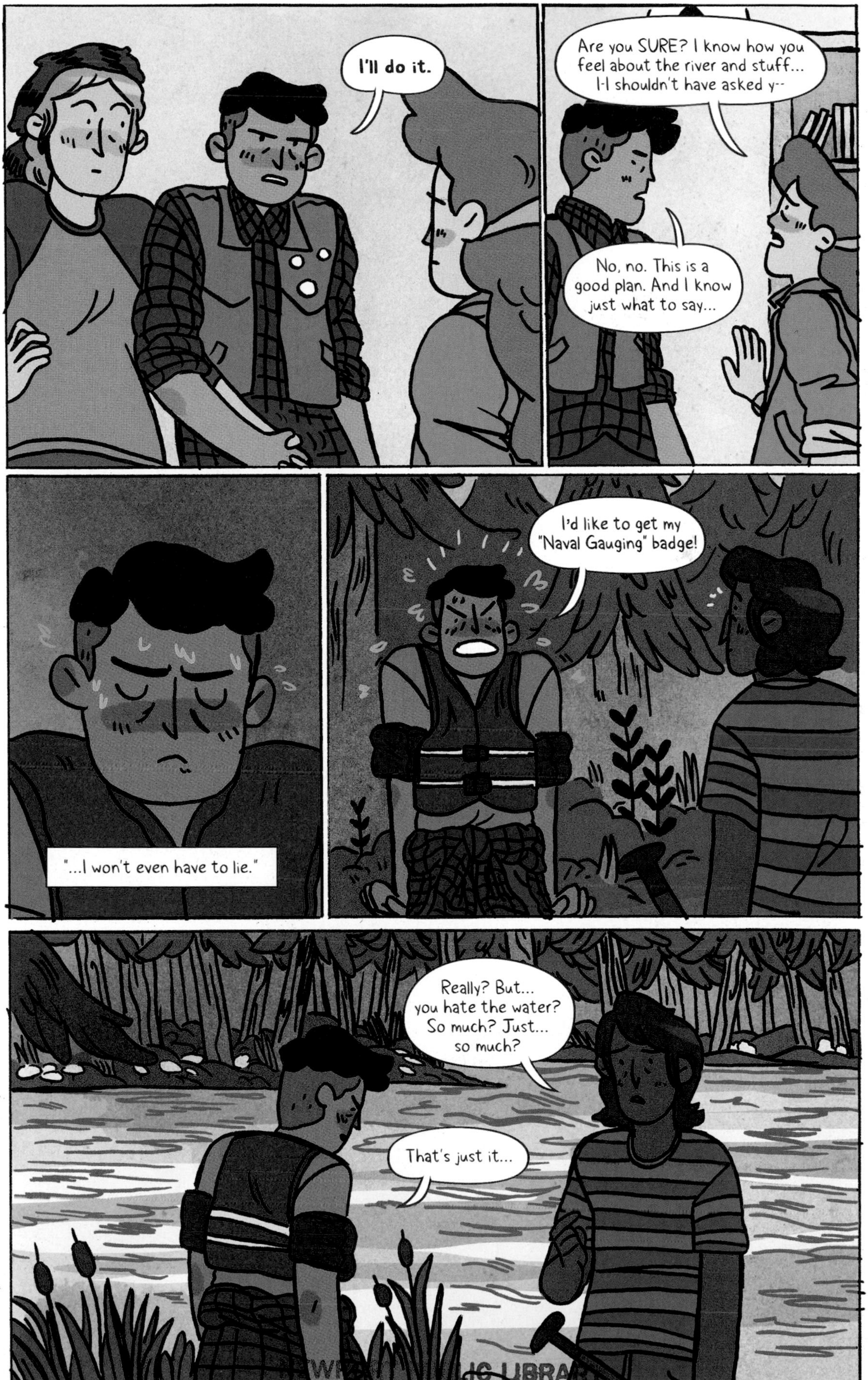
I'll do it.
Are you SURE? I know how you feel about the river and stuff... I-I shouldn't have asked y--
No, no. This is a good plan. And I know just what to say...
"...I won't even have to lie."
I'd like to get my "Naval Gauging" badge!
Really? But... you hate the water? So much? Just... so much?
That's just it...

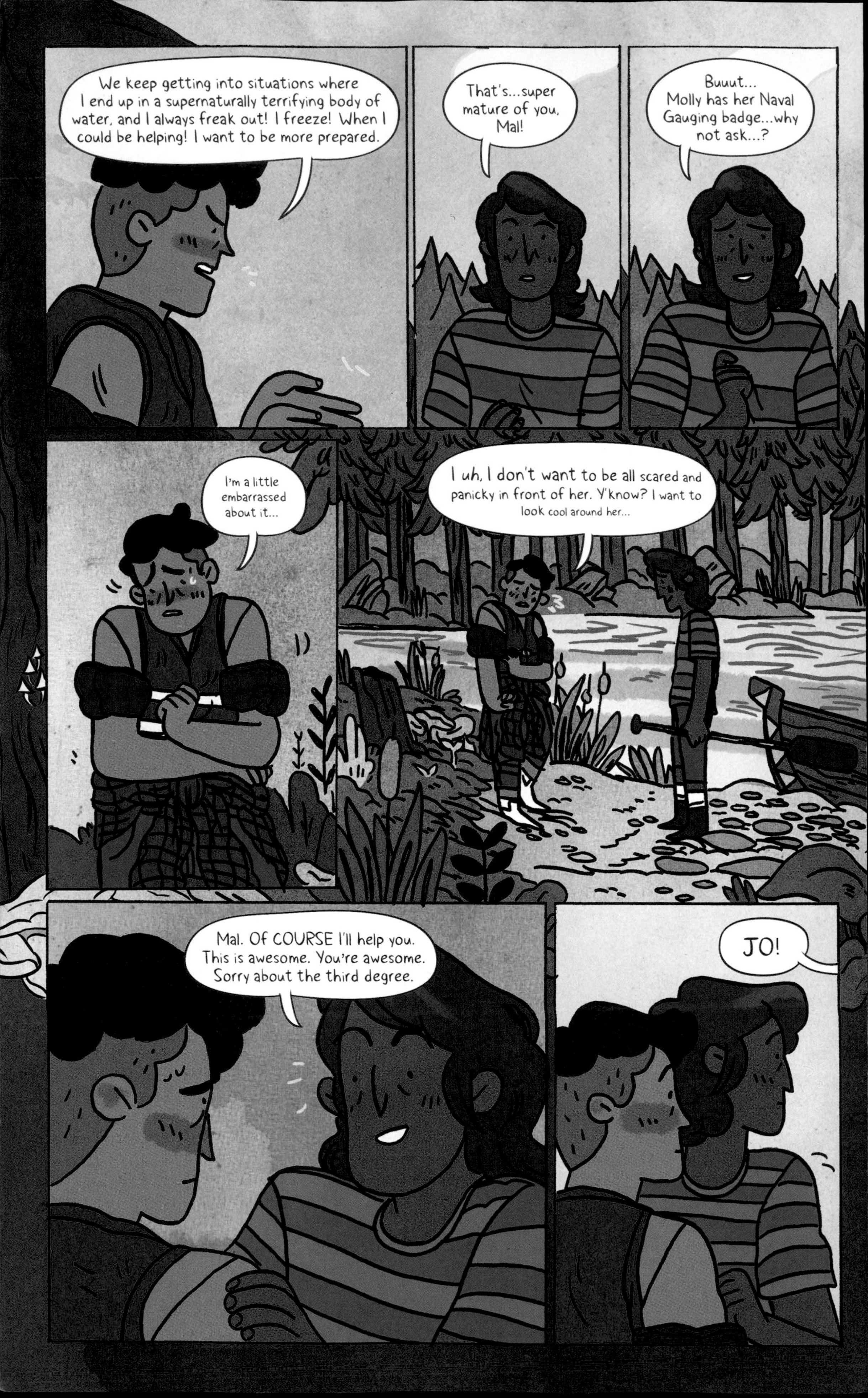
We keep getting into situations where I end up in a supernaturally terrifying body of water, and I always freak out! I freeze! When I could be helping! I want to be more prepared.
That's...super mature of you, Mal!
Buuut... Molly has her Naval Gauging badge...why not ask...?
I'm a little embarrassed about it...
I uh, I don't want to be all scared and panicky in front of her. Y'know? I want to look cool around her...
Mal. Of COURSE I'll help you. This is awesome. You're awesome. Sorry about the third degree.
JO!

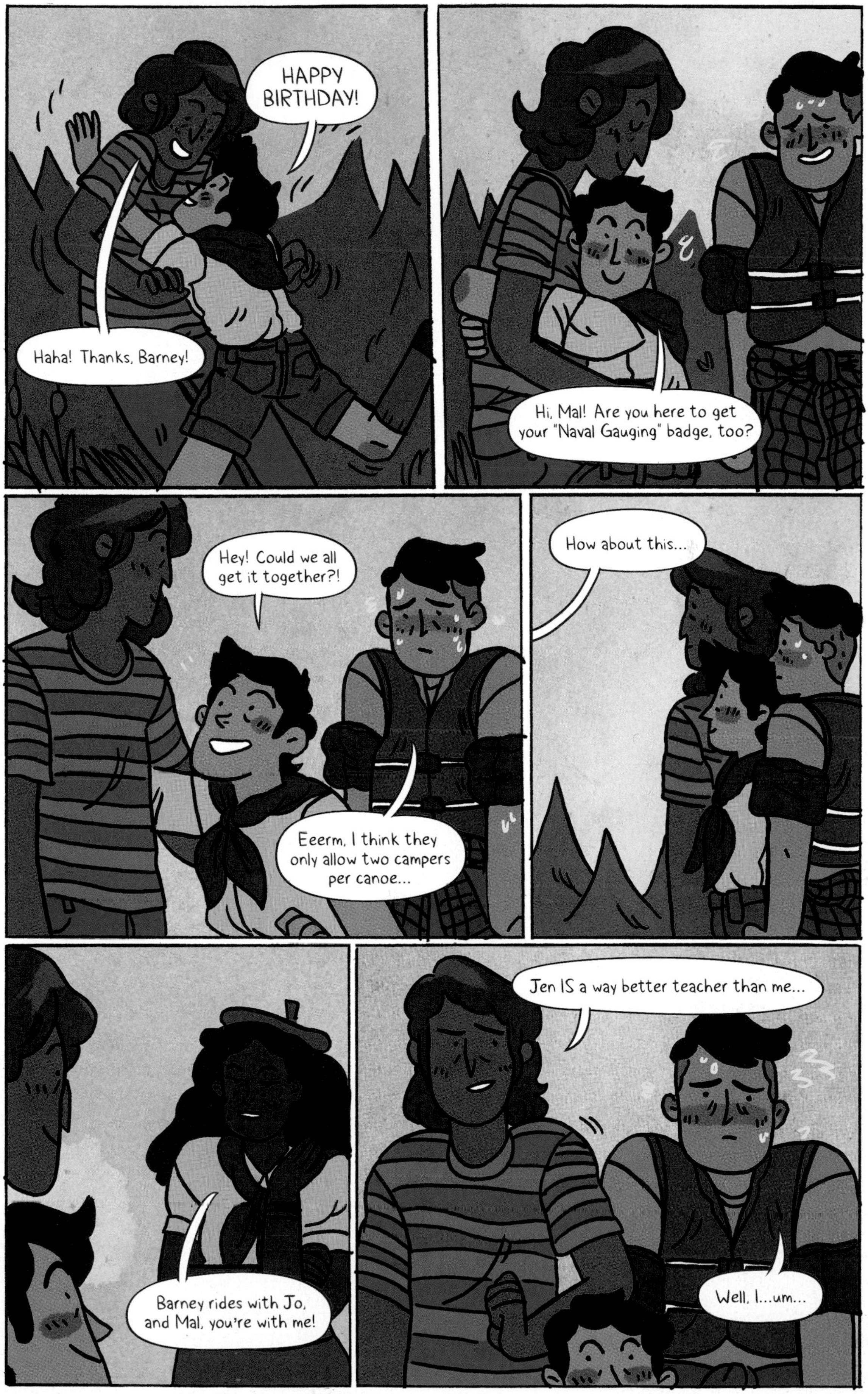
HAPPY BIRTHDAY!
Haha! Thanks, Barney!
Hi, Mal! Are you here to get your "Naval Gauging" badge, too?
Hey! Could we all get it together?!
Eeerm, I think they only allow two campers per canoe...
How about this...
Barney rides with Jo, and Mal, you're with me!
Jen IS a way better teacher than me...
Well, I...um...

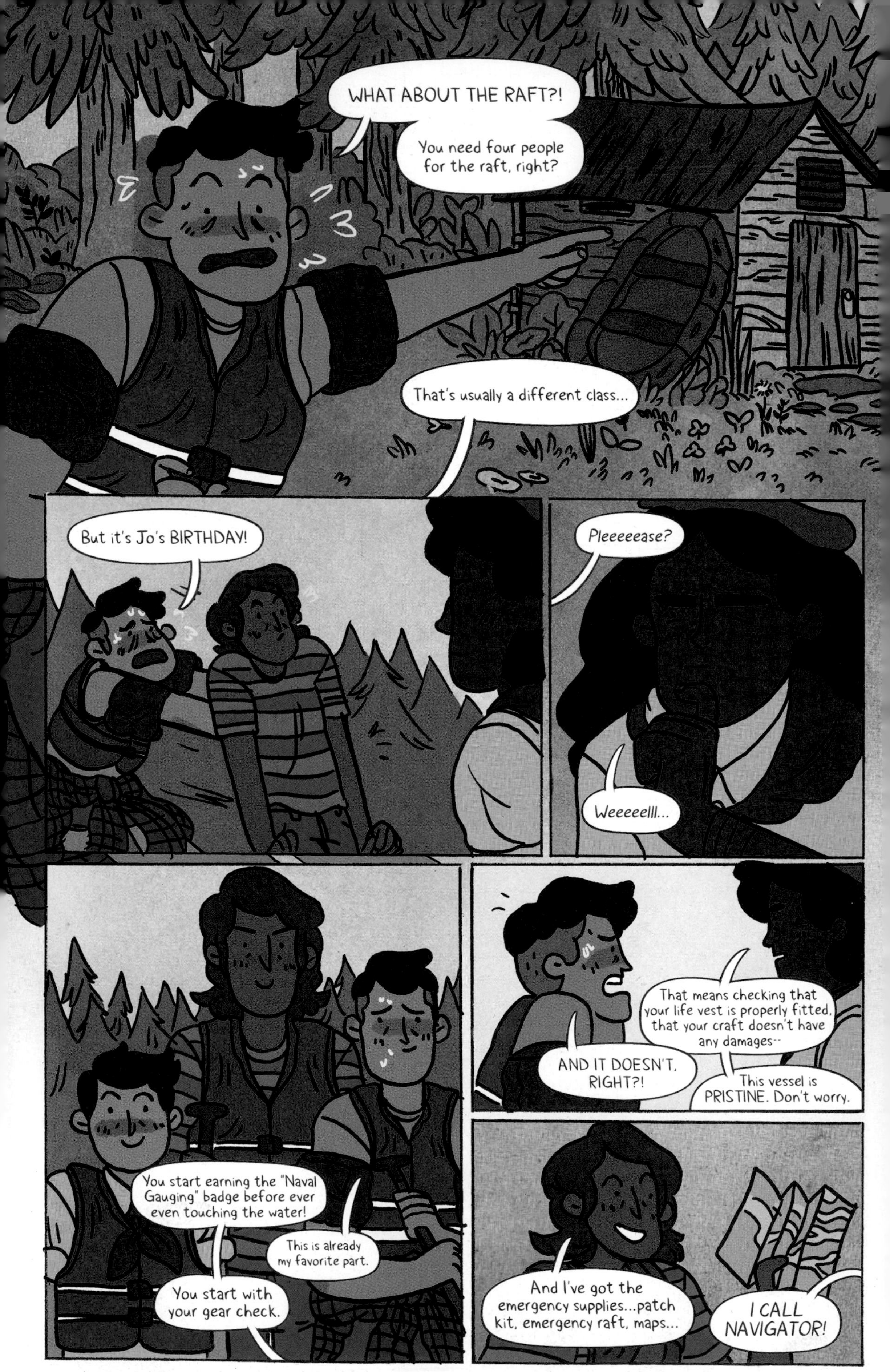
WHAT ABOUT THE RAFT?!
You need four people for the raft, right?
That's usually a different class...
But it's Jo's BIRTHDAY!
Pleeeeease?
Weeeeelll...
You start earning the "Naval Gauging" badge before ever even touching the water!
This is already my favorite part.
You start with your gear check.
That means checking that your life vest is properly fitted, that your craft doesn't have any damages--
AND IT DOESN'T, RIGHT?!
This vessel is PRISTINE. Don't worry.
And I've got the emergency supplies...patch kit, emergency raft, maps...
I CALL NAVIGATOR!

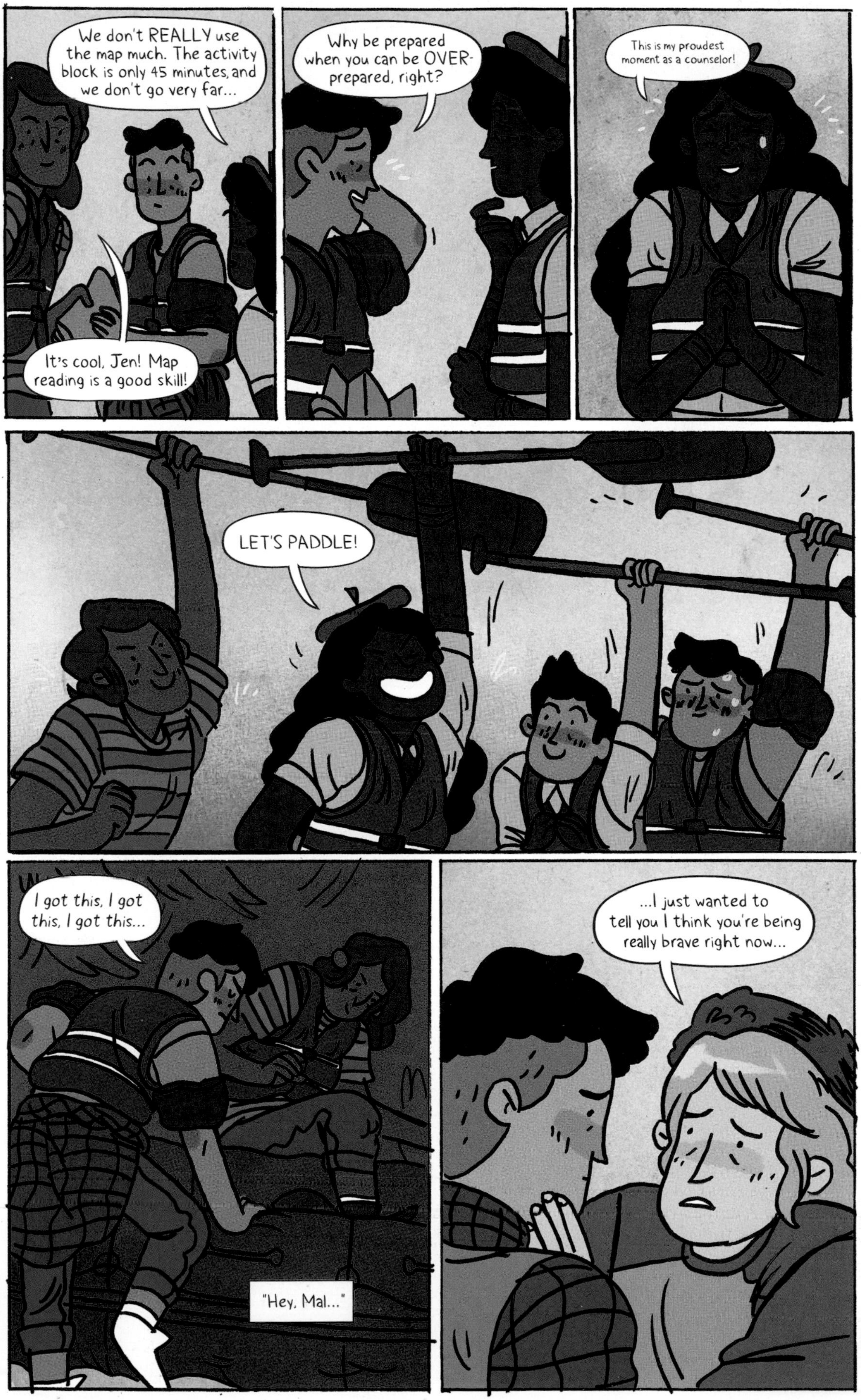
We don't REALLY use the map much. The activity block is only 45 minutes, and we don't go very far...
It's cool, Jen! Map reading is a good skill!
Why be prepared when you can be OVER-prepared, right?
This is my proudest moment as a counselor!
LET'S PADDLE!
I got this, I got this, I got this...
"Hey, Mal..."
...I just wanted to tell you I think you're being really brave right now...

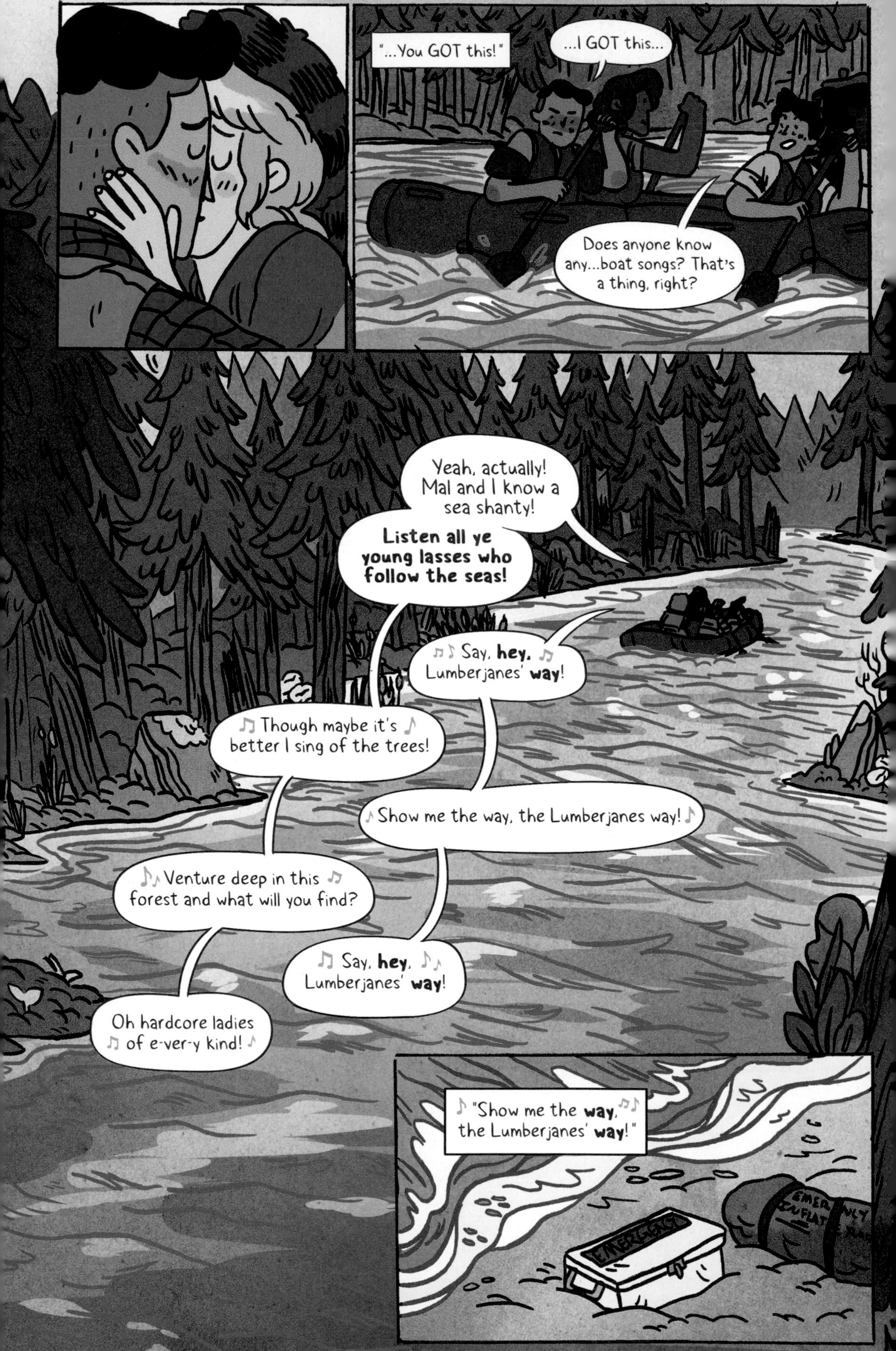
"...You GOT this!"
...I GOT this...
Does anyone know any...boat songs? That's a thing, right?
Yeah, actually! Mal and I know a sea shanty!
Listen all ye young lasses who follow the seas!
♫♪ Say, hey. ♫ Lumberjanes' way!
♫ Though maybe it's ♪ better I sing of the trees!
♪ Show me the way, the Lumberjanes way! ♪
♪♪ Venture deep in this ♫ forest and what will you find?
♫ Say, hey, ♪♪ Lumberjanes' way!
Oh hardcore ladies ♫ of e-ver-y kind! ♪
♪ "Show me the way, ♫♪ the Lumberjanes' way!"
EMERGENCY
EMERGENCY INFLATA

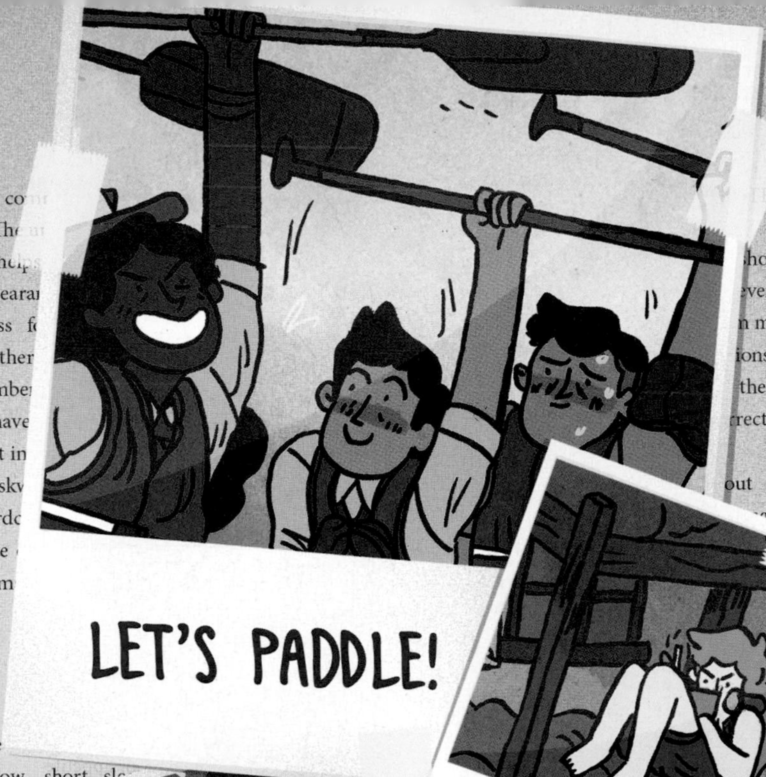
LET'S PADDLE!

will co

The

It h

appeara

dress f

Further

Lumbe

to have

part in

Thiskv

Hardc

have

them

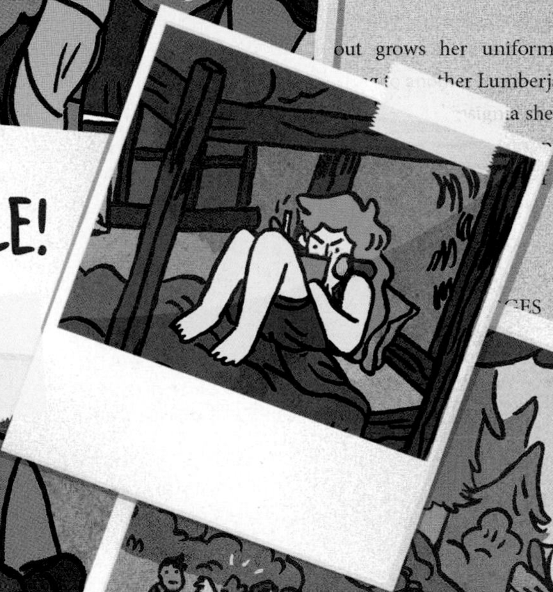

THE UNIFORM

should be worn at camp events when Lumberjanes n may also be worn at other ions. It should be worn as a the uniform dress with rrect shoes, and stocking or

out grows her uniform or ther Lumberjane. a she has her her

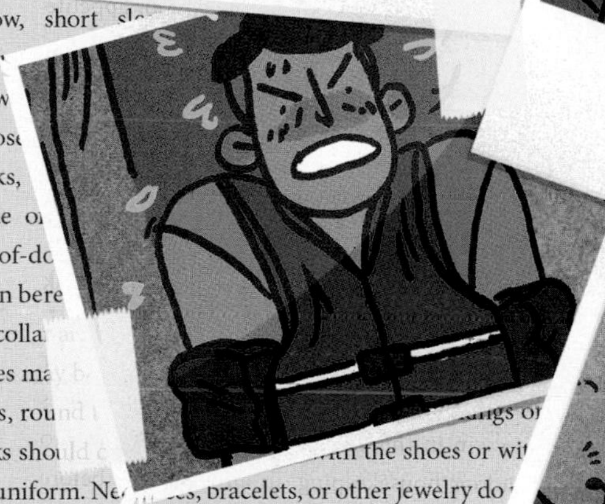

The yellow, short sl emb the w choose slacks, made o out-of-do green bere the colla Shoes ma heels, rou kings or socks shou ith the shoes or wi the uniform. Ne es, bracelets, or other jewelry do belong with a Lumberjane uniform.

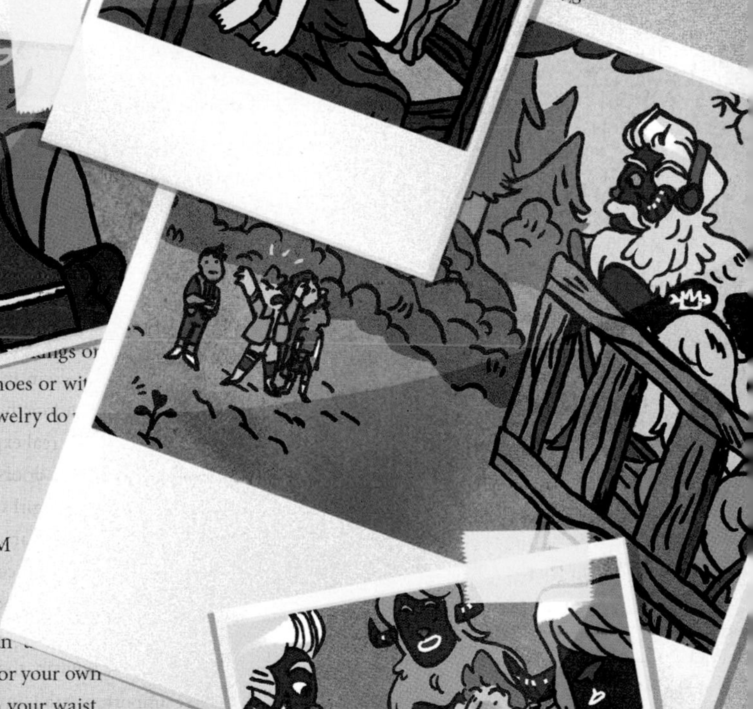

HOW TO WEAR THE UNIFORM

To look well in a uniform demands first of uniform be kept in good condition—clean pressed. See that the skirt is the right length for your own height and build, that the belt is adjusted to your waist, that your shoes and stockings are in keeping with the uniform, that you watch your posture and carry yourself with dignity and grace. If the beret is removed indoors, be sure that your hair is neat and kept in place with an inconspicuous clip or ribbon. When you wear a Lumberjane uniform you are identified as a member of this organization and you should be doubly careful to conduct yourself in a way that will show everyone that courtesy and thoughtfulness are part of being a Lumberjane. People are likely to judge a whole nation by the selfishness of a few individuals, to criticize a whole family because of the misconduct of one member, and to feel unkindly toward an organization because of the

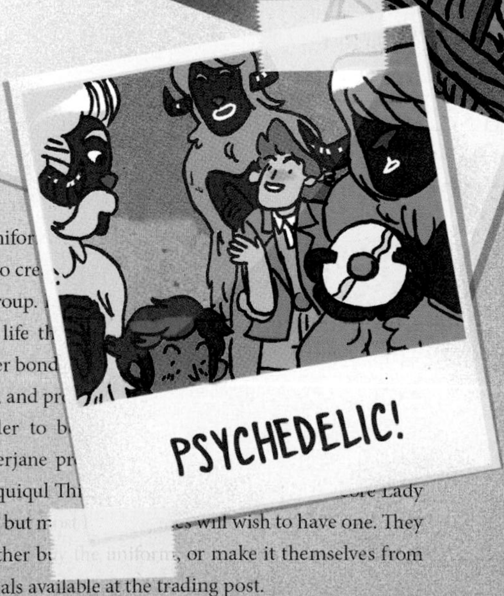
PSYCHEDELIC!

The unifor helps to cre in a group. active life th another bond future, and pr in order to b Lumberjane pr Penniquiqul Thi ore Lady Types, but m es will wish to have one. They can either bu , or make it themselves from materials available at the trading post.

LUMBERJANES FIELD MANUAL

CHAPTER
FIFTY-EIGHT

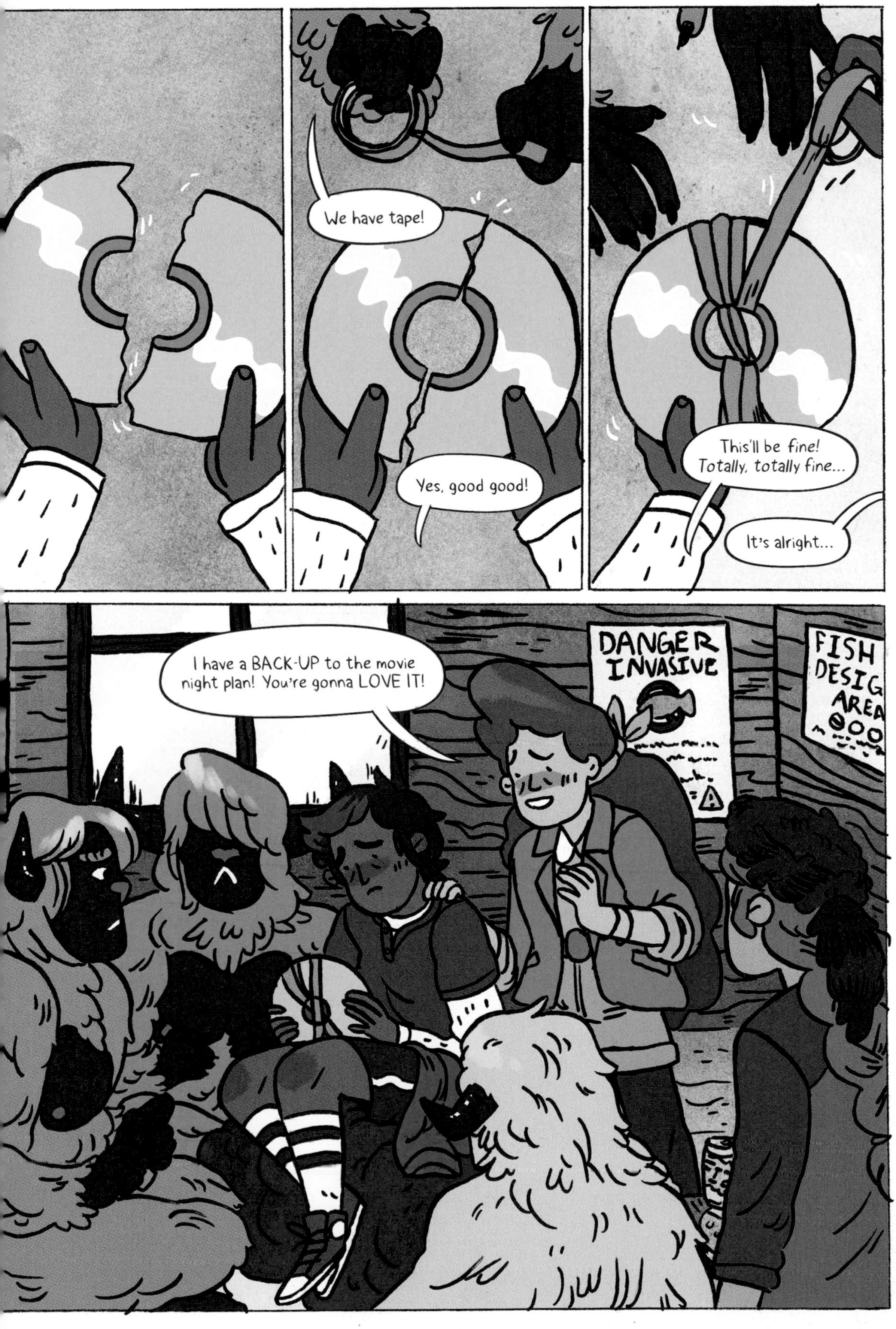
We have tape!
Yes, good good!
This'll be fine! Totally, totally fine...
It's alright...
I have a BACK-UP to the movie night plan! You're gonna LOVE IT!
DANGER INVASIVE
FISH DESIG AREA

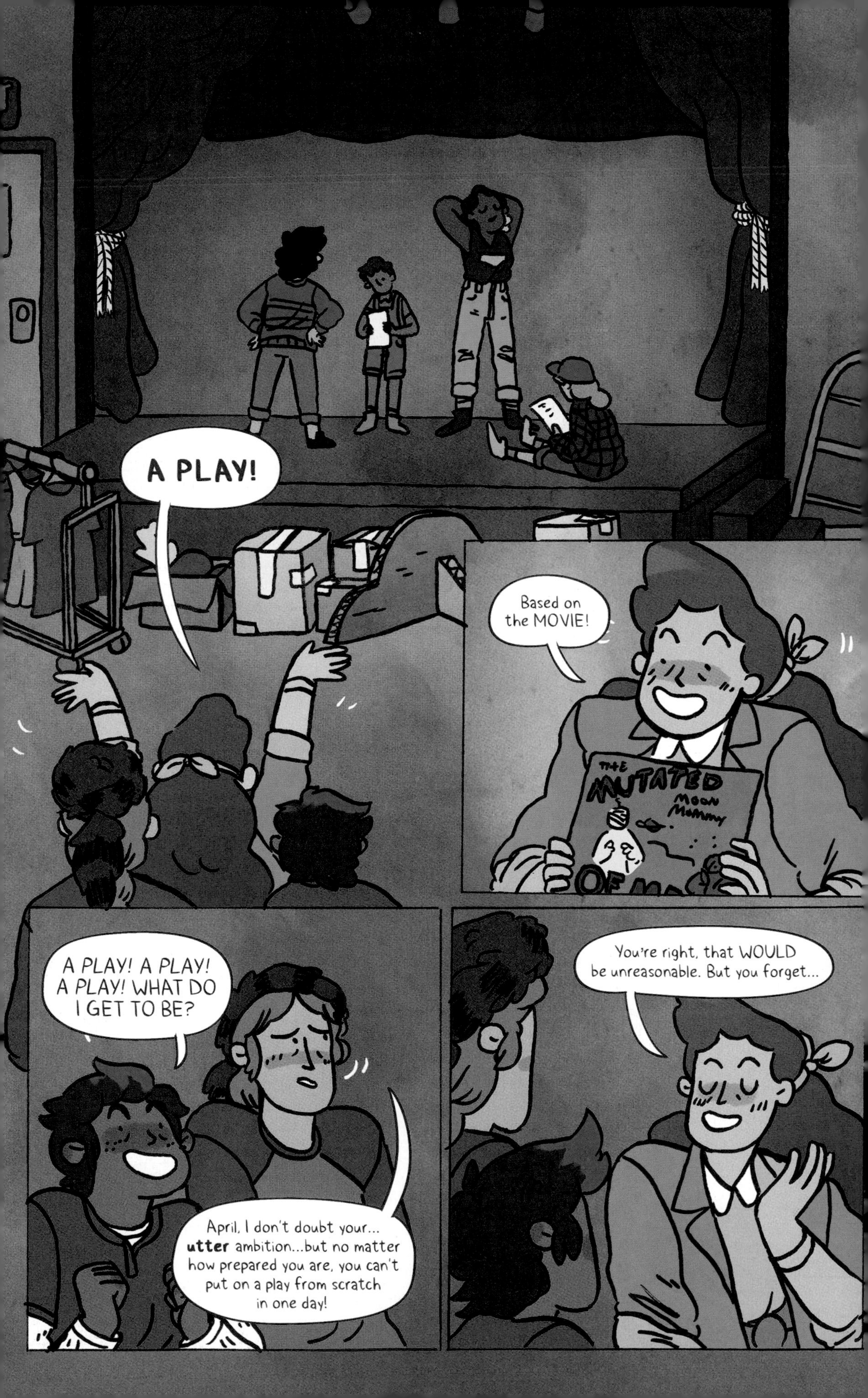
A PLAY!
Based on the MOVIE!
THE MUTATED MOON MUMMY OF M
A PLAY! A PLAY! A PLAY! WHAT DO I GET TO BE?
April, I don't doubt your... **utter** ambition...but no matter how prepared you are, you can't put on a play from scratch in one day!
You're right, that WOULD be unreasonable. But you forget...

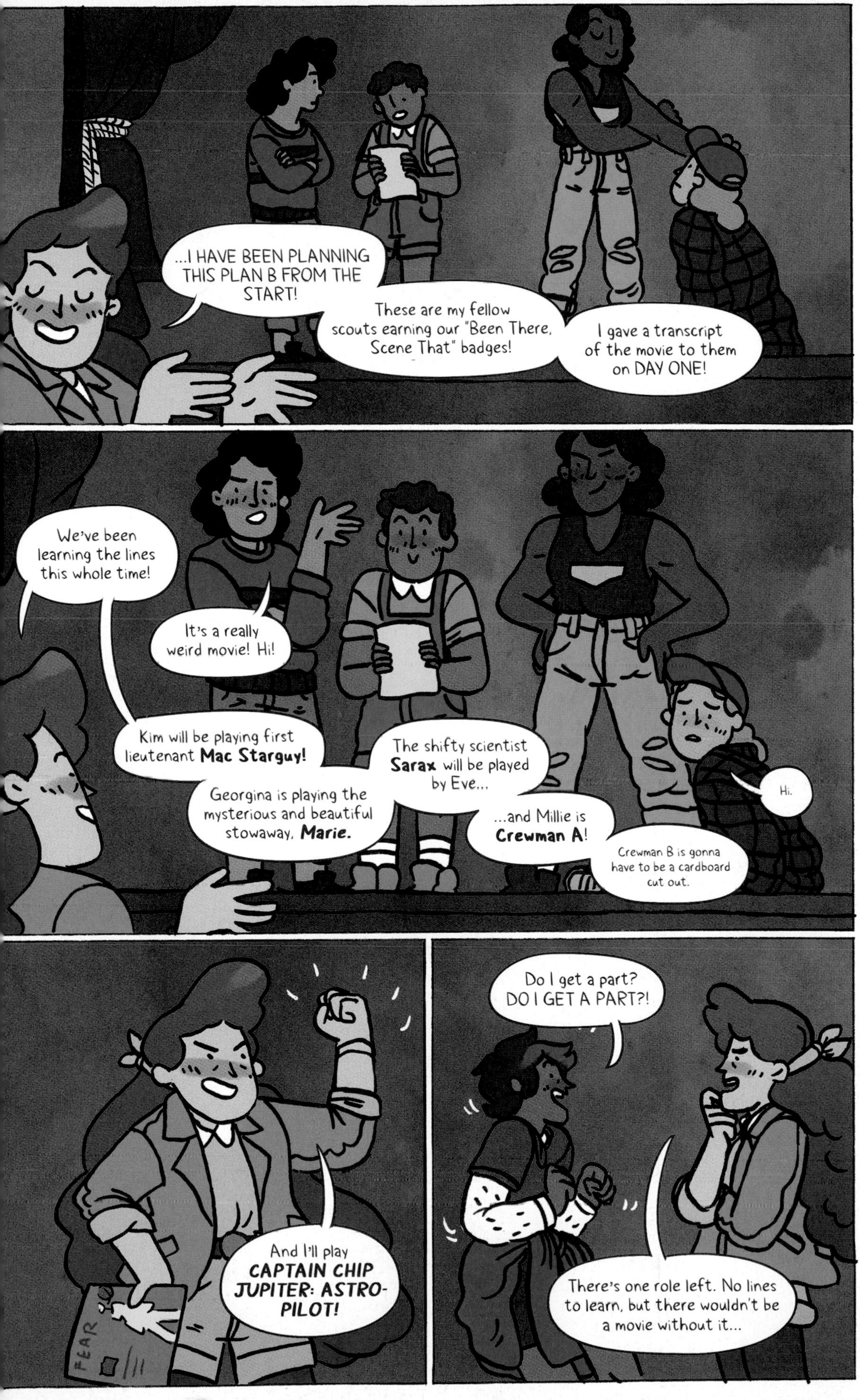
...I HAVE BEEN PLANNING THIS PLAN B FROM THE START!
These are my fellow scouts earning our "Been There, Scene That" badges!
I gave a transcript of the movie to them on DAY ONE!
We've been learning the lines this whole time!
It's a really weird movie! Hi!
Kim will be playing first lieutenant **Mac Starguy!**
Georgina is playing the mysterious and beautiful stowaway, **Marie.**
The shifty scientist **Sarax** will be played by Eve...
...and Millie is **Crewman A**!
Hi.
Crewman B is gonna have to be a cardboard cut out.
And I'll play **CAPTAIN CHIP JUPITER: ASTRO-PILOT!**
FEAR
Do I get a part? DO I GET A PART?!
There's one role left. No lines to learn, but there wouldn't be a movie without it...

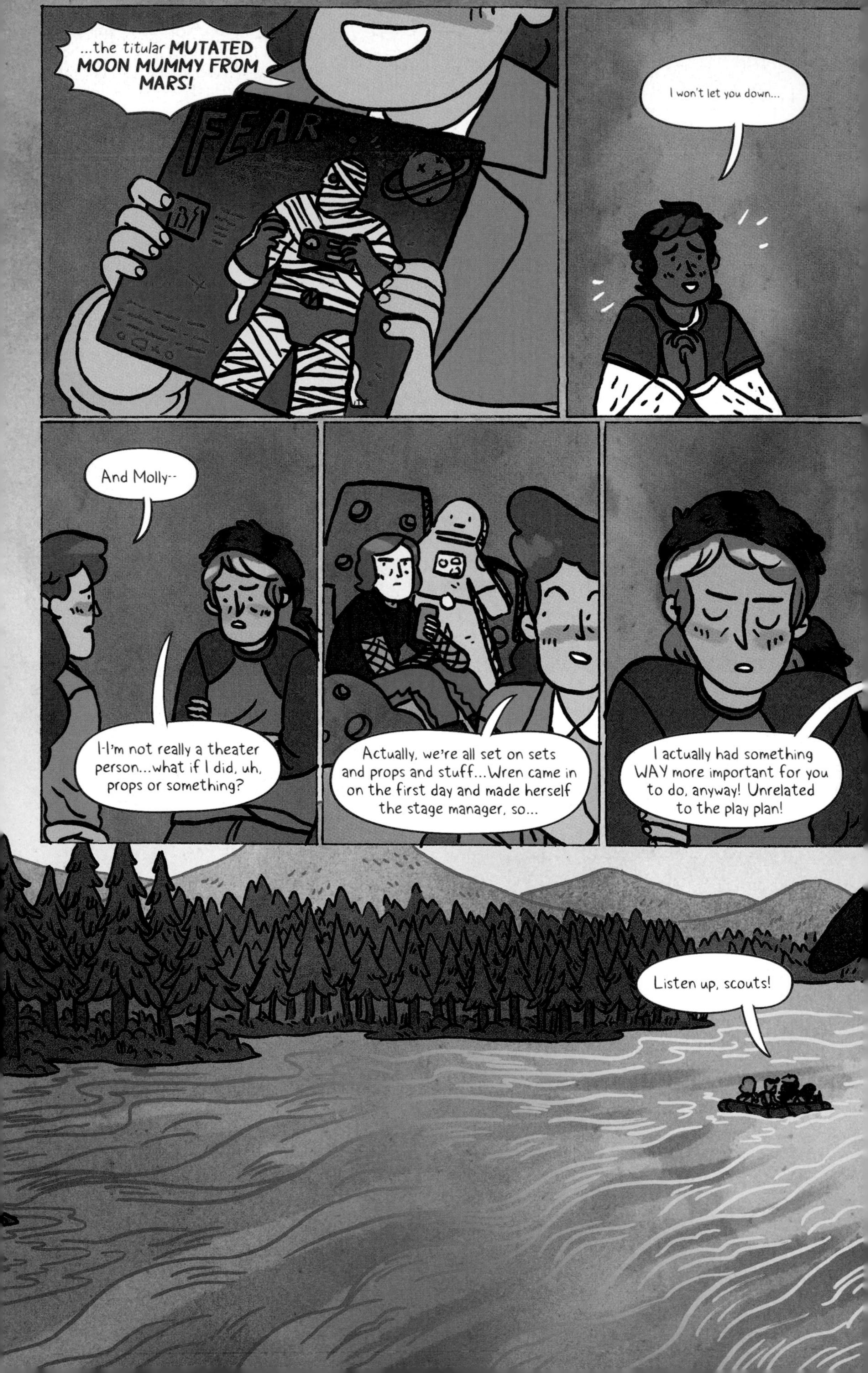
...the titular MUTATED MOON MUMMY FROM MARS!
FEAR
I won't let you down...
And Molly--
I-I'm not really a theater person...what if I did, uh, props or something?
Actually, we're all set on sets and props and stuff...Wren came in on the first day and made herself the stage manager, so...
I actually had something WAY more important for you to do, anyway! Unrelated to the play plan!
Listen up, scouts!

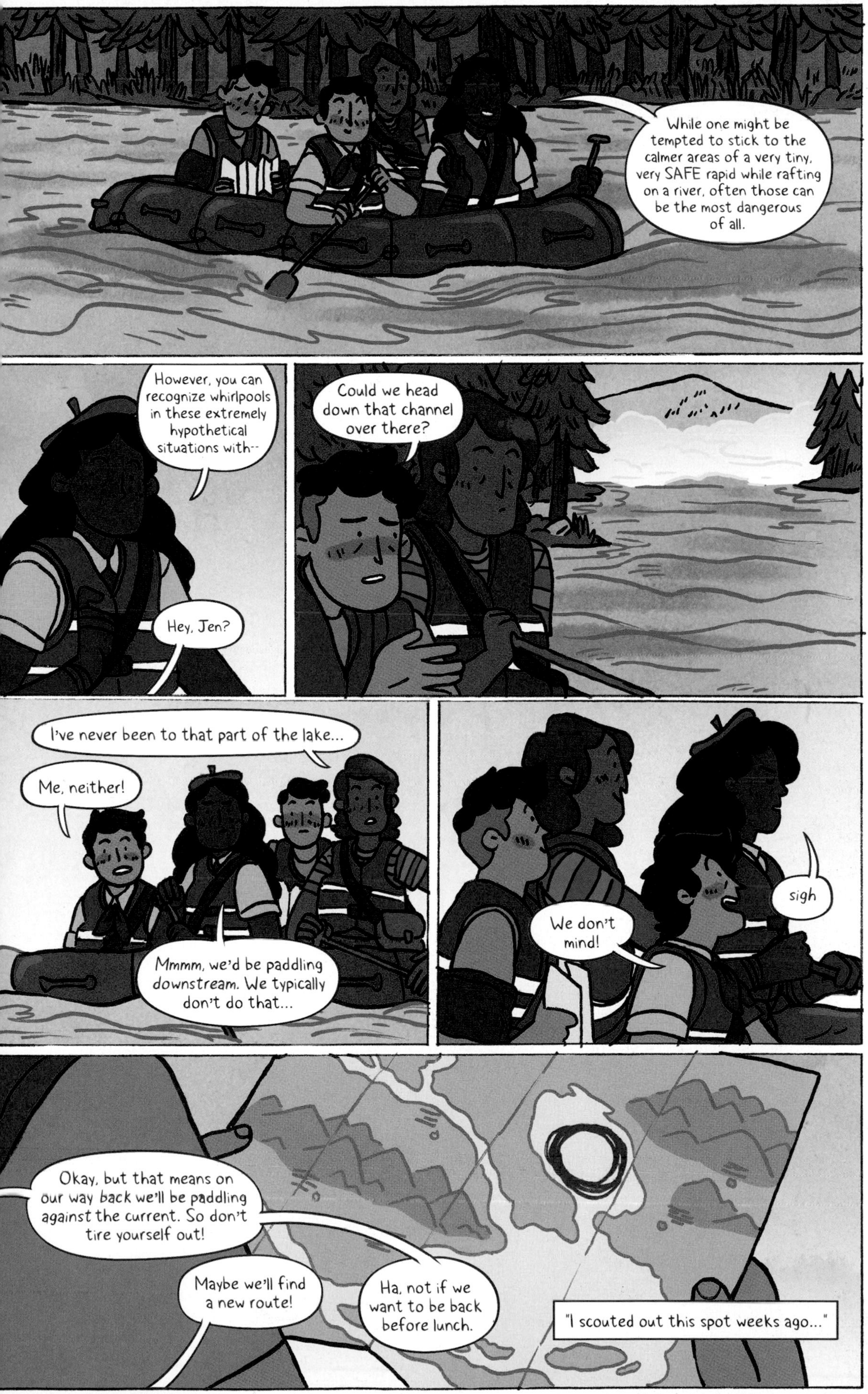
While one might be tempted to stick to the calmer areas of a very tiny, very SAFE rapid while rafting on a river, often those can be the most dangerous of all.
However, you can recognize whirlpools in these extremely hypothetical situations with--
Hey, Jen?
Could we head down that channel over there?
I've never been to that part of the lake...
Me, neither!
Mmmm, we'd be paddling downstream. We typically don't do that...
We don't mind!
sigh
Okay, but that means on our way *back* we'll be paddling against the current. So don't tire yourself out!
Maybe we'll find a new route!
Ha, not if we want to be back before lunch.
"I scouted out this spot weeks ago..."

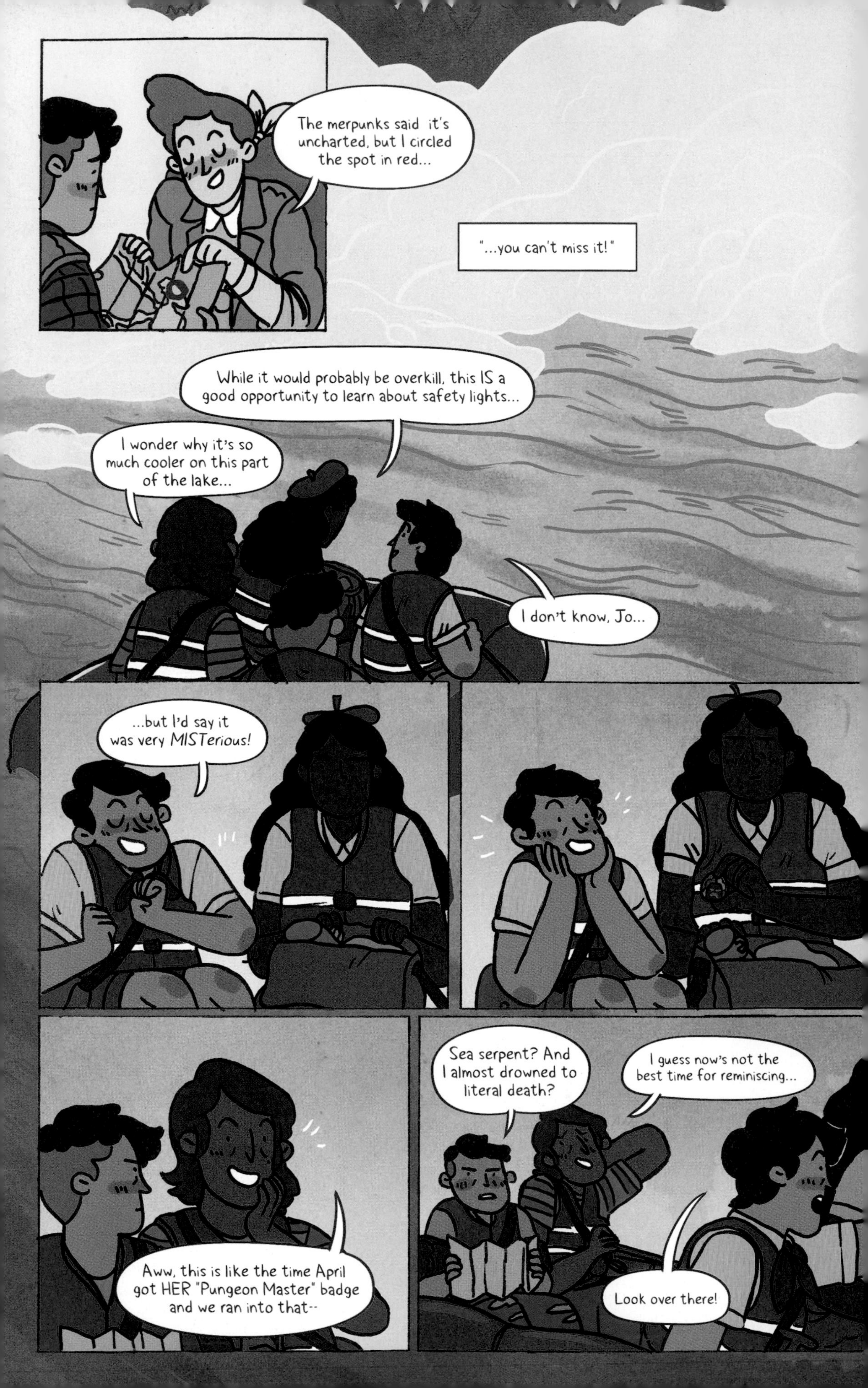
The merpunks said it's uncharted, but I circled the spot in red...
"...you can't miss it!"
While it would probably be overkill, this IS a good opportunity to learn about safety lights...
I wonder why it's so much cooler on this part of the lake...
I don't know, Jo...
...but I'd say it was very MISTerious!
Aww, this is like the time April got HER "Pungeon Master" badge and we ran into that--
Sea serpent? And I almost drowned to literal death?
I guess now's not the best time for reminiscing...
Look over there!

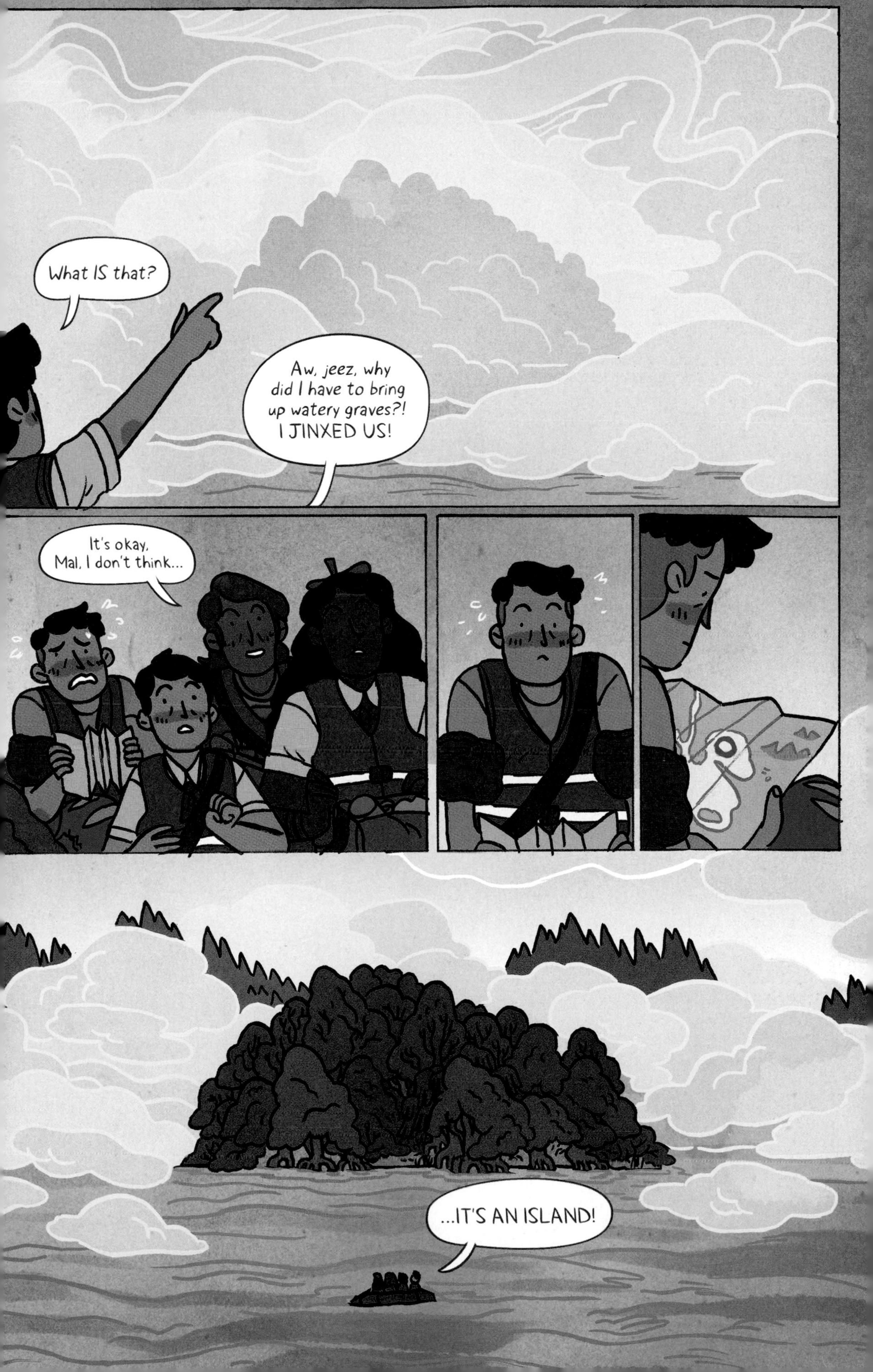
What IS that?
Aw, jeez, why did I have to bring up watery graves?! I JINXED US!
It's okay, Mal, I don't think...
...IT'S AN ISLAND!

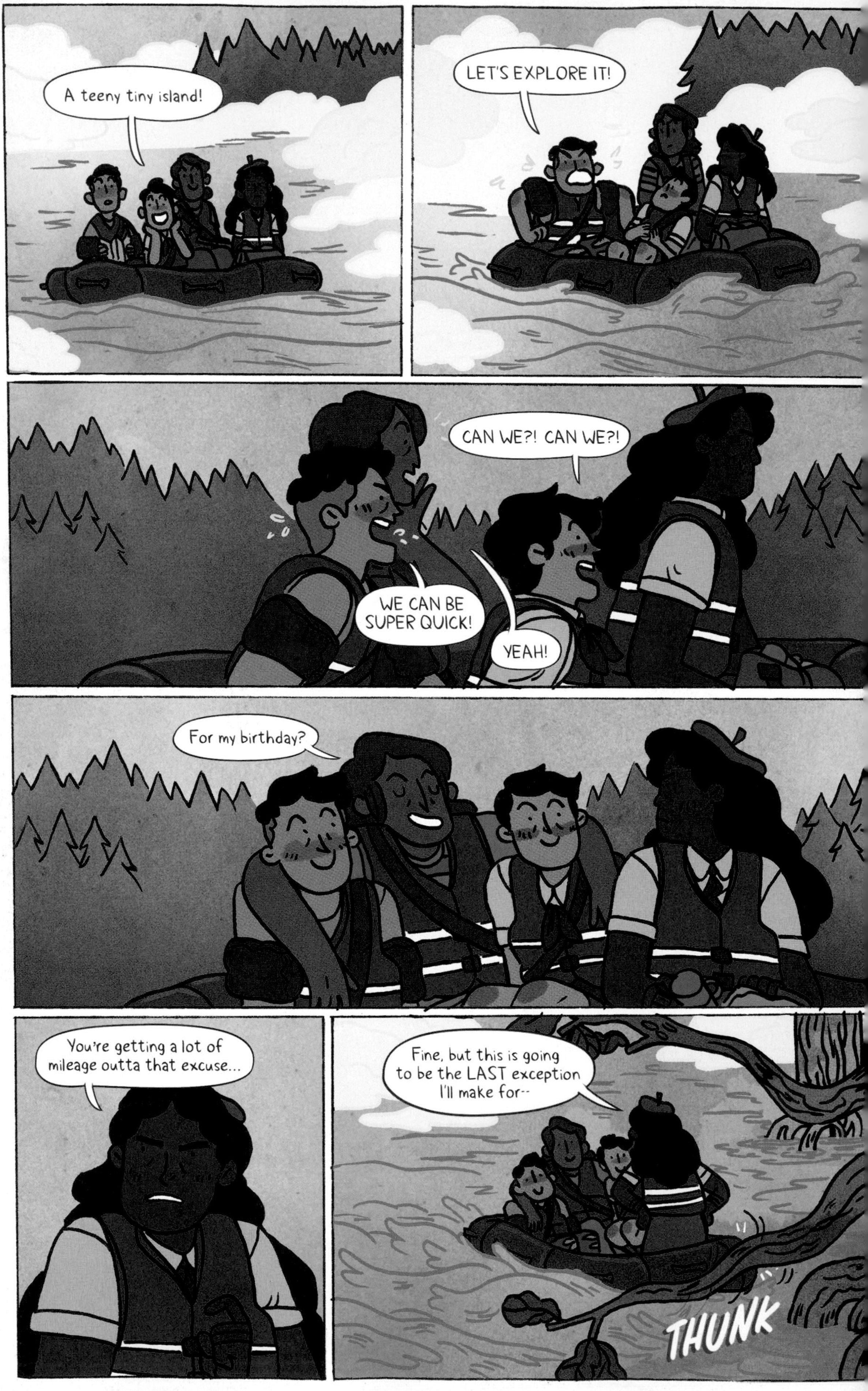
A teeny tiny island!
LET'S EXPLORE IT!
CAN WE?! CAN WE?!
WE CAN BE SUPER QUICK!
YEAH!
For my birthday?
You're getting a lot of mileage outta that excuse...
Fine, but this is going to be the LAST exception I'll make for--
THUNK

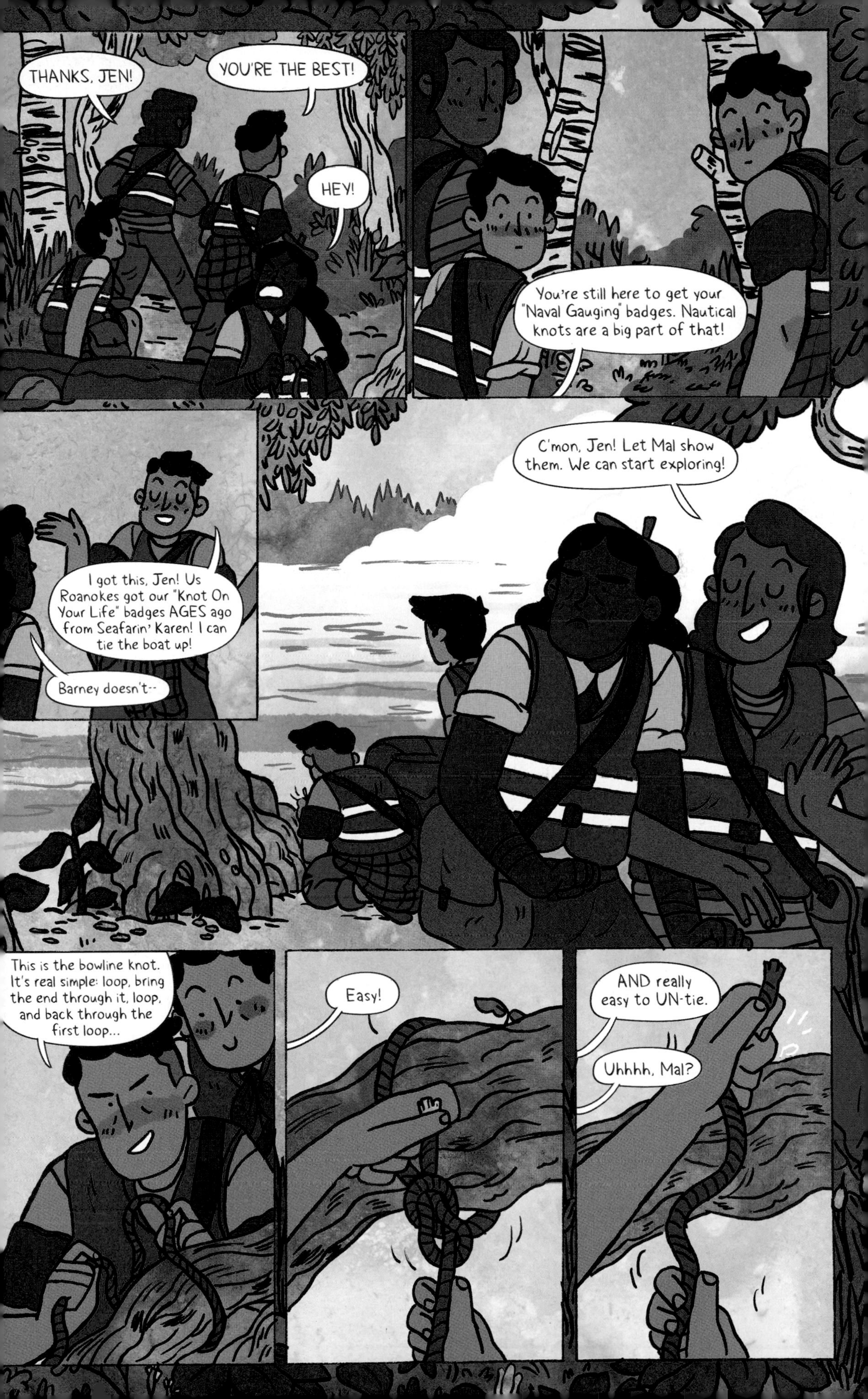
THANKS, JEN!
YOU'RE THE BEST!
HEY!
You're still here to get your "Naval Gauging" badges. Nautical knots are a big part of that!
I got this, Jen! Us Roanokes got our "Knot On Your Life" badges AGES ago from Seafarin' Karen! I can tie the boat up!
Barney doesn't--
C'mon, Jen! Let Mal show them. We can start exploring!
This is the bowline knot. It's real simple: loop, bring the end through it, loop, and back through the first loop...
Easy!
AND really easy to UN-tie.
Uhhhh, Mal?

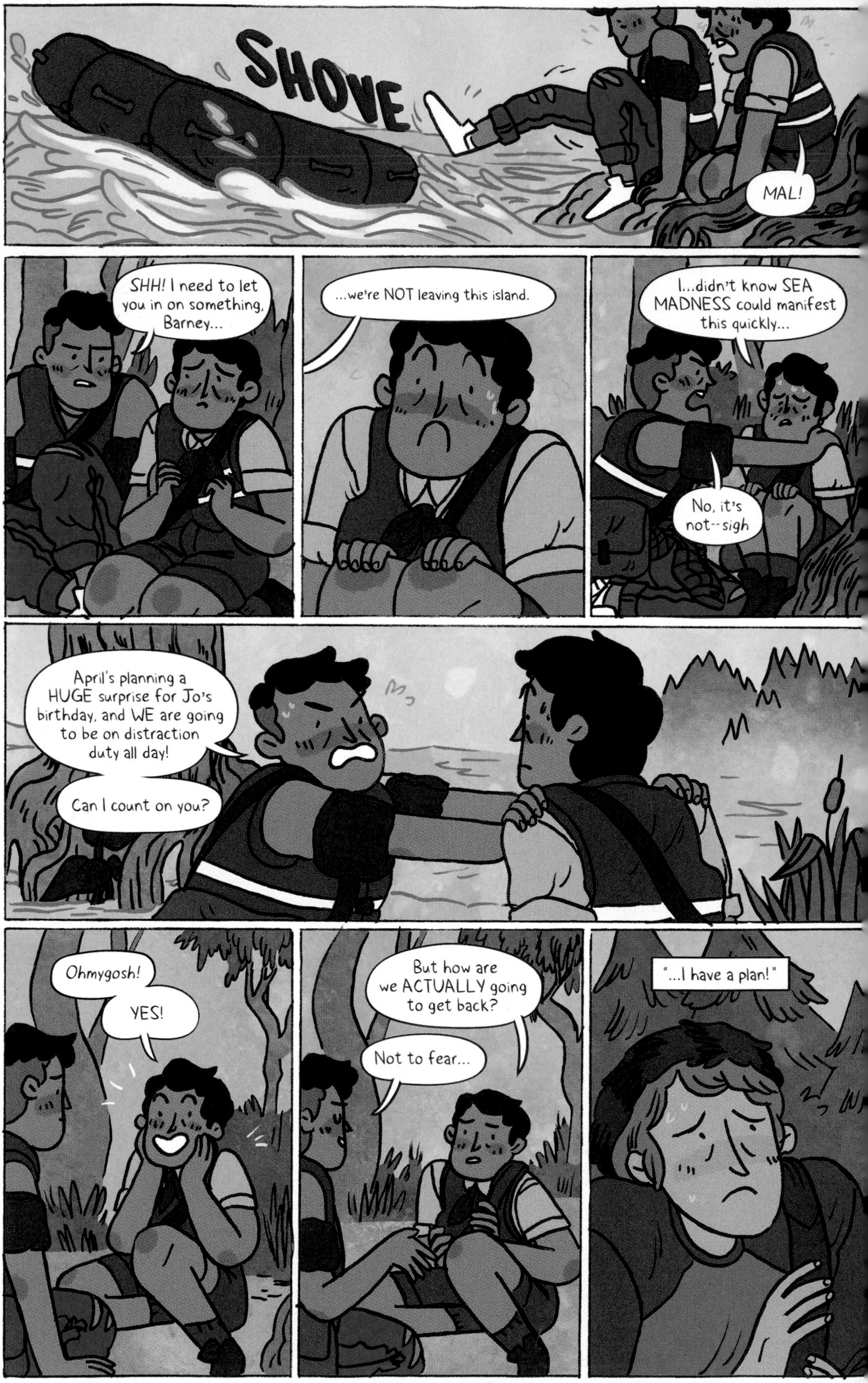
SHOVE
MAL!
SHH! I need to let you in on something, Barney...
...we're NOT leaving this island.
I...didn't know SEA MADNESS could manifest this quickly...
No, it's not--sigh
April's planning a HUGE surprise for Jo's birthday, and WE are going to be on distraction duty all day!
Can I count on you?
Ohmygosh!
YES!
But how are we ACTUALLY going to get back?
Not to fear...
"...I have a plan!"

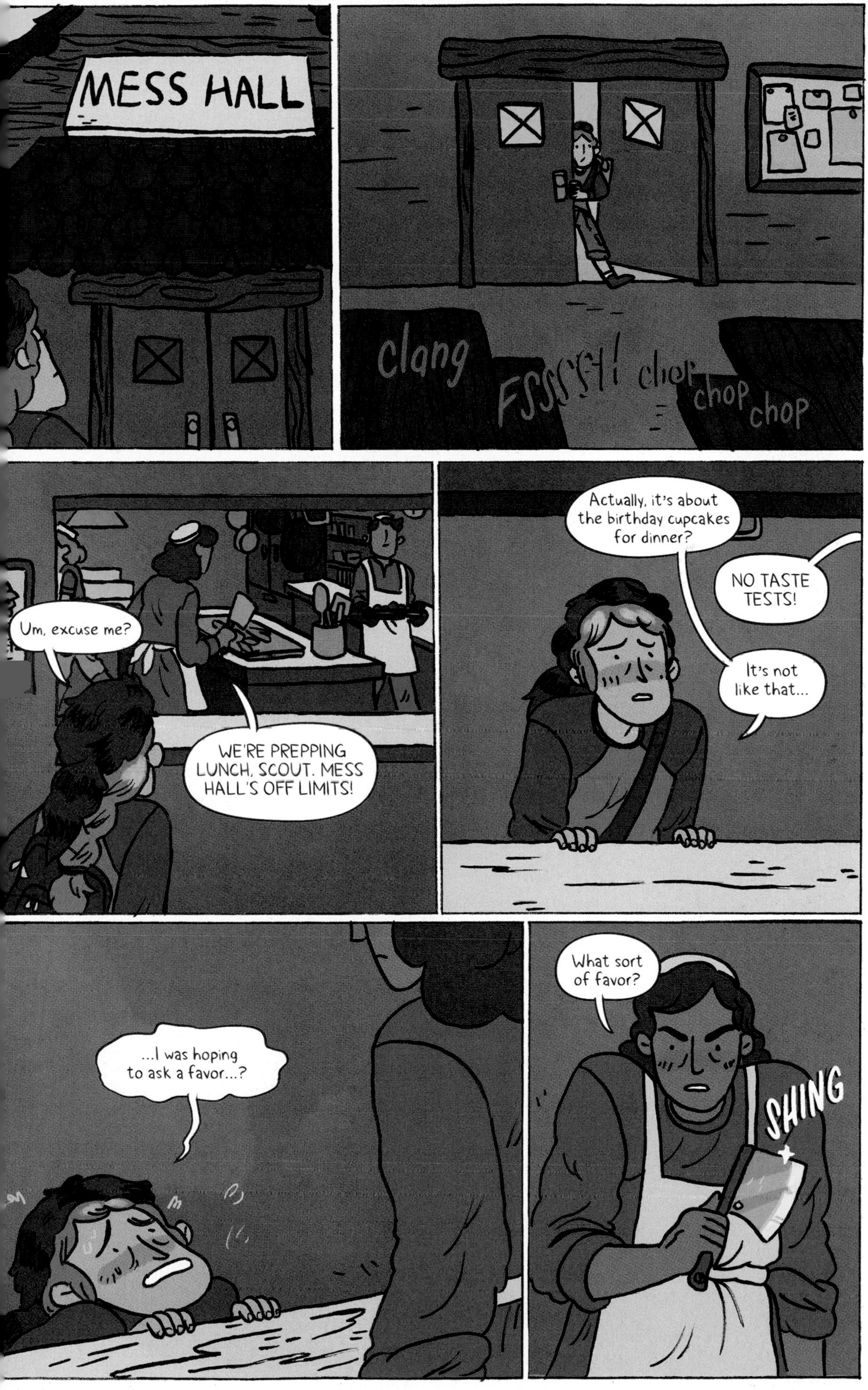
MESS HALL
clang
FSSSSH!
chop
chop
chop
Um, excuse me?
WE'RE PREPPING LUNCH, SCOUT. MESS HALL'S OFF LIMITS!
Actually, it's about the birthday cupcakes for dinner?
NO TASTE TESTS!
It's not like that...
...I was hoping to ask a favor...?
What sort of favor?
SHING

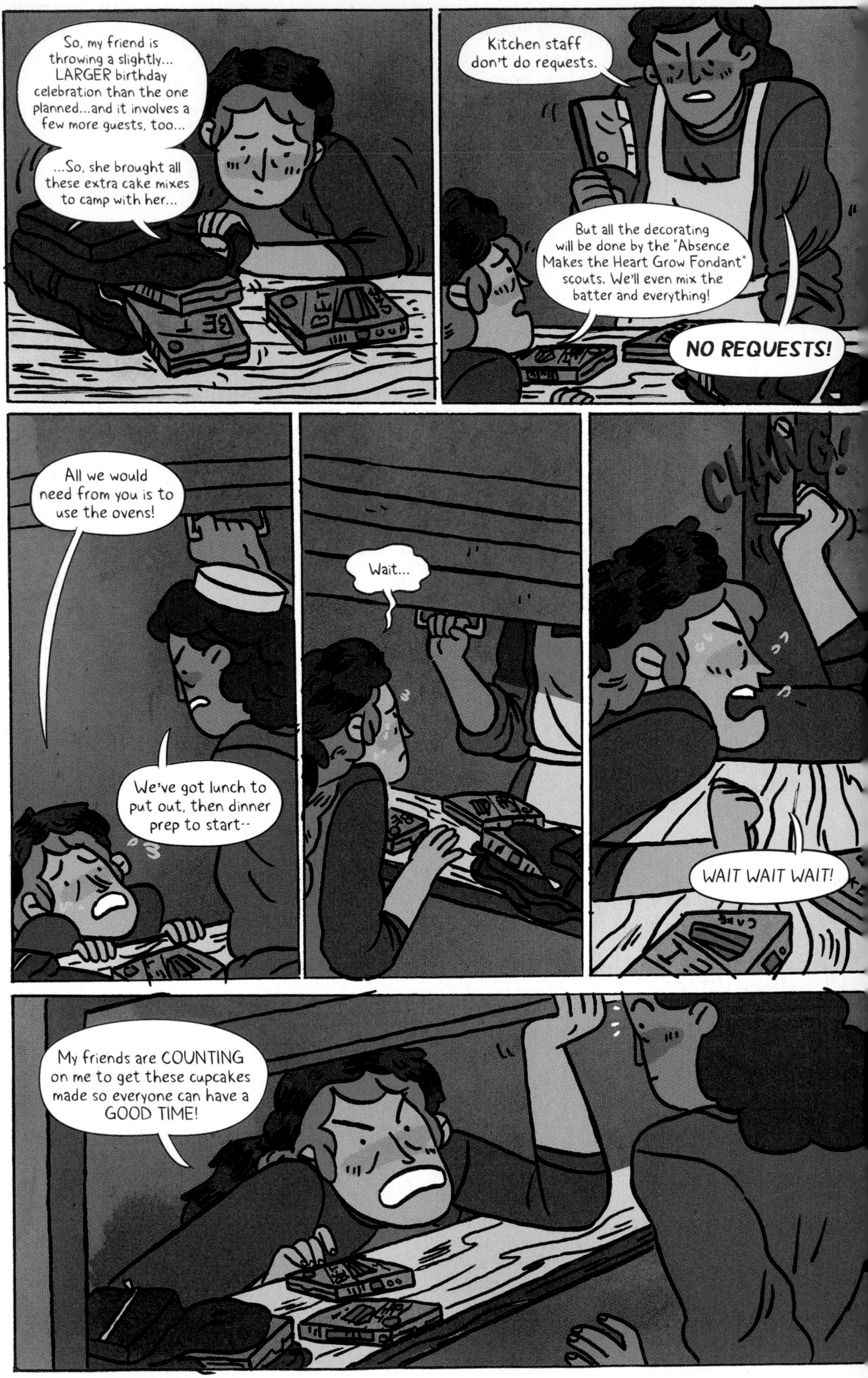
So, my friend is throwing a slightly... LARGER birthday celebration than the one planned...and it involves a few more guests, too...
...So, she brought all these extra cake mixes to camp with her...
Kitchen staff don't do requests.
But all the decorating will be done by the "Absence Makes the Heart Grow Fondant" scouts. We'll even mix the batter and everything!
NO REQUESTS!
All we would need from you is to use the ovens!
We've got lunch to put out, then dinner prep to start--
Wait...
CLANG!
WAIT WAIT WAIT!
My friends are COUNTING on me to get these cupcakes made so everyone can have a GOOD TIME!

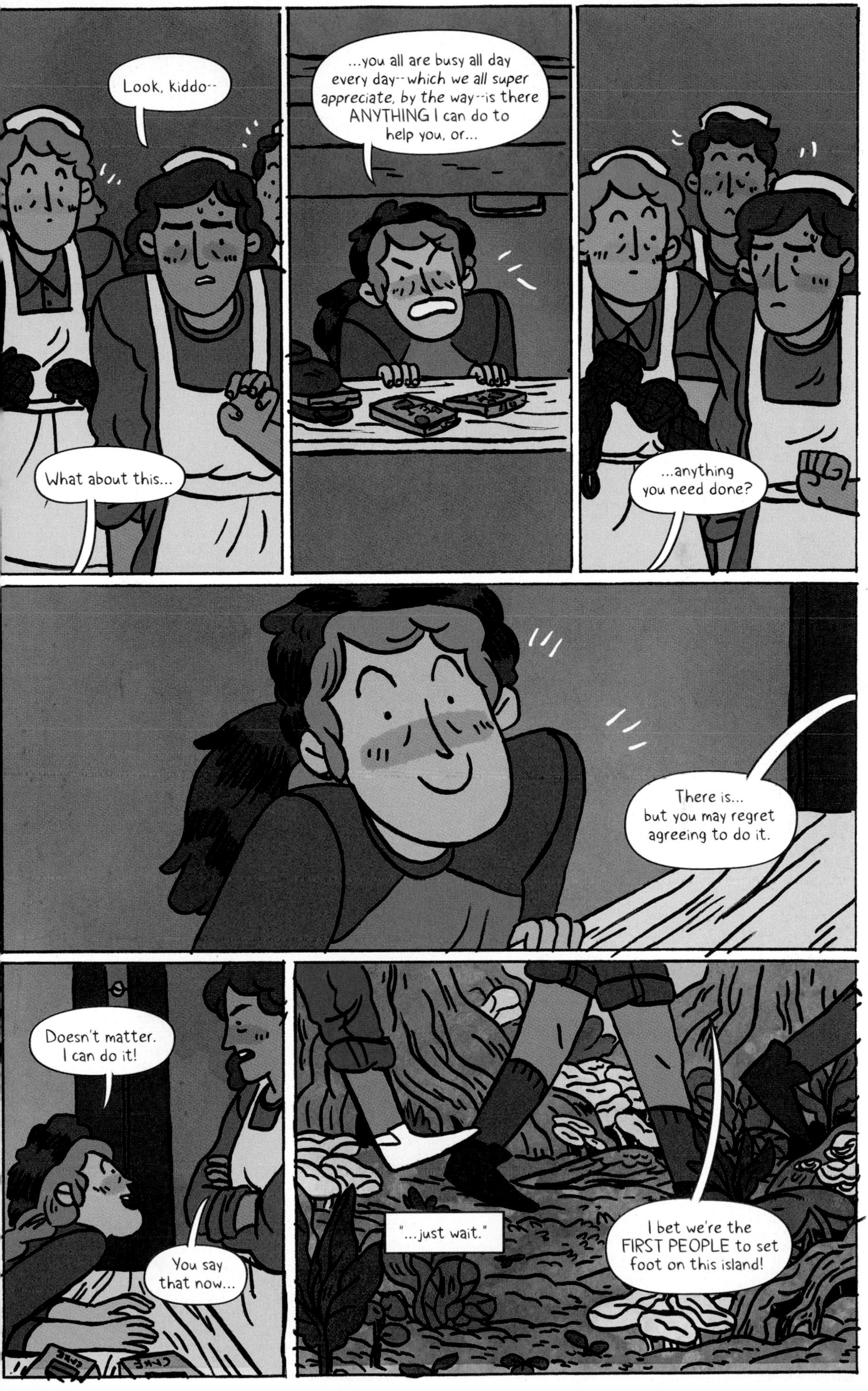
Look, kiddo--
What about this...
...you all are busy all day every day--which we all super appreciate, by the way--is there ANYTHING I can do to help you, or...
...anything you need done?
There is... but you may regret agreeing to do it.
Doesn't matter. I can do it!
You say that now...
"...just wait."
I bet we're the FIRST PEOPLE to set foot on this island!

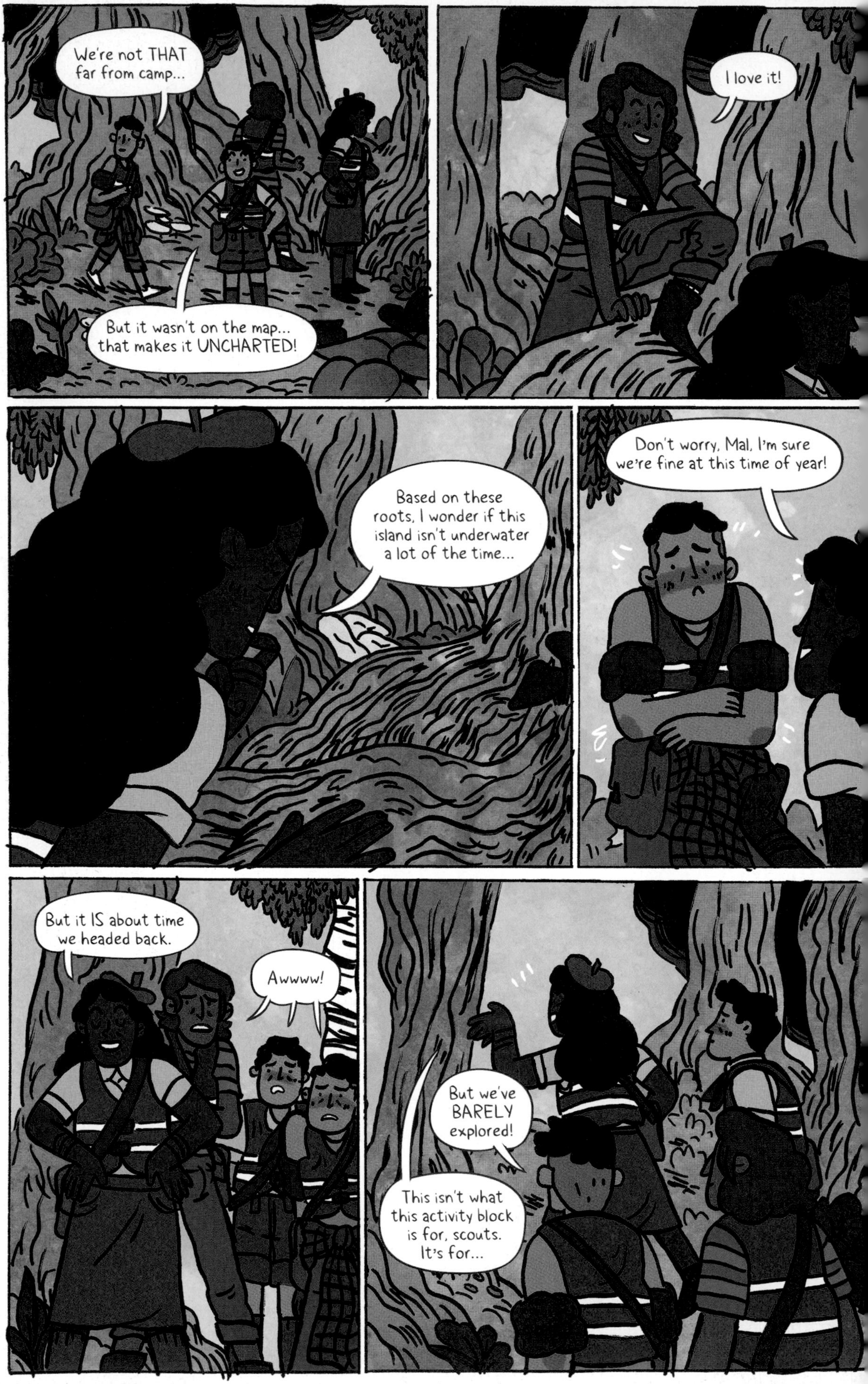
We're not THAT far from camp...
But it wasn't on the map... that makes it UNCHARTED!
I love it!
Based on these roots, I wonder if this island isn't underwater a lot of the time...
Don't worry, Mal, I'm sure we're fine at this time of year!
But it IS about time we headed back.
Awwww!
But we've BARELY explored!
This isn't what this activity block is for, scouts. It's for...

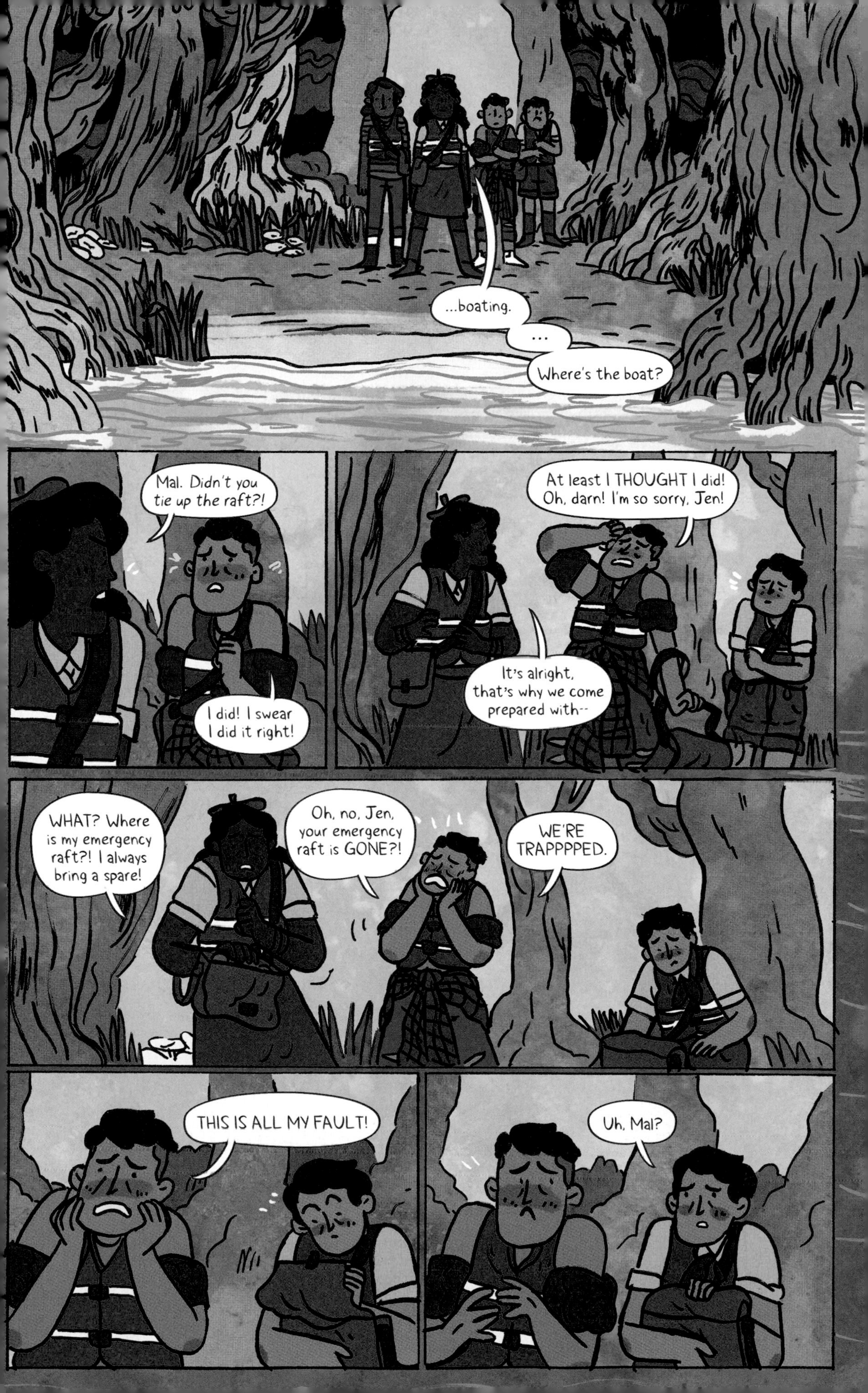
...boating.
...
Where's the boat?
Mal. Didn't you tie up the raft?!
I did! I swear I did it right!
At least I THOUGHT I did! Oh, darn! I'm so sorry, Jen!
It's alright, that's why we come prepared with--
WHAT? Where is my emergency raft?! I always bring a spare!
Oh, no, Jen, your emergency raft is GONE?!
WE'RE TRAPPPPED.
THIS IS ALL MY FAULT!
Uh, Mal?

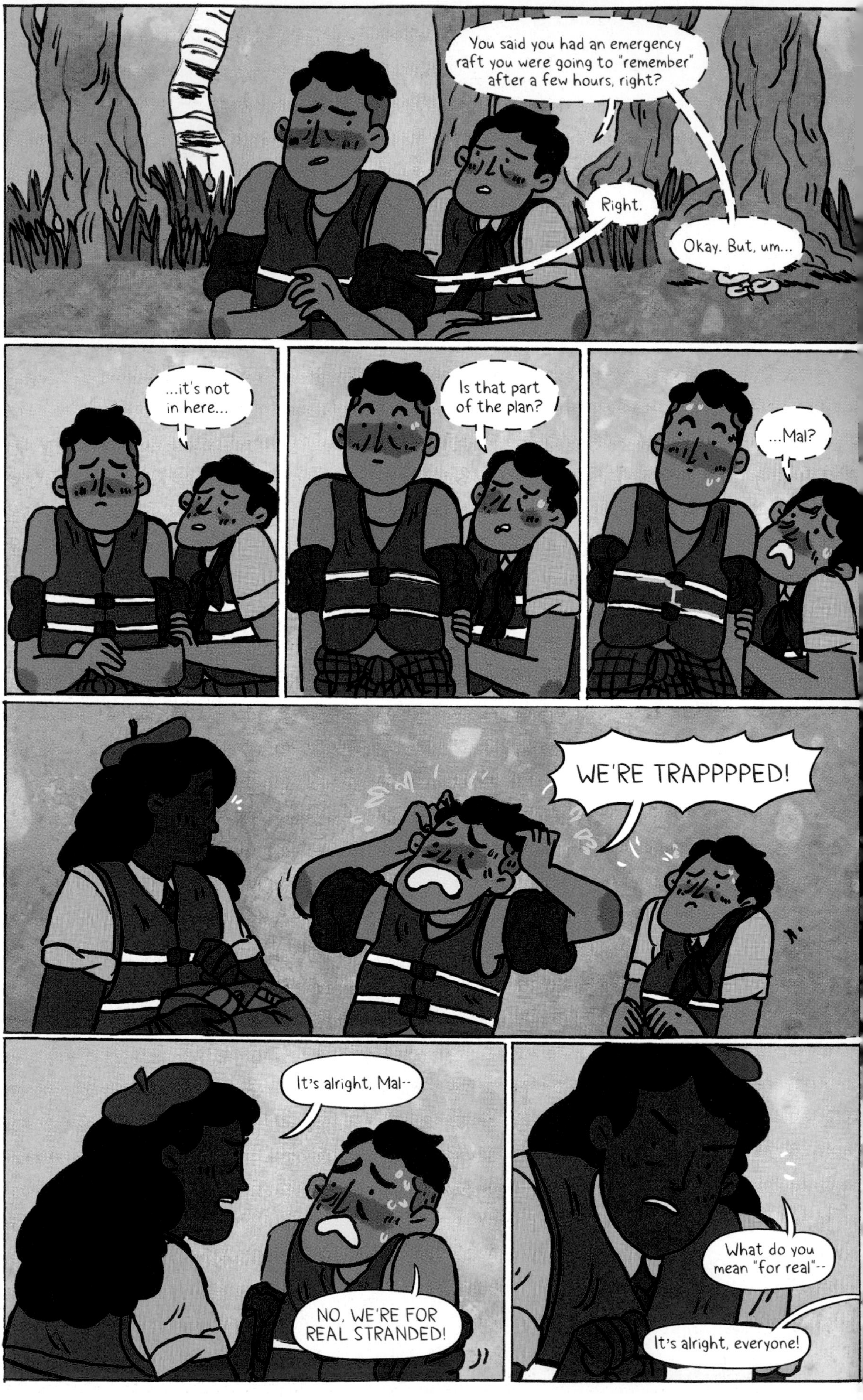
You said you had an emergency raft you were going to "remember" after a few hours, right?
Right.
Okay. But, um...
...it's not in here...
Is that part of the plan?
...Mal?
WE'RE TRAPPPPED!
It's alright, Mal--
NO, WE'RE FOR REAL STRANDED!
What do you mean "for real"--
It's alright, everyone!

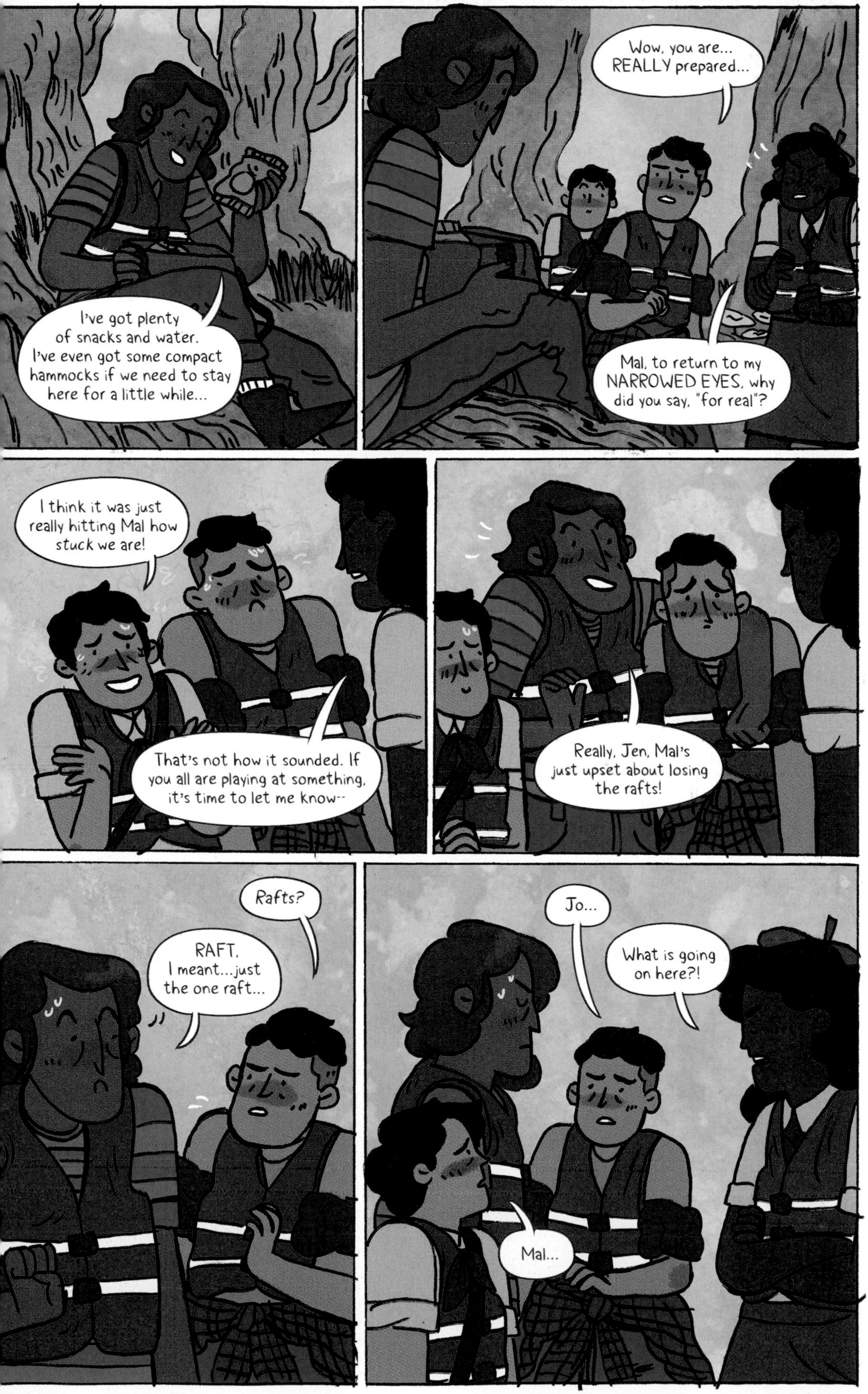
I've got plenty of snacks and water. I've even got some compact hammocks if we need to stay here for a little while...
Wow, you are... REALLY prepared...
Mal, to return to my NARROWED EYES, why did you say, "for real"?
I think it was just really hitting Mal how *stuck* we are!
That's not how it sounded. If you all are playing at something, it's time to let me know--
Really, Jen, Mal's just upset about losing the rafts!
Rafts?
RAFT, I meant...just the one raft...
Jo...
What is going on here?!
Mal...

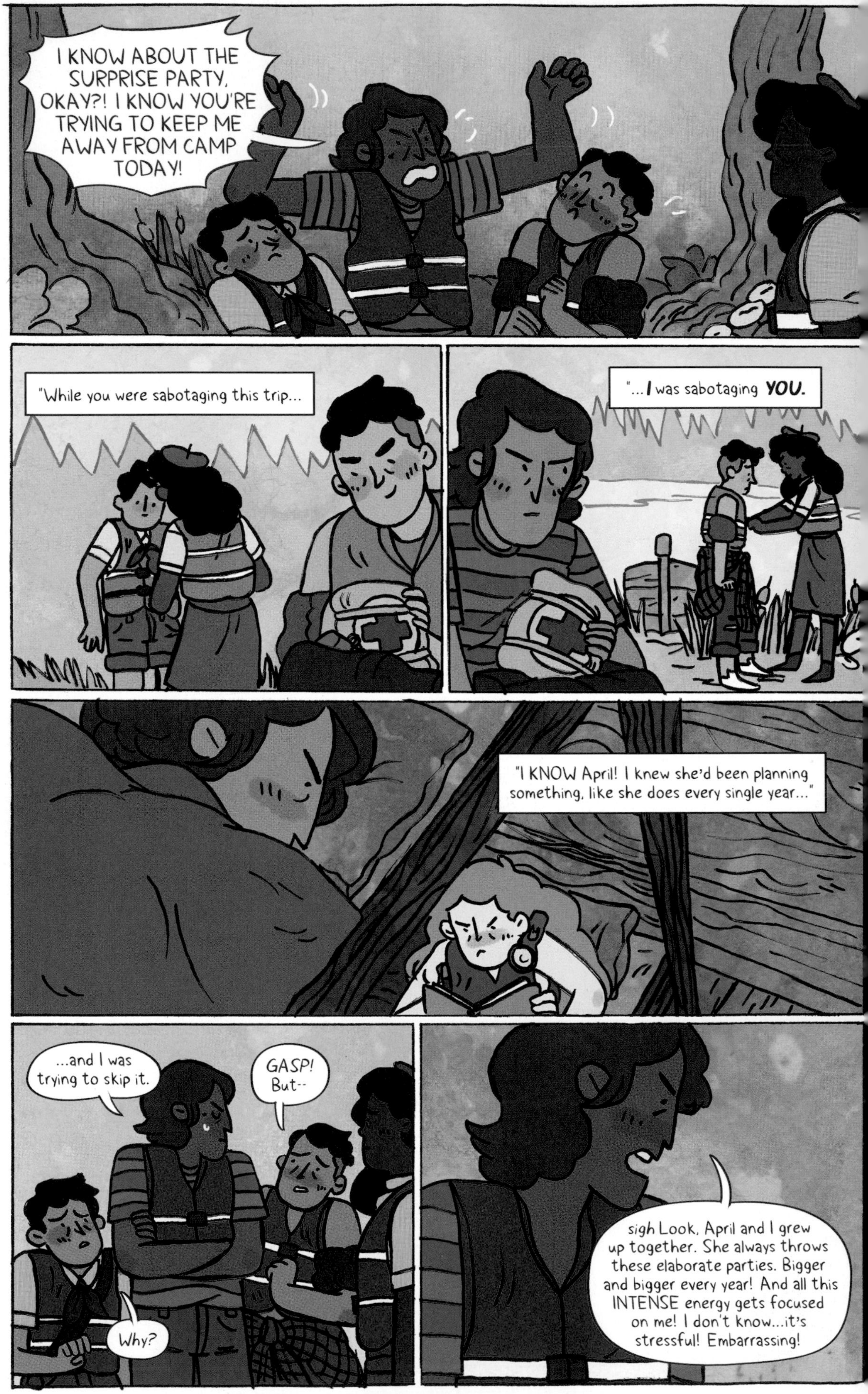
I KNOW ABOUT THE SURPRISE PARTY, OKAY?! I KNOW YOU'RE TRYING TO KEEP ME AWAY FROM CAMP TODAY!
"While you were sabotaging this trip...
"...I was sabotaging YOU.
"I KNOW April! I knew she'd been planning something, like she does every single year..."
...and I was trying to skip it.
GASP! But--
Why?
sigh Look, April and I grew up together. She always throws these elaborate parties. Bigger and bigger every year! And all this INTENSE energy gets focused on me! I don't know...it's stressful! Embarrassing!

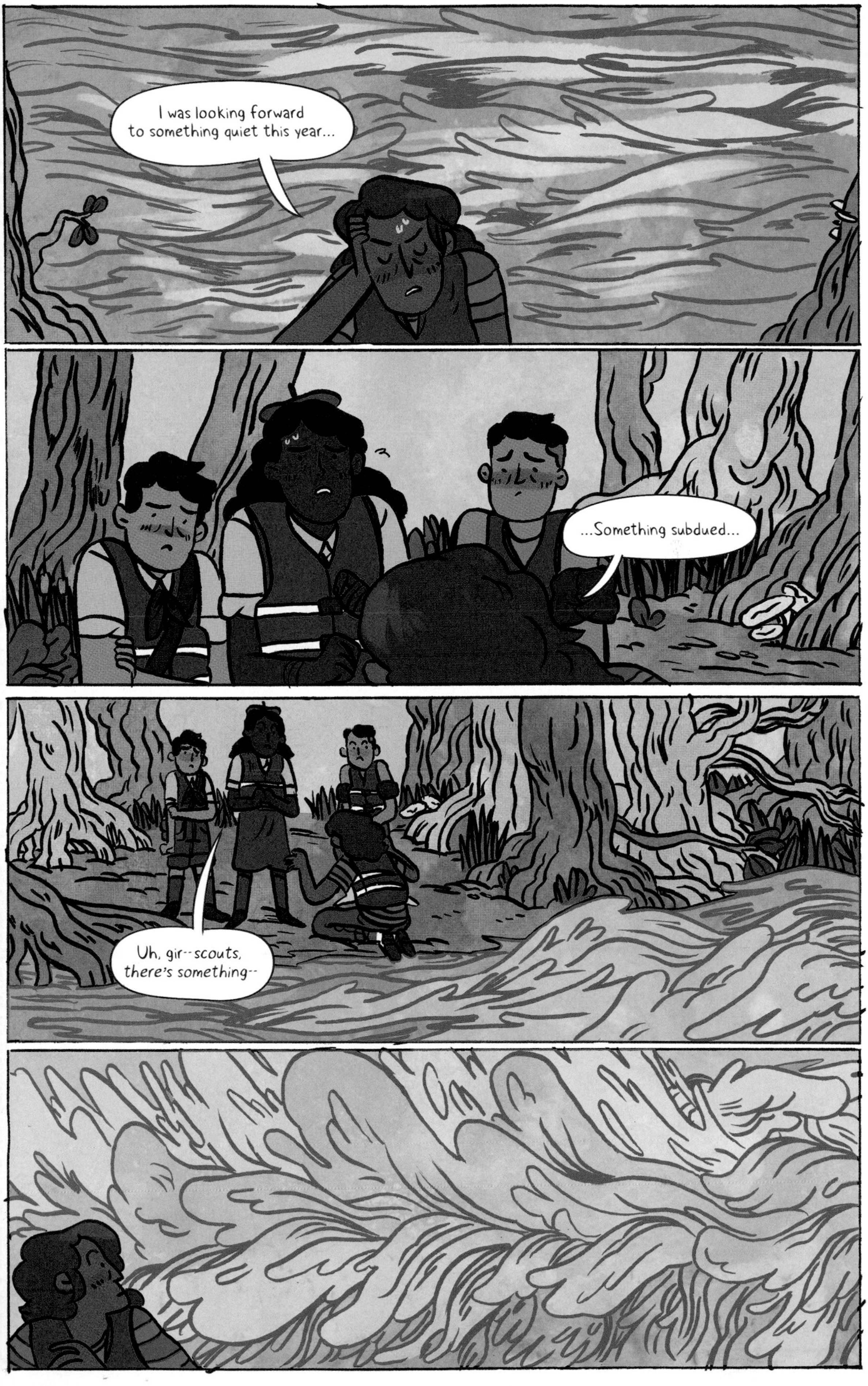
I was looking forward to something quiet this year...
...Something subdued...
Uh, gir--scouts, there's something--

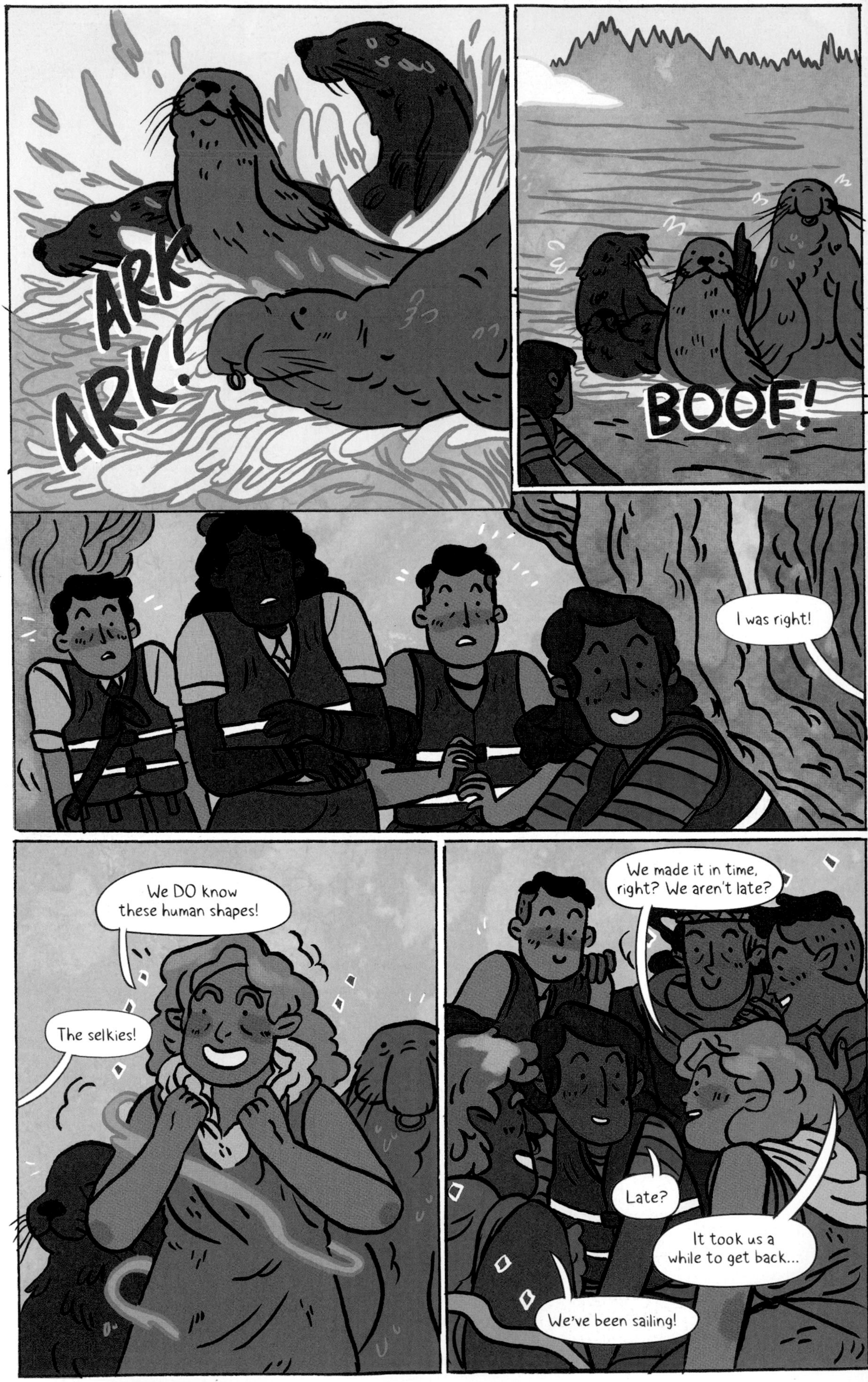
ARK ARK!
BOOF!
I was right!
We DO know these human shapes!
The selkies!
We made it in time, right? We aren't late?
Late?
It took us a while to get back...
We've been sailing!

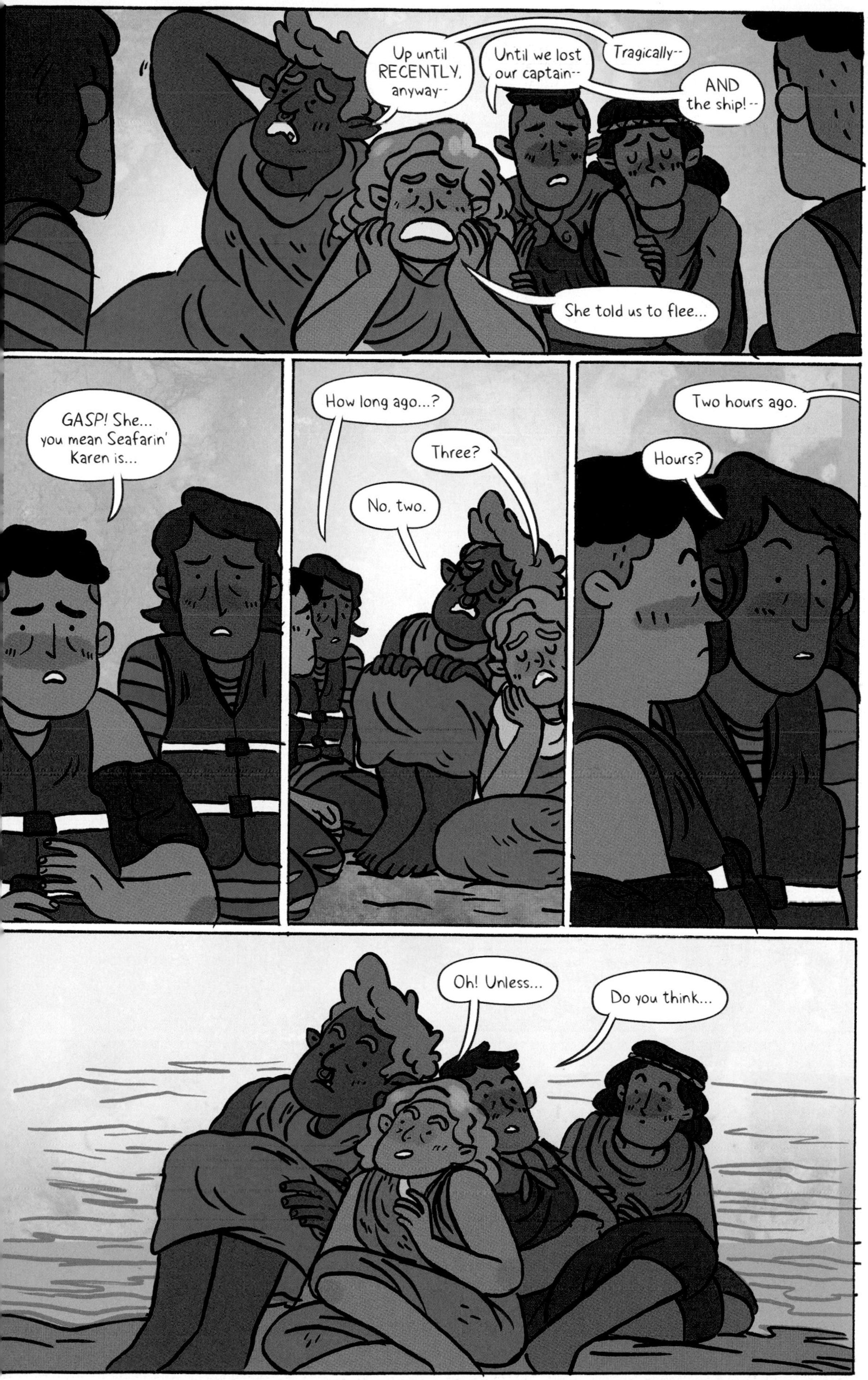
Up until RECENTLY, anyway--
Until we lost our captain--
Tragically--
AND the ship!--
She told us to flee...
GASP! She... you mean Seafarin' Karen is...
How long ago...?
Three?
No, two.
Two hours ago.
Hours?
Oh! Unless...
Do you think...

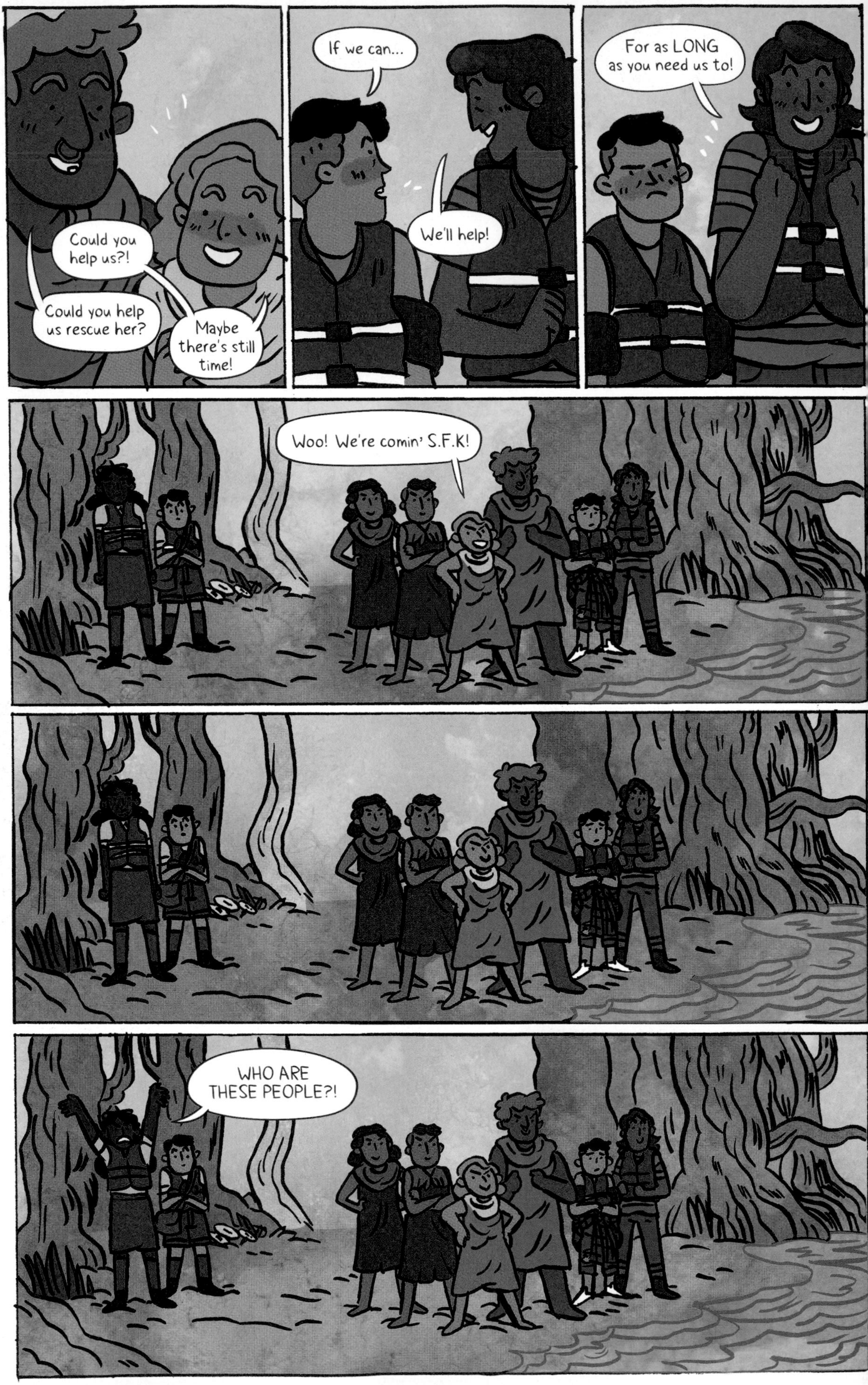
Could you help us?!
Could you help us rescue her?
Maybe there's still time!
If we can...
We'll help!
For as LONG as you need us to!
Woo! We're comin' S.F.K!
WHO ARE THESE PEOPLE?!

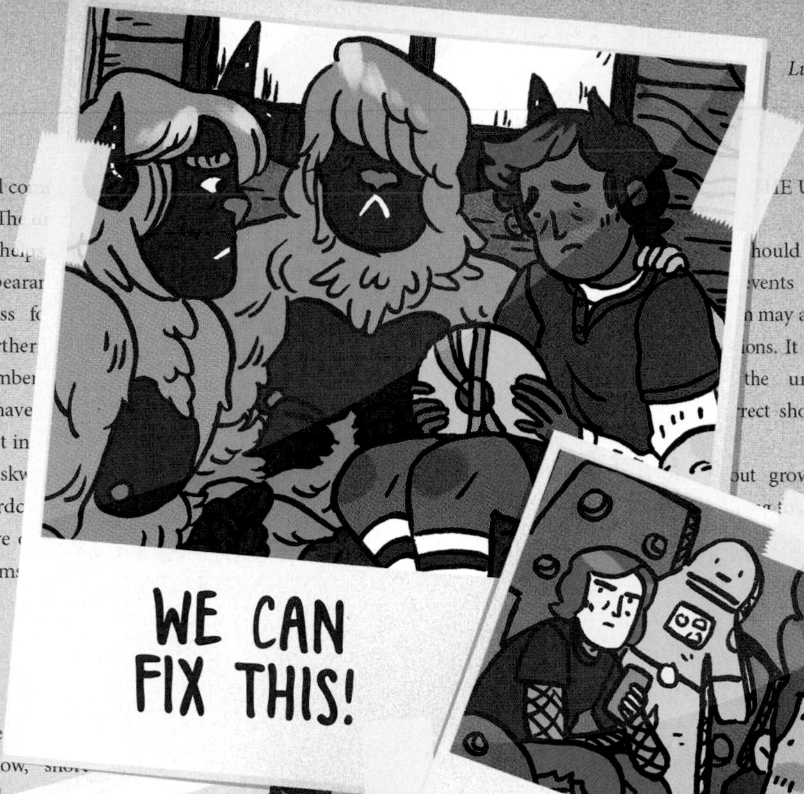
WE CAN
FIX THIS!

will co
The
It h
appearan
dress f
Further
Lumbe
to have
part in
Thiskw
Hardc
have
thems

IE UNIFORM

hould be worn at camp
events when Lumberjanes
n may also be worn at other
ions. It should be worn as a
the uniform dress with
rect shoes, and stocking or

out grows her uniform or
other Lumberjane.
a she has
her
her

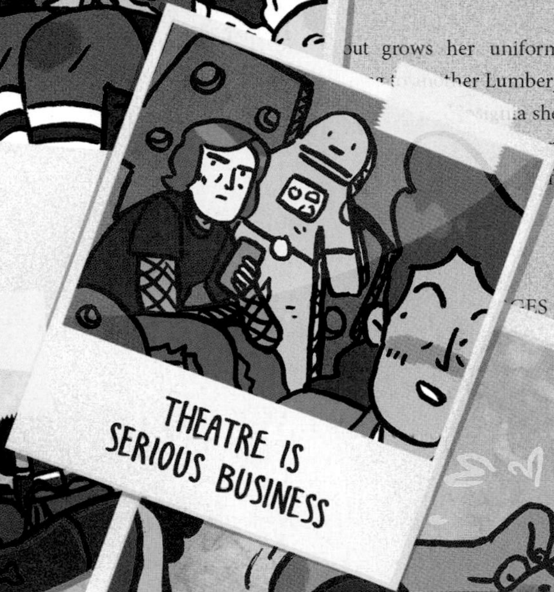
THEATRE IS
SERIOUS BUSINESS

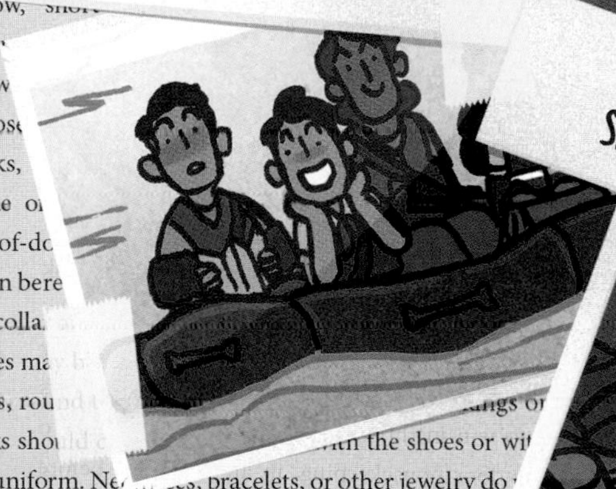

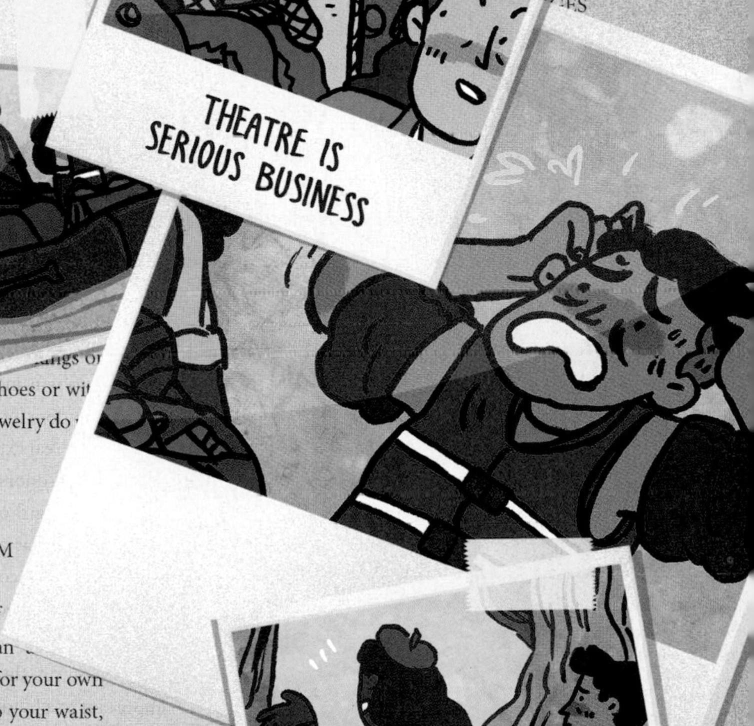

The
yellow,
emb
the w
choose
slacks,
made o
out-of-do
green bere
the colla
Shoes ma
heels, rou … ings or
socks shou … with the shoes or wi
the uniform. Ne … es, bracelets, or other jewelry do
belong with a Lumberjane uniform.

GES

HOW TO WEAR THE UNIFORM

To look well in a uniform demands first of … uniform be kept in good condition—clean … pressed. See that the skirt is the right length for your own height and build, that the belt is adjusted to your waist, that your shoes and stockings are in keeping with the uniform, that you watch your posture and carry yourself with dignity and grace. If the beret is removed indoors, be sure that your hair is neat and kept in place with an inconspicuous clip or ribbon. When you wear a Lumberjane uniform you are identified as a member of this organization and you should be doubly careful to conduct yourself in a way that will show everyone that courtesy and thoughtfulness are part of being a Lumberjane. People are likely to judge a whole nation by the selfishness of a few individuals, to criticize a whole family because of the misconduct of one member, and to feel unkindly toward an organization because of the

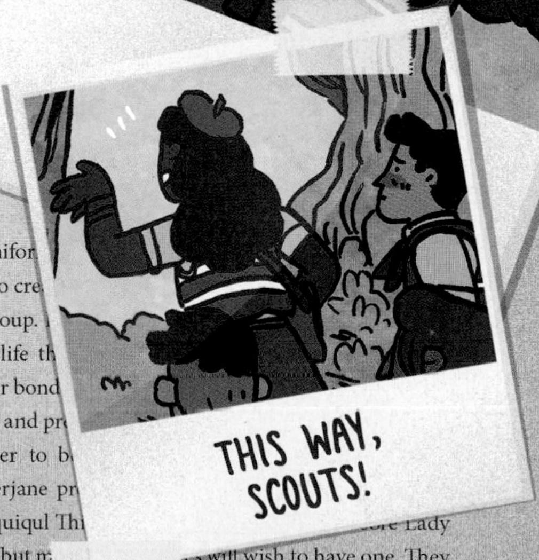
THIS WAY,
SCOUTS!

The unifor
helps to cre
in a group.
active life th
another bond
future, and pr
in order to b
Lumberjane pr
Penniquiqul Thi … ore Lady
Types, but m … s will wish to have one. They
can either b … , or make it themselves from
materials available at the trading post.

LUMBERJANES FIELD MANUAL

CHAPTER FIFTY-NINE

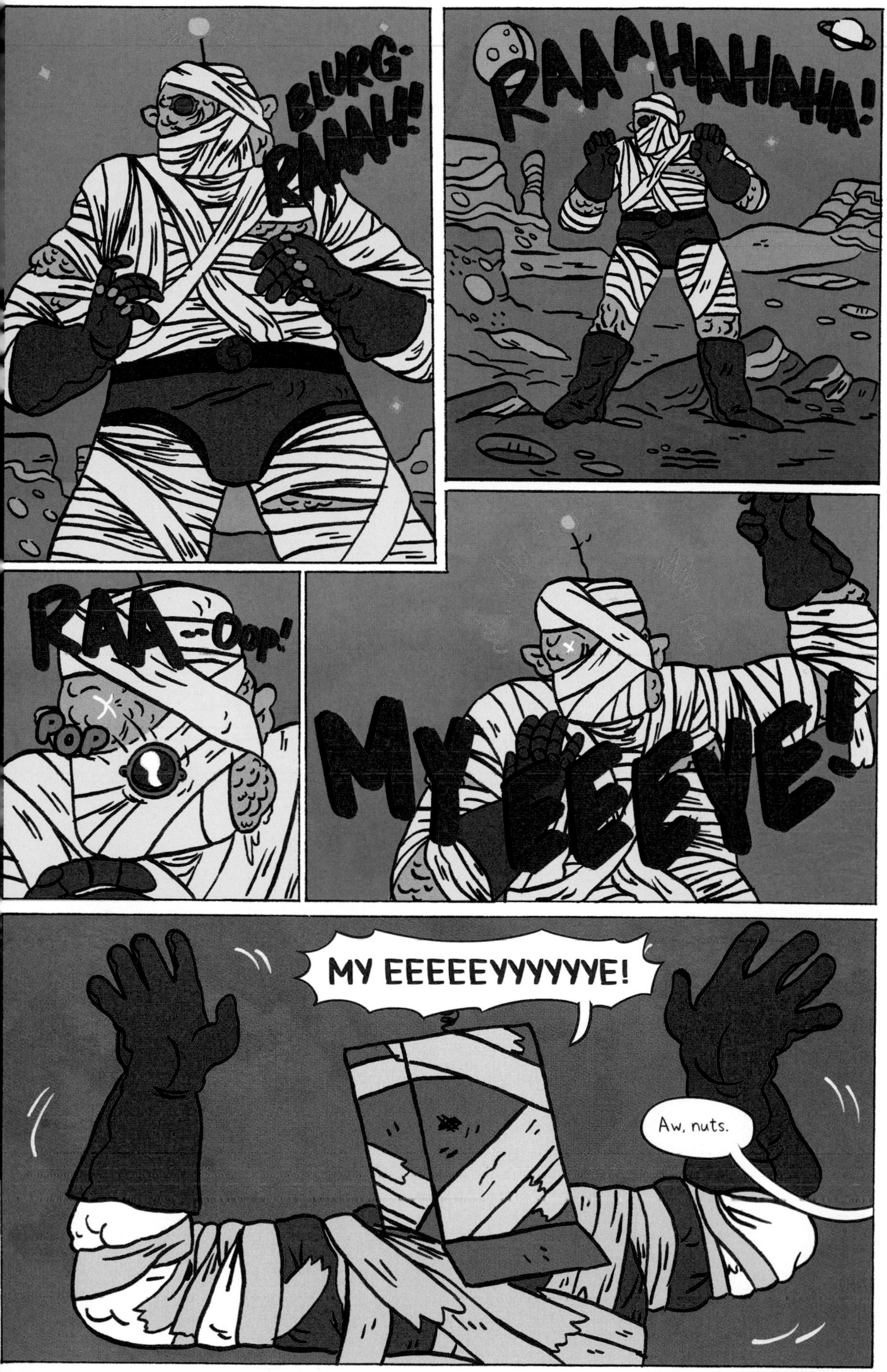
BLURG-RAAAH!
RAAAHAHAHAHA!
RAA--OOP!
POP
MY EEEYE!
MY EEEEEYYYYYYE!
Aw, nuts.

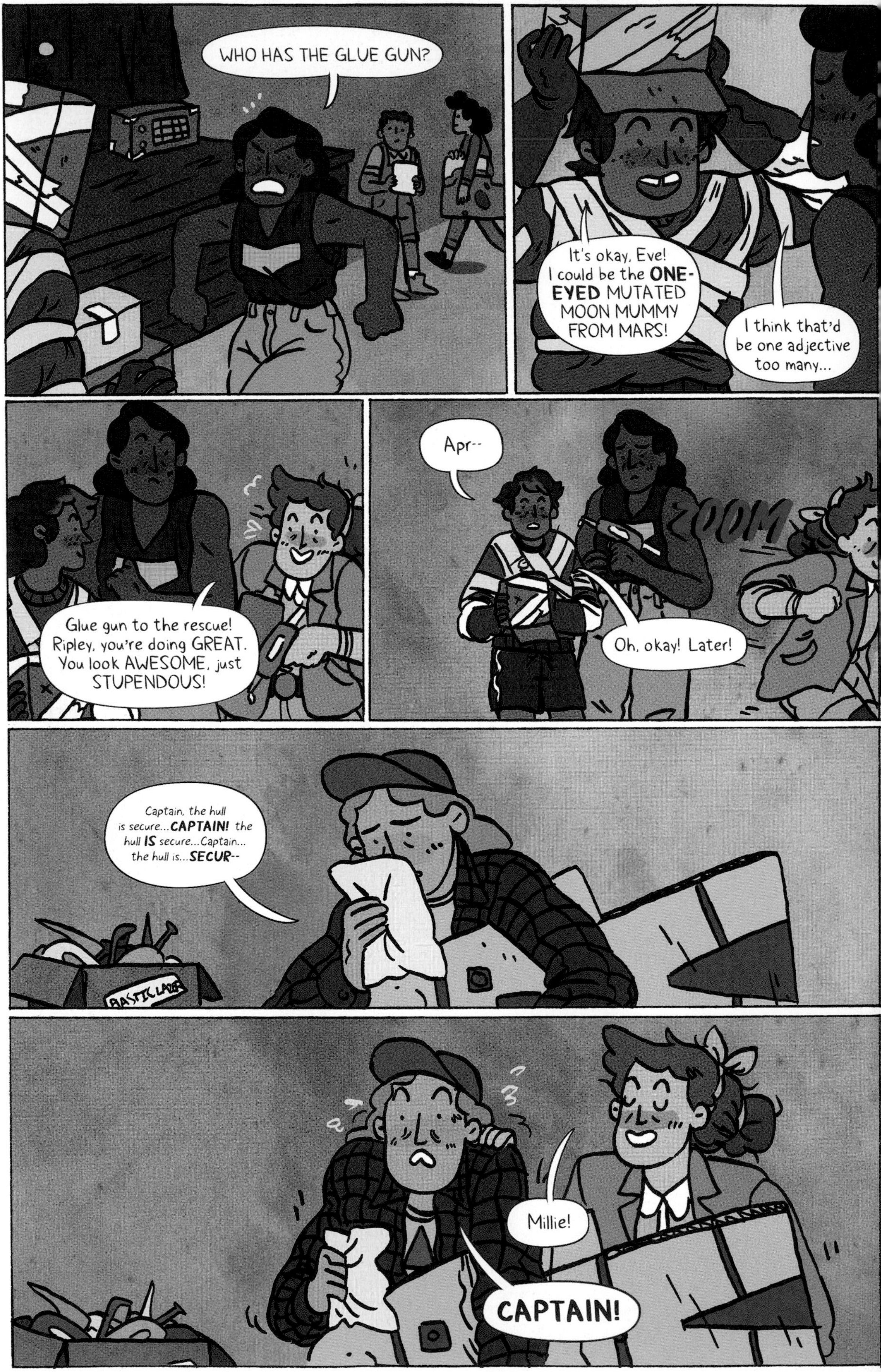
WHO HAS THE GLUE GUN?
It's okay, Eve! I could be the **ONE-EYED** MUTATED MOON MUMMY FROM MARS!
I think that'd be one adjective too many...
Glue gun to the rescue! Ripley, you're doing GREAT. You look AWESOME, just STUPENDOUS!
Apr--
ZOOM
Oh, okay! Later!
Captain, the hull is secure...**CAPTAIN!** the hull **IS** secure...Captain... the hull is...**SECUR**--
Millie!
CAPTAIN!

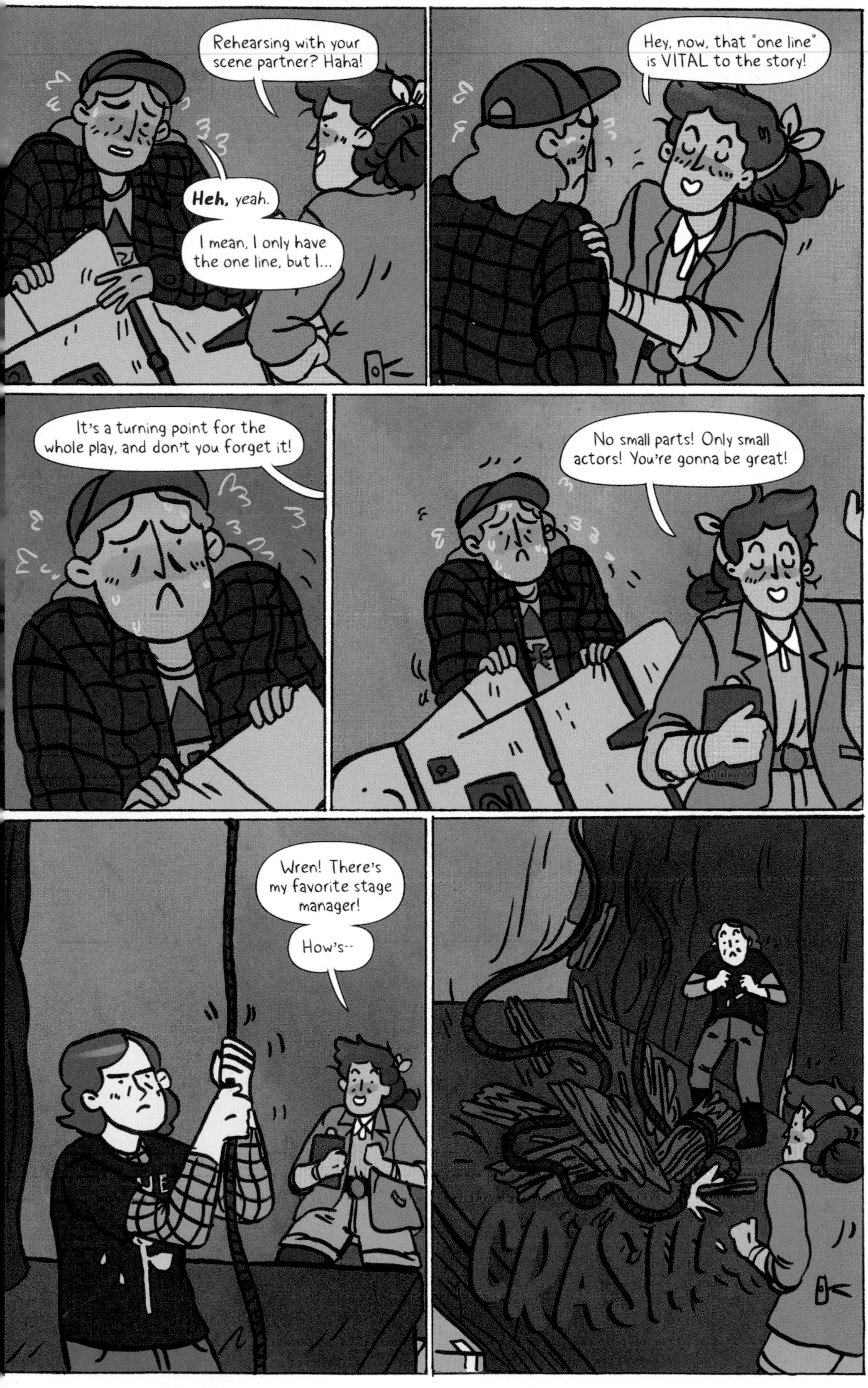
Rehearsing with your scene partner? Haha!
Heh, yeah.
I mean, I only have the one line, but I...
Hey, now, that "one line" is VITAL to the story!
It's a turning point for the whole play, and don't you forget it!
No small parts! Only small actors! You're gonna be great!
Wren! There's my favorite stage manager!
How's--
CRASH!

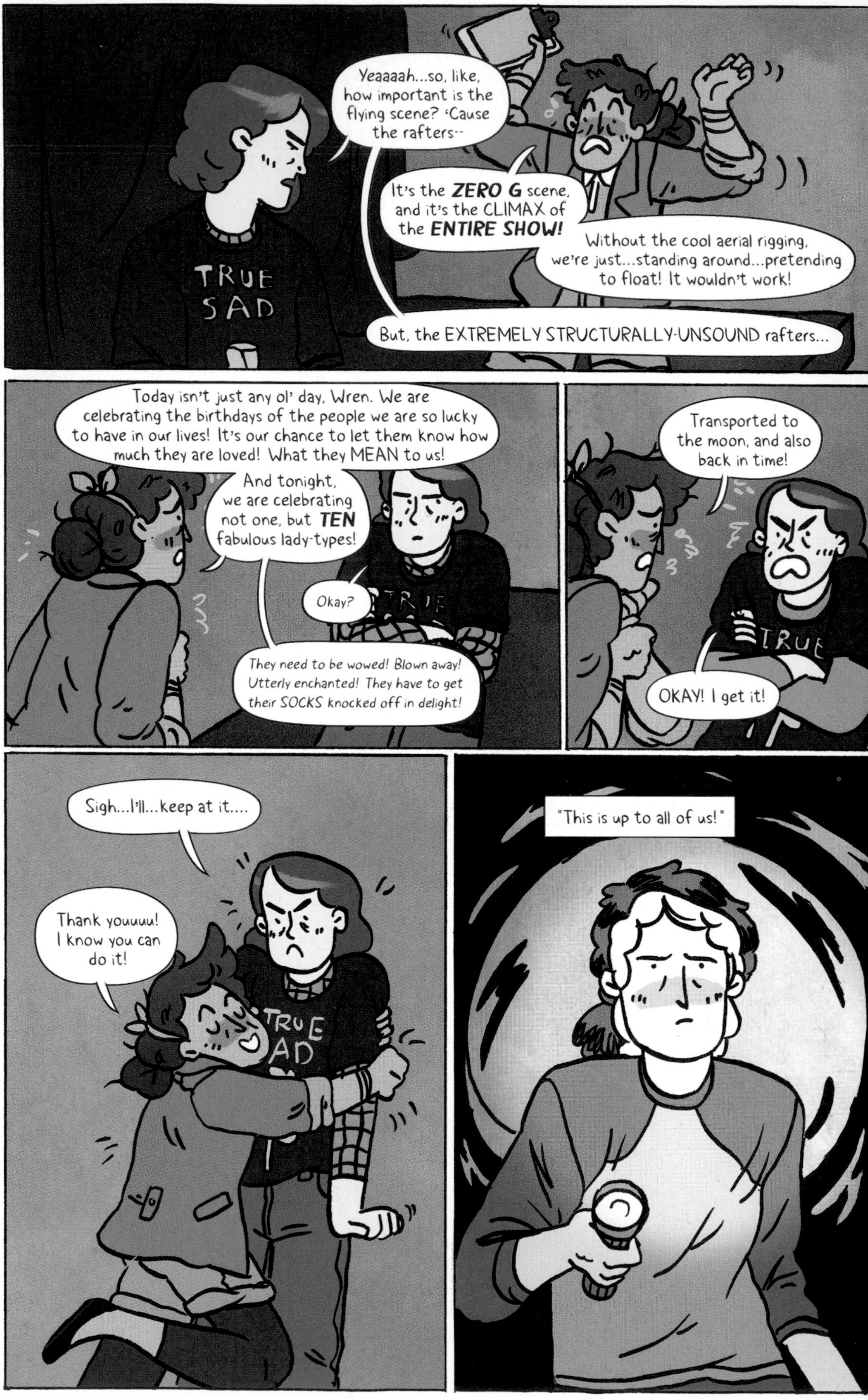
Yeaaaah...so, like, how important is the flying scene? 'Cause the rafters--
It's the **ZERO G** scene, and it's the CLIMAX of the **ENTIRE SHOW!**
Without the cool aerial rigging, we're just...standing around...pretending to float! It wouldn't work!
But, the EXTREMELY STRUCTURALLY-UNSOUND rafters...
TRUE SAD
Today isn't just any ol' day, Wren. We are celebrating the birthdays of the people we are so lucky to have in our lives! It's our chance to let them know how much they are loved! What they MEAN to us!
And tonight, we are celebrating not one, but **TEN** fabulous lady-types!
Okay?
They need to be wowed! Blown away! Utterly enchanted! They have to get their SOCKS knocked off in delight!
Transported to the moon, and also back in time!
OKAY! I get it!
Sigh...I'll...keep at it....
Thank youuuu! I know you can do it!
"This is up to all of us!"

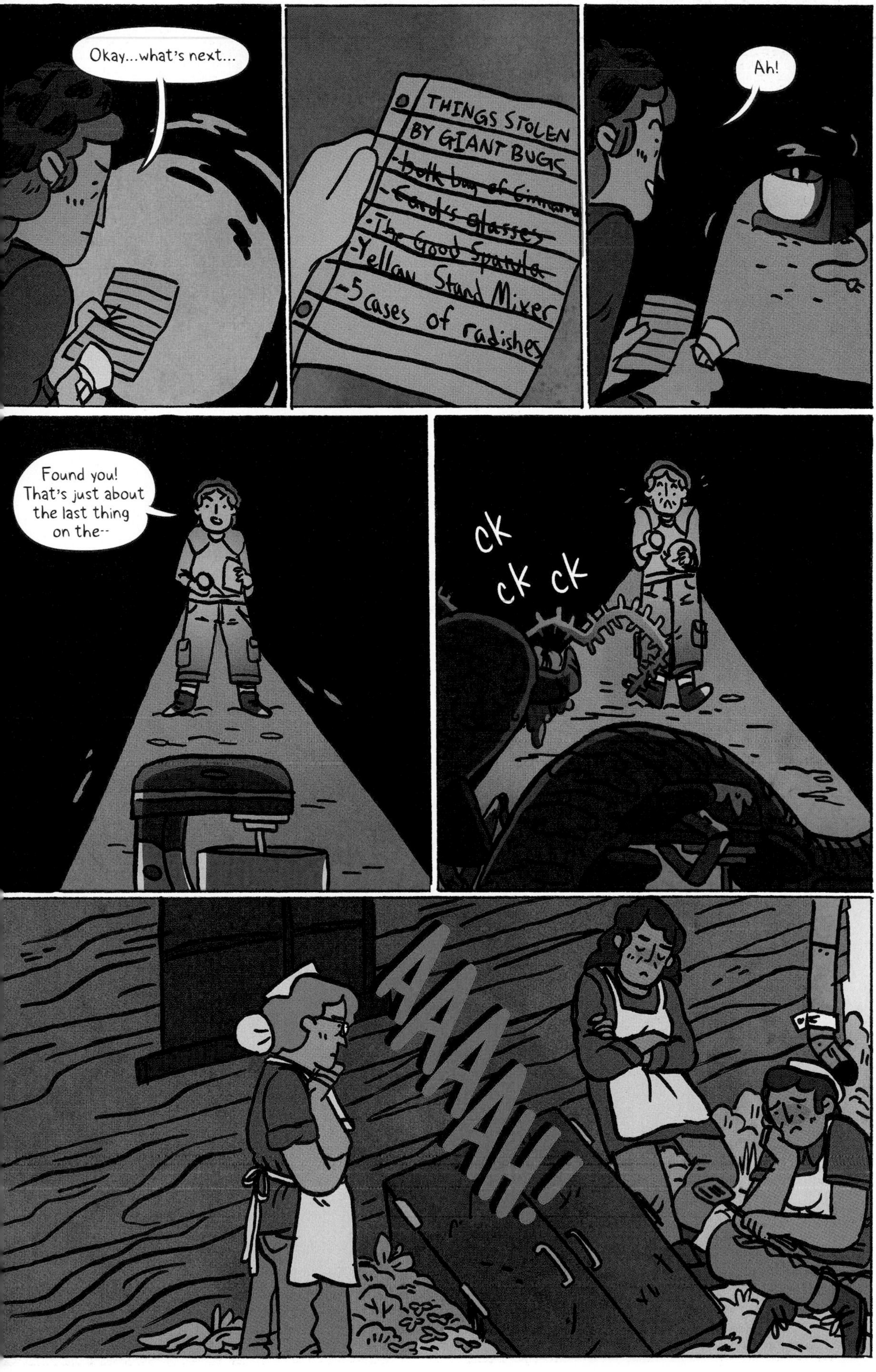

Okay...what's next...
THINGS STOLEN
BY GIANT BUGS
-bulk bag of
-Carol's glasses
-The Good Spatula
-Yellow Stand Mixer
-5 cases of radishes
Ah!
Found you! That's just about the last thing on the--
ck
ck ck
AAAAAH!

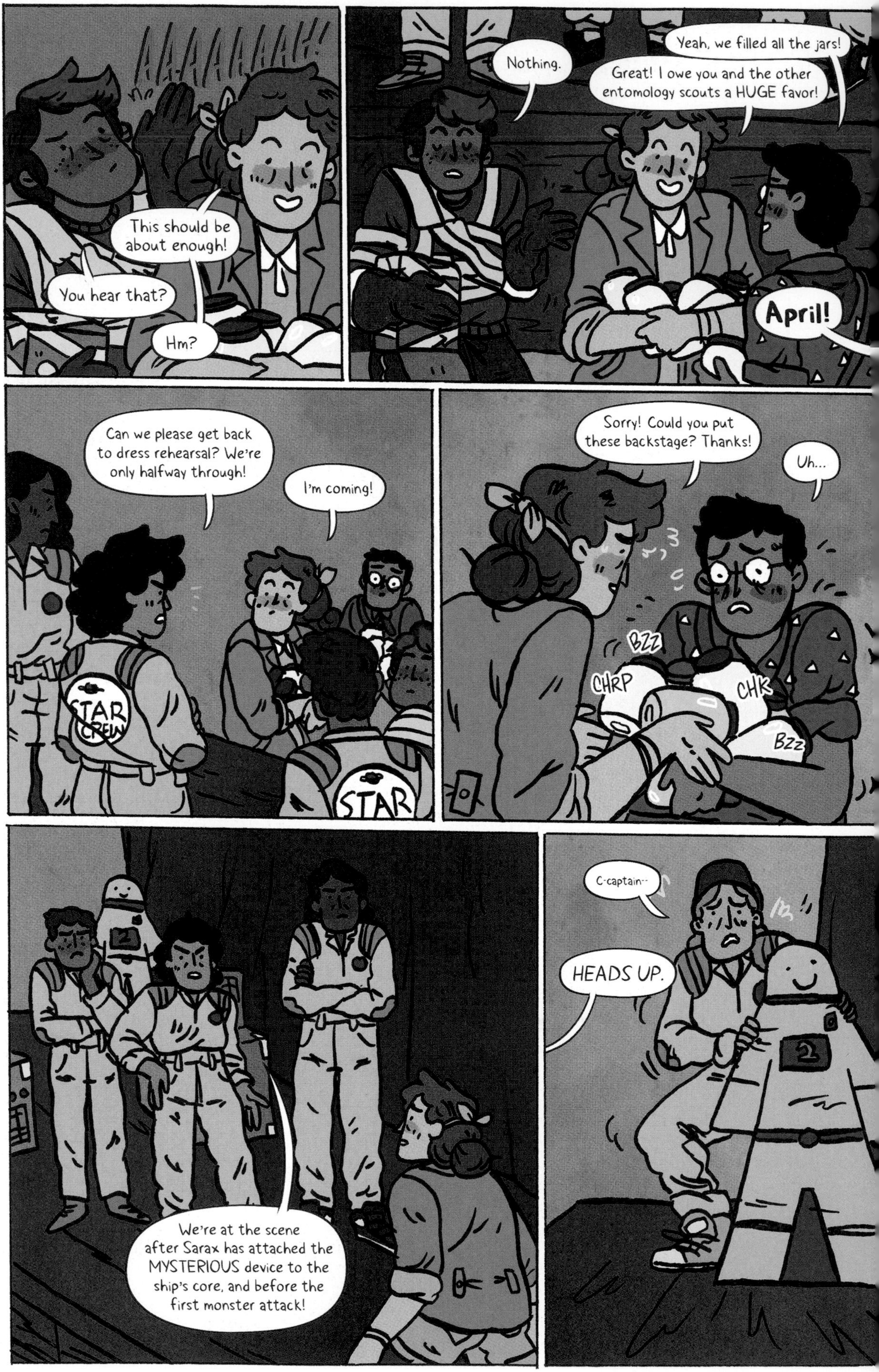
AAAAAAAH!
This should be about enough!
You hear that?
Hm?
Nothing.
Yeah, we filled all the jars!
Great! I owe you and the other entomology scouts a HUGE favor!
April!
Can we please get back to dress rehearsal? We're only halfway through!
I'm coming!
STAR CREW
STAR
Sorry! Could you put these backstage? Thanks!
Uh...
BZZ
CHRP
CHK
BZZ
We're at the scene after Sarax has attached the MYSTERIOUS device to the ship's core, and before the first monster attack!
C-captain--
HEADS UP.

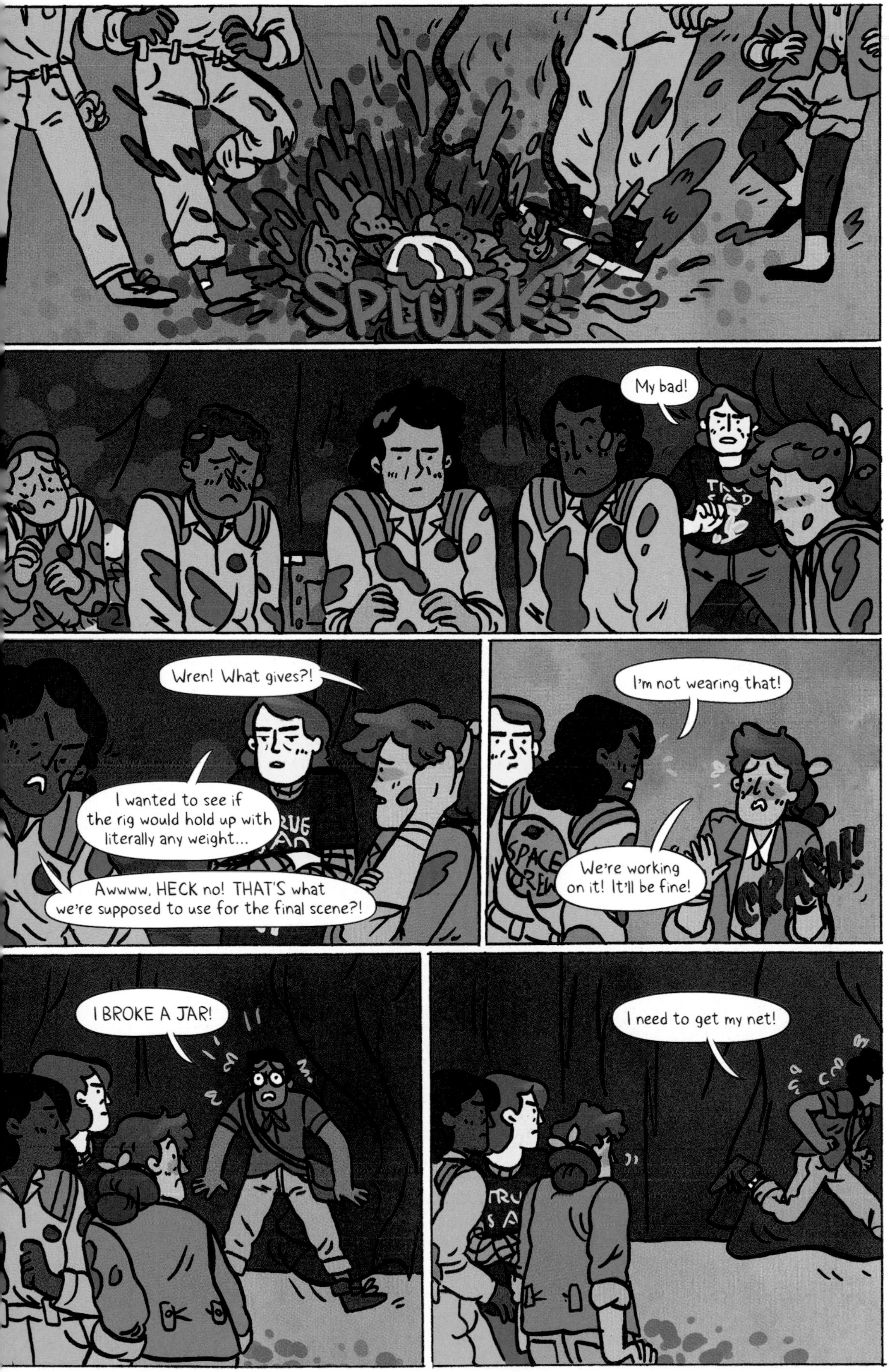
SPLURK!
My bad!
TRUE SAD
Wren! What gives?!
I wanted to see if the rig would hold up with literally any weight...
Awwww, HECK no! THAT'S what we're supposed to use for the final scene?!
I'm not wearing that!
SPACE CREW
We're working on it! It'll be fine!
CRASH!
I BROKE A JAR!
I need to get my net!

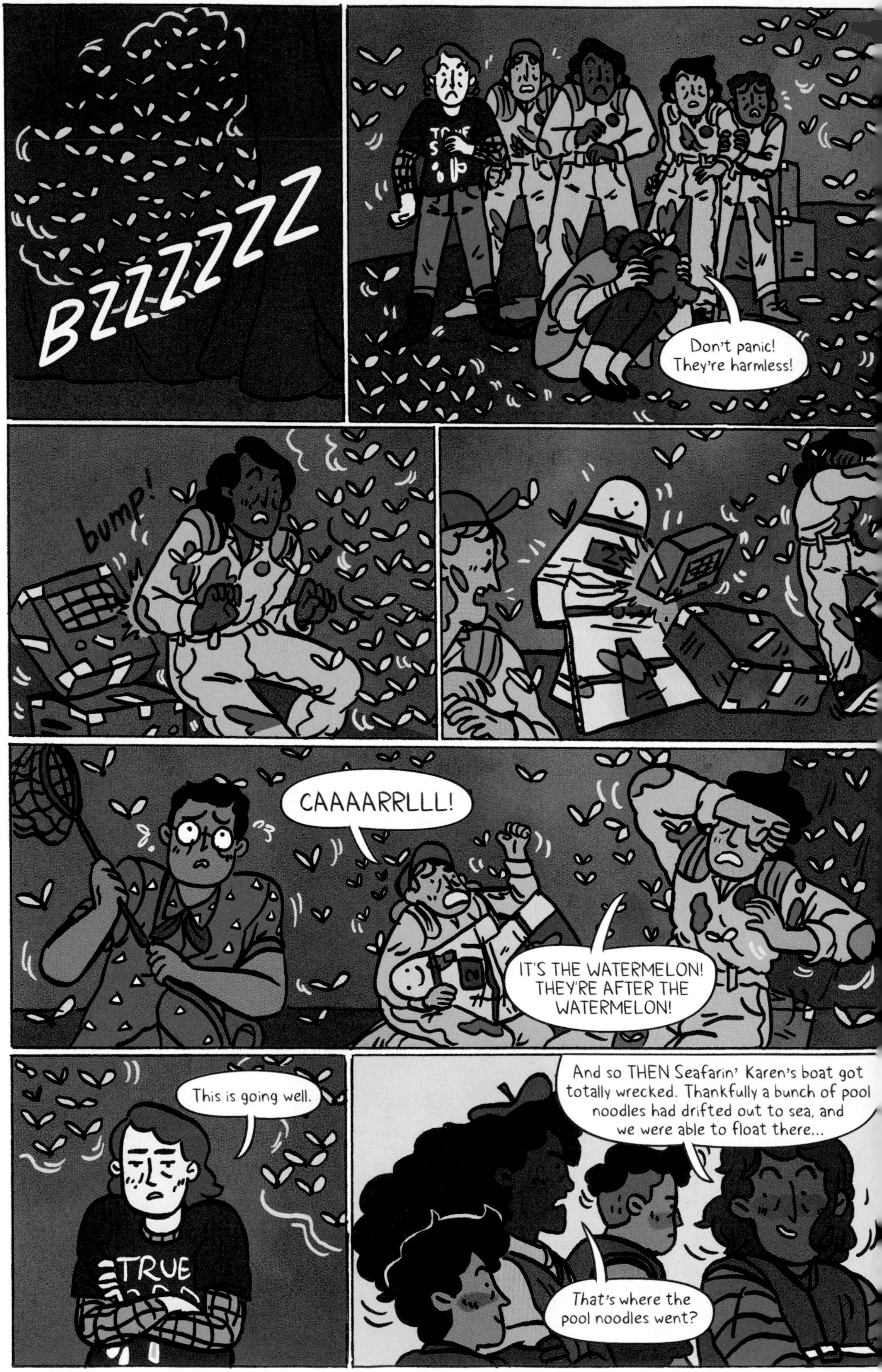
BZZZZZZZ
Don't panic! They're harmless!
bump!
CAAAARRLLL!
IT'S THE WATERMELON! THEY'RE AFTER THE WATERMELON!
This is going well.
And so THEN Seafarin' Karen's boat got totally wrecked. Thankfully a bunch of pool noodles had drifted out to sea, and we were able to float there...
That's where the pool noodles went?

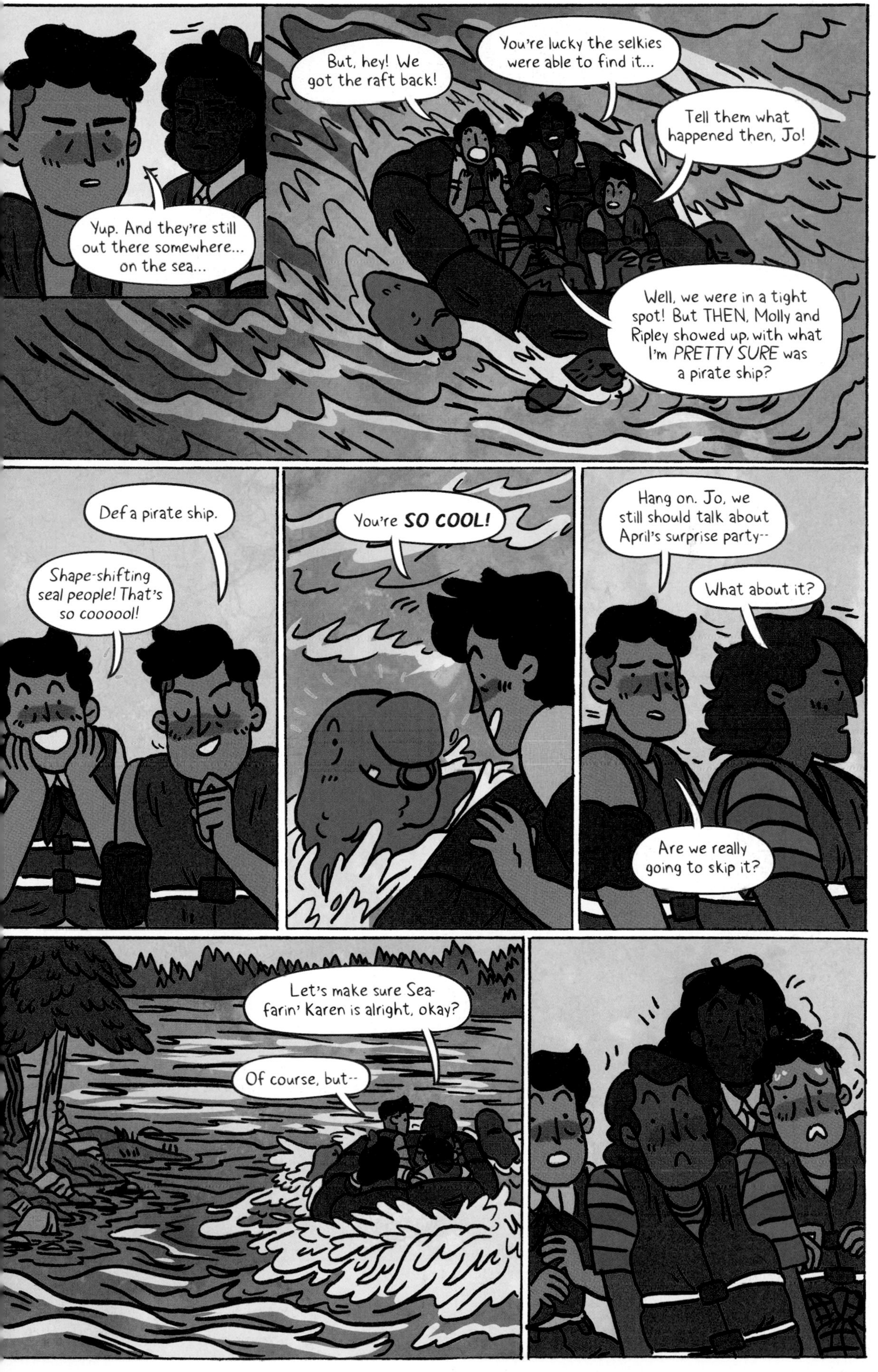
Yup. And they're still out there somewhere... on the sea...
But, hey! We got the raft back!
You're lucky the selkies were able to find it...
Tell them what happened then, Jo!
Well, we were in a tight spot! But THEN, Molly and Ripley showed up, with what I'm *PRETTY SURE* was a pirate ship?
Def a pirate ship.
Shape-shifting seal people! That's so coooool!
You're **SO COOL!**
Hang on. Jo, we still should talk about April's surprise party--
What about it?
Are we really going to skip it?
Let's make sure Sea-farin' Karen is alright, okay?
Of course, but--

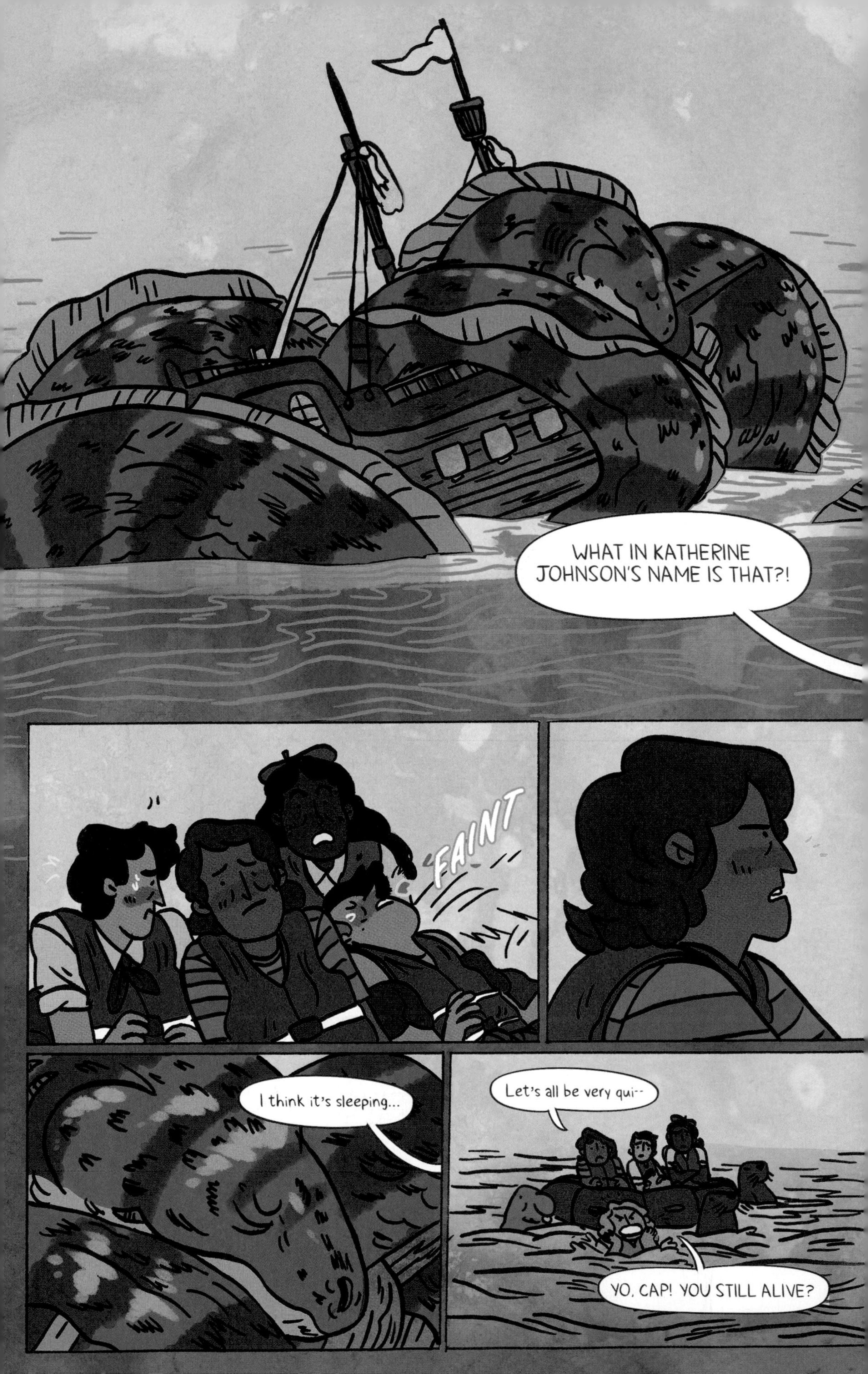

WHAT IN KATHERINE JOHNSON'S NAME IS THAT?!
FAINT
I think it's sleeping...
Let's all be very qui--
YO, CAP! YOU STILL ALIVE?

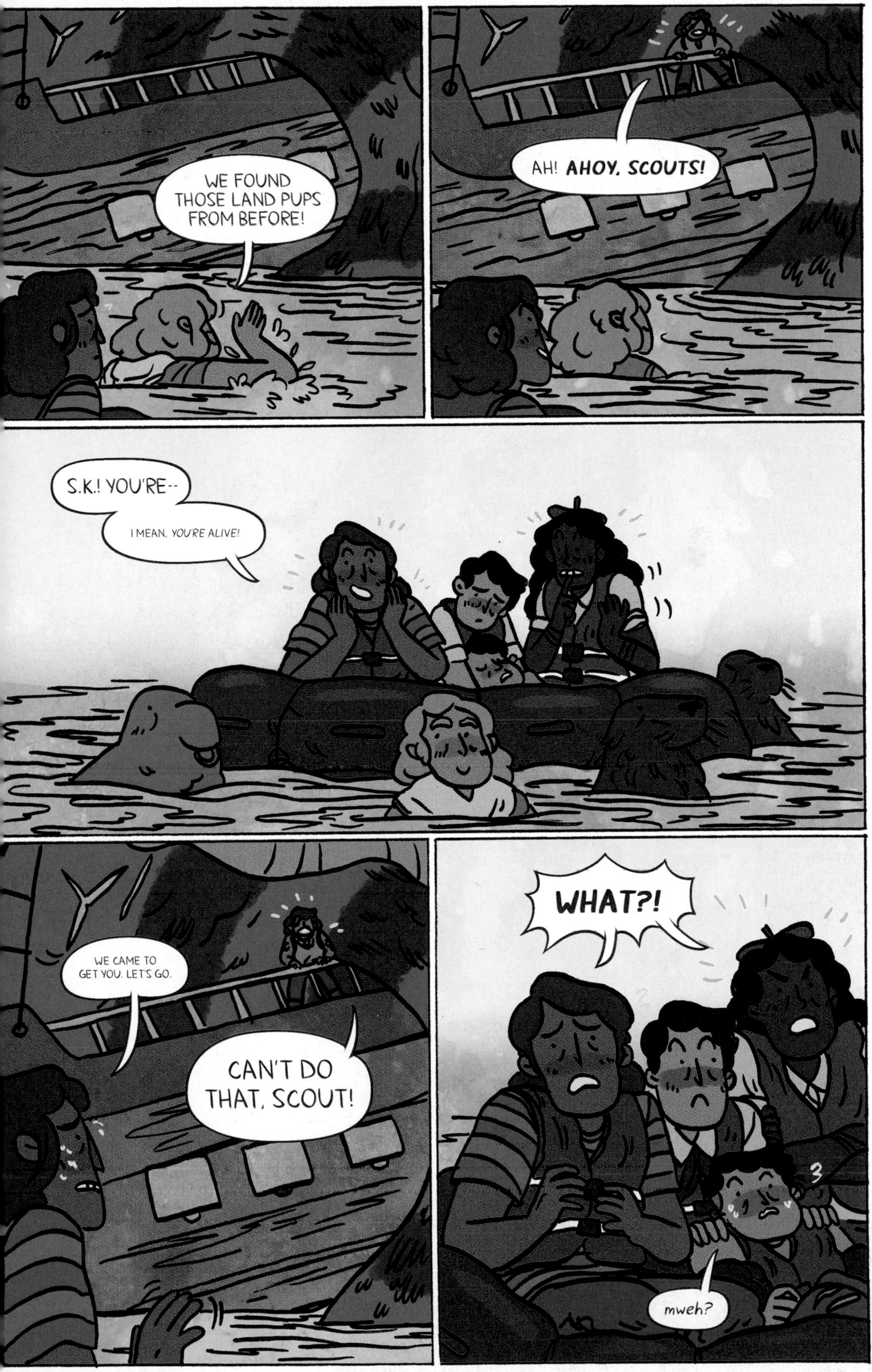
WE FOUND THOSE LAND PUPS FROM BEFORE!
AH! AHOY, SCOUTS!
S.K.! YOU'RE--
I MEAN, YOU'RE ALIVE!
WE CAME TO GET YOU. LET'S GO.
CAN'T DO THAT, SCOUT!
WHAT?!
mweh?

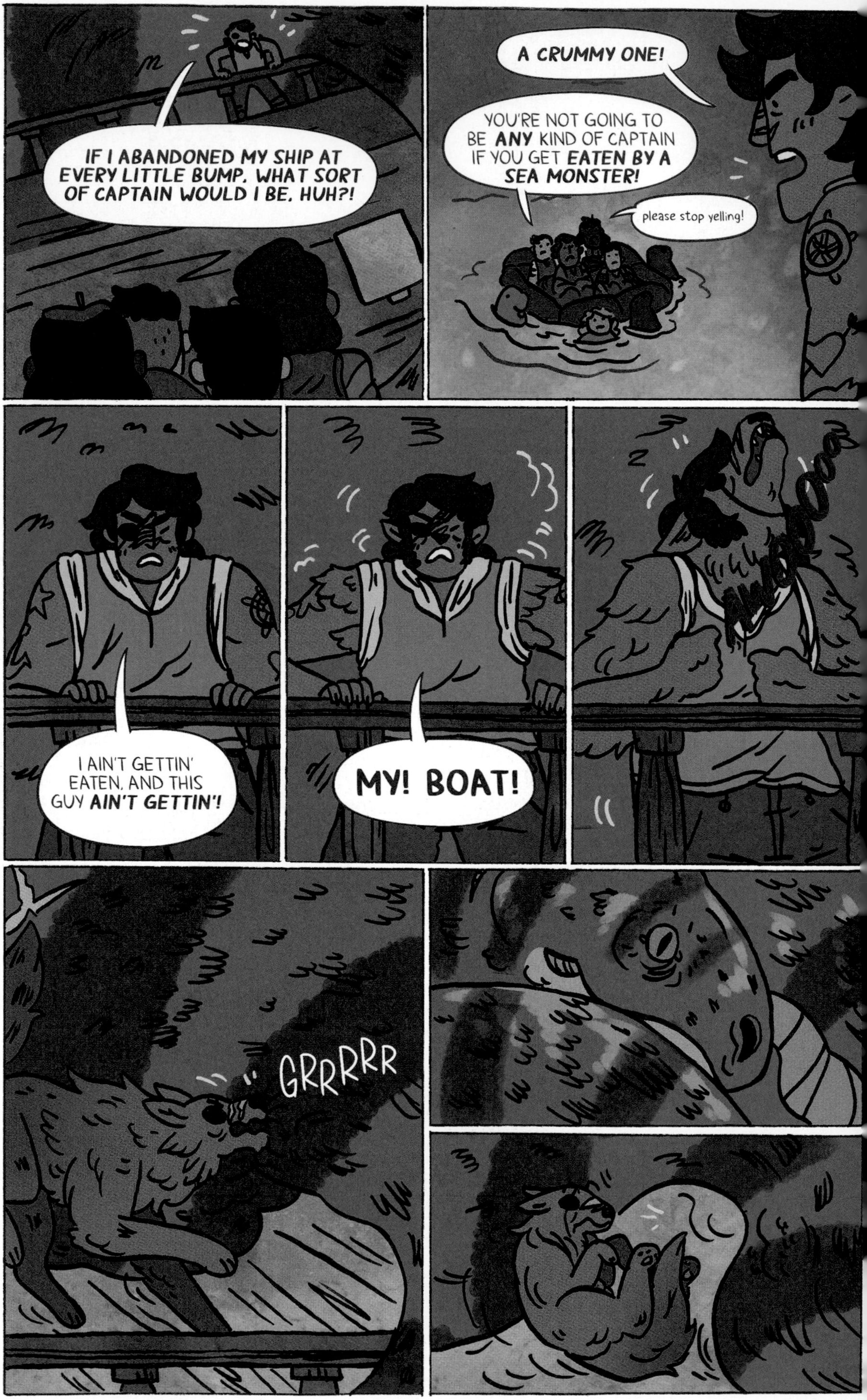
IF I ABANDONED MY SHIP AT EVERY LITTLE BUMP, WHAT SORT OF CAPTAIN WOULD I BE, HUH?!
A CRUMMY ONE!
YOU'RE NOT GOING TO BE ANY KIND OF CAPTAIN IF YOU GET EATEN BY A SEA MONSTER!
please stop yelling!
I AIN'T GETTIN' EATEN, AND THIS GUY AIN'T GETTIN'!
MY! BOAT!
GRRRRR

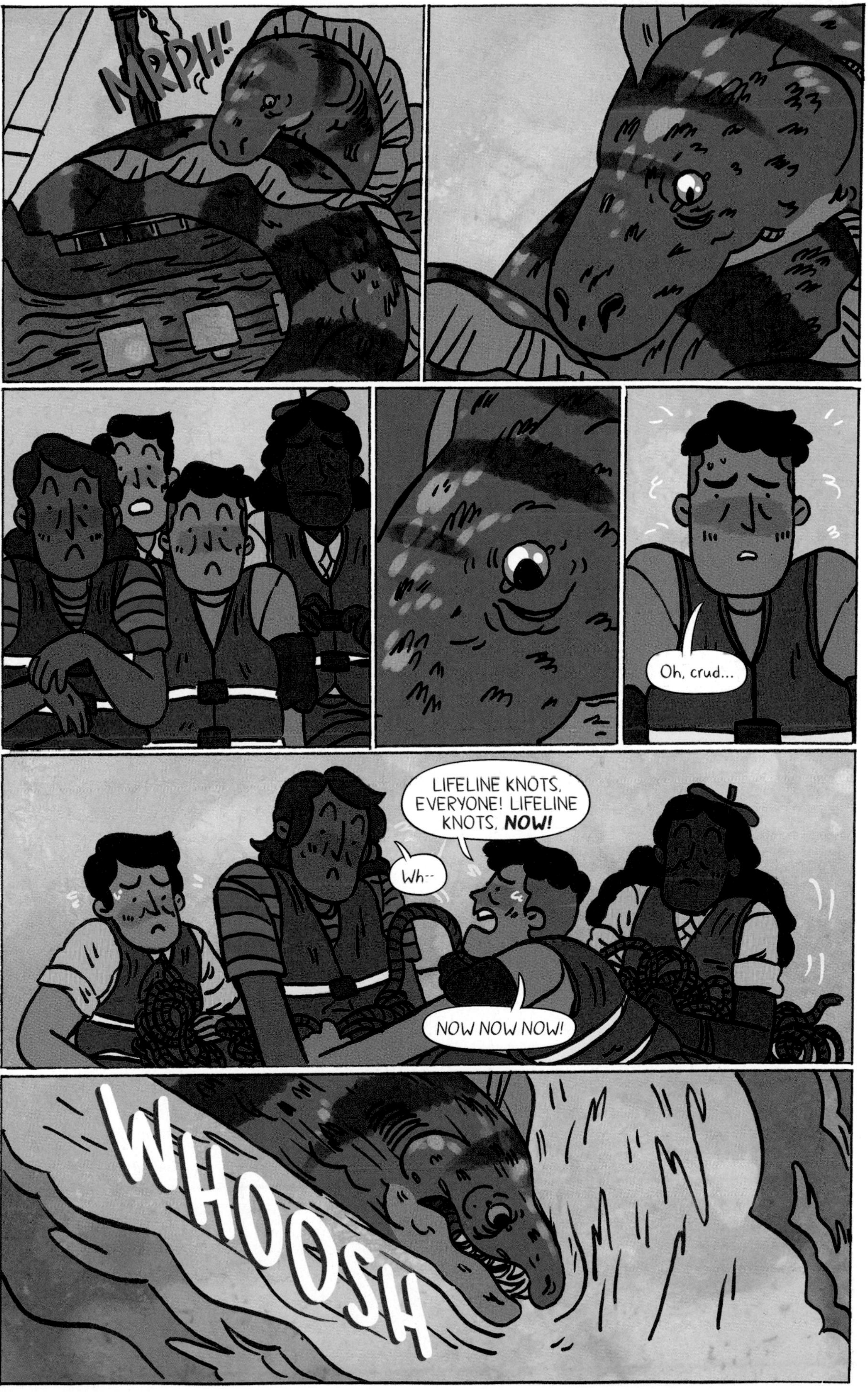
MRPH!
Oh, crud...
LIFELINE KNOTS, EVERYONE! LIFELINE KNOTS, **NOW!**
Wh--
NOW NOW NOW!
WHOOSH

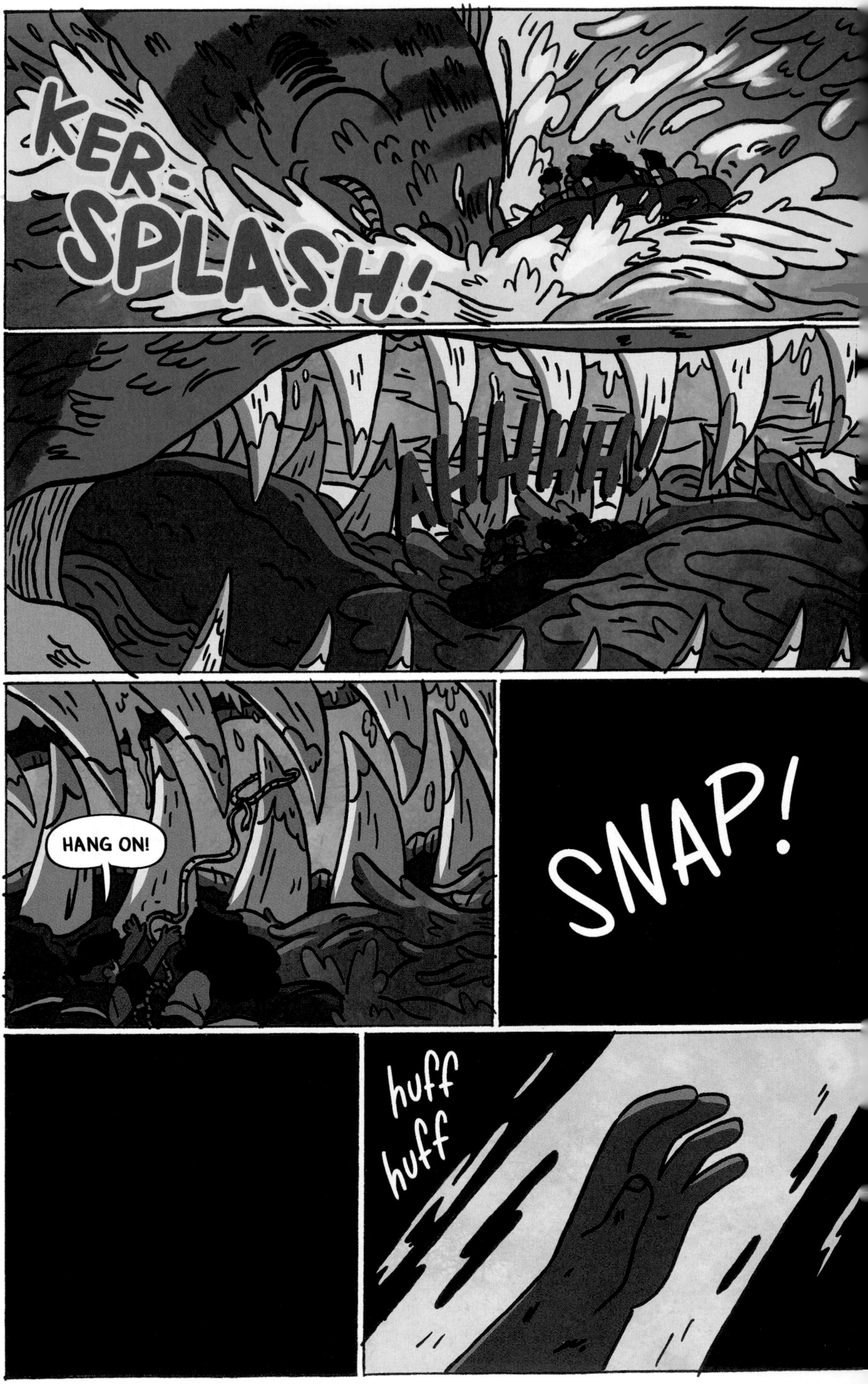
KER-SPLASH!
AHHHHH!
HANG ON!
SNAP!
huff
huff

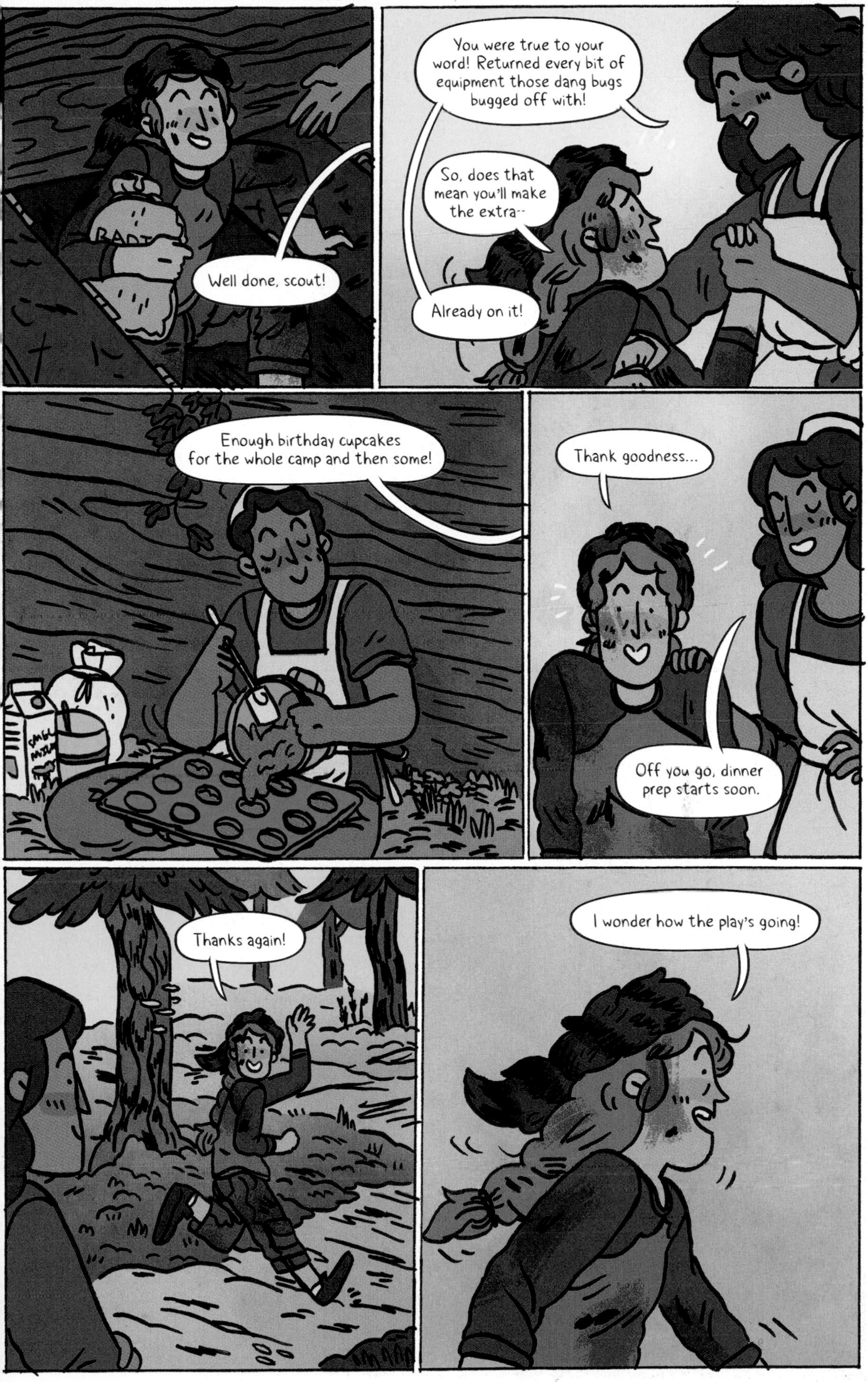
Well done, scout!
You were true to your word! Returned every bit of equipment those dang bugs bugged off with!
So, does that mean you'll make the extra--
Already on it!
Enough birthday cupcakes for the whole camp and then some!
Thank goodness...
Off you go, dinner prep starts soon.
Thanks again!
I wonder how the play's going!

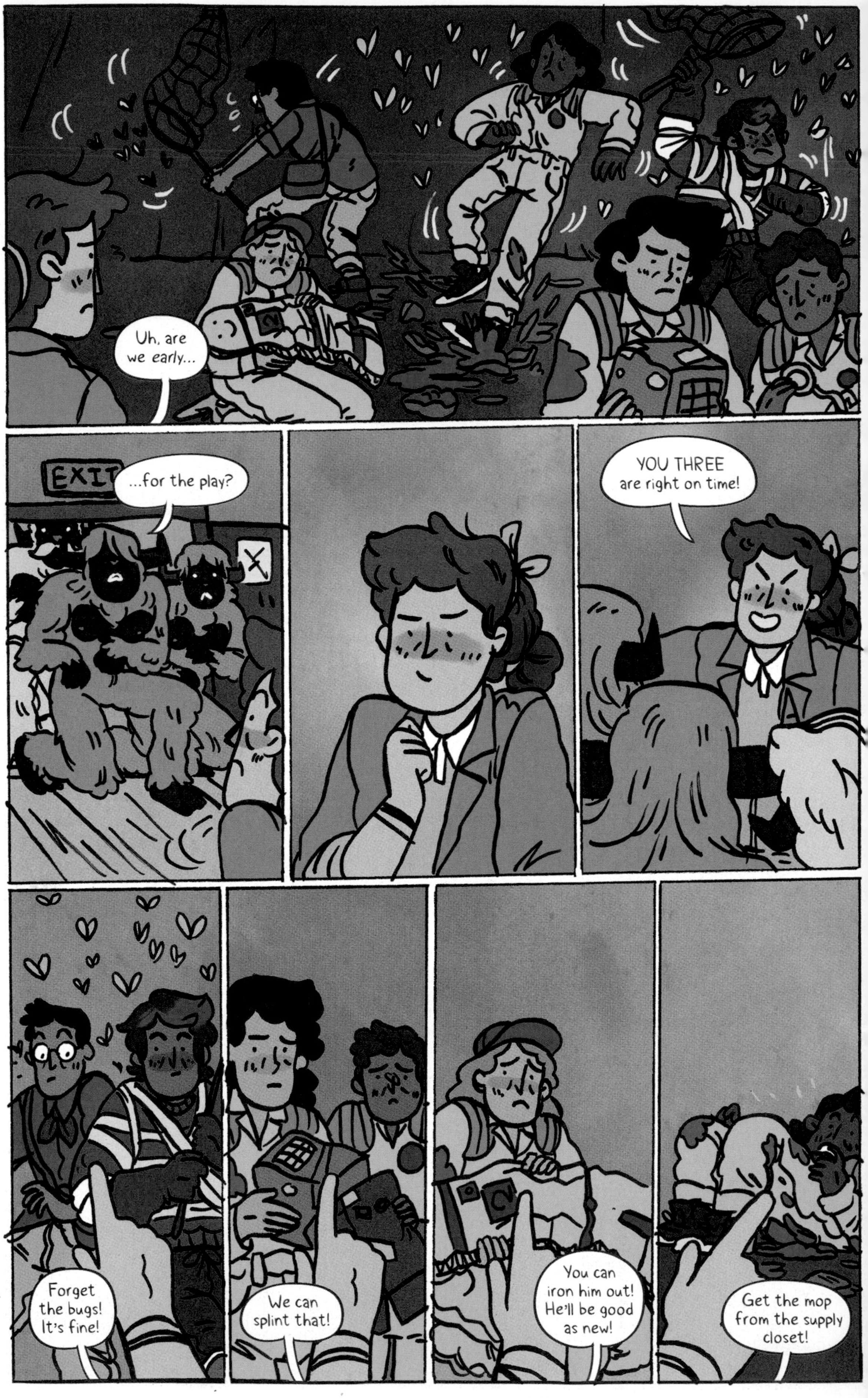
Uh, are we early...
EXIT
...for the play?
YOU THREE are right on time!
Forget the bugs! It's fine!
We can splint that!
You can iron him out! He'll be good as new!
Get the mop from the supply closet!

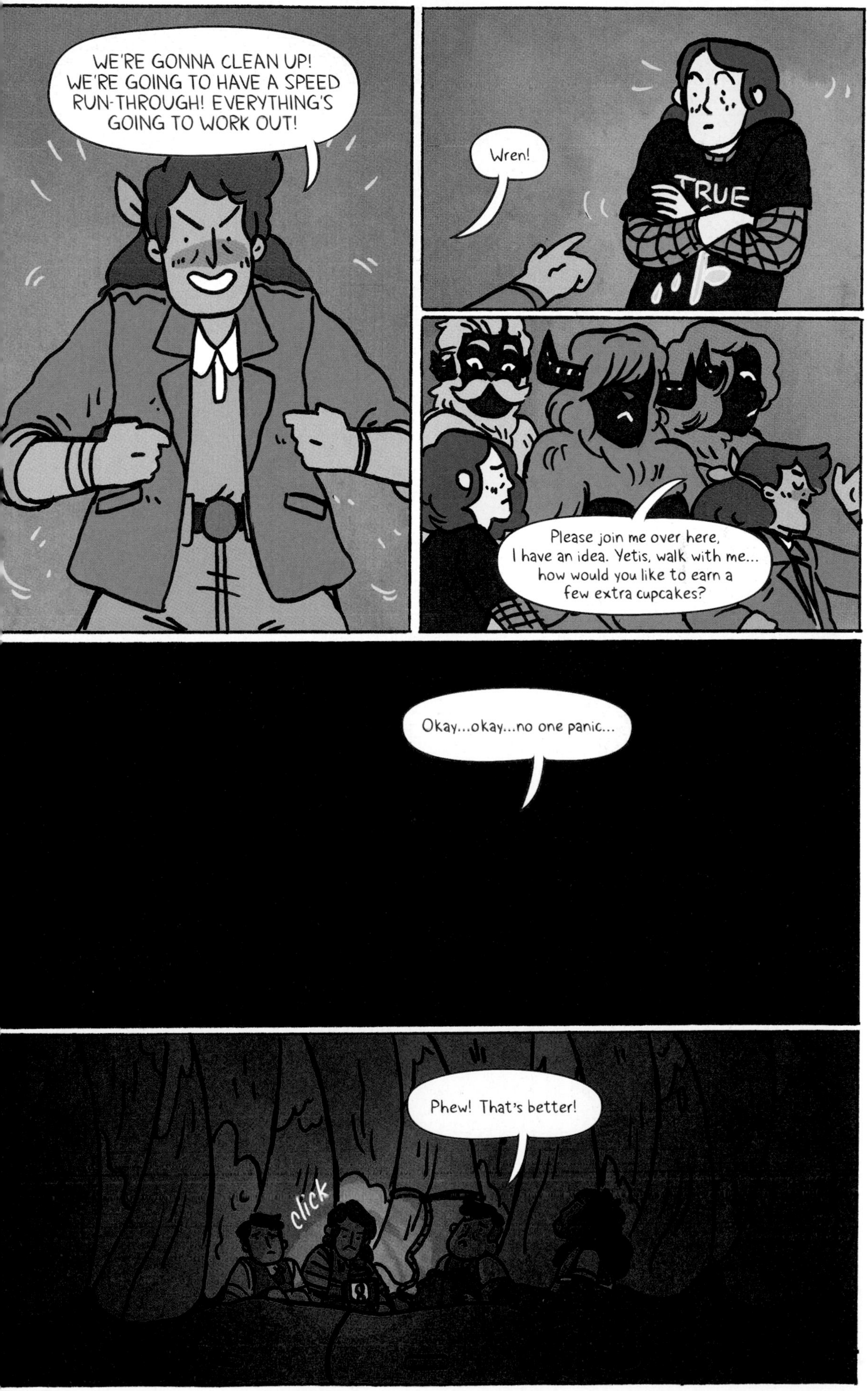
WE'RE GONNA CLEAN UP! WE'RE GOING TO HAVE A SPEED RUN-THROUGH! EVERYTHING'S GOING TO WORK OUT!
Wren!
TRUE
Please join me over here, I have an idea. Yetis, walk with me... how would you like to earn a few extra cupcakes?
Okay...okay...no one panic...
Phew! That's better!
click

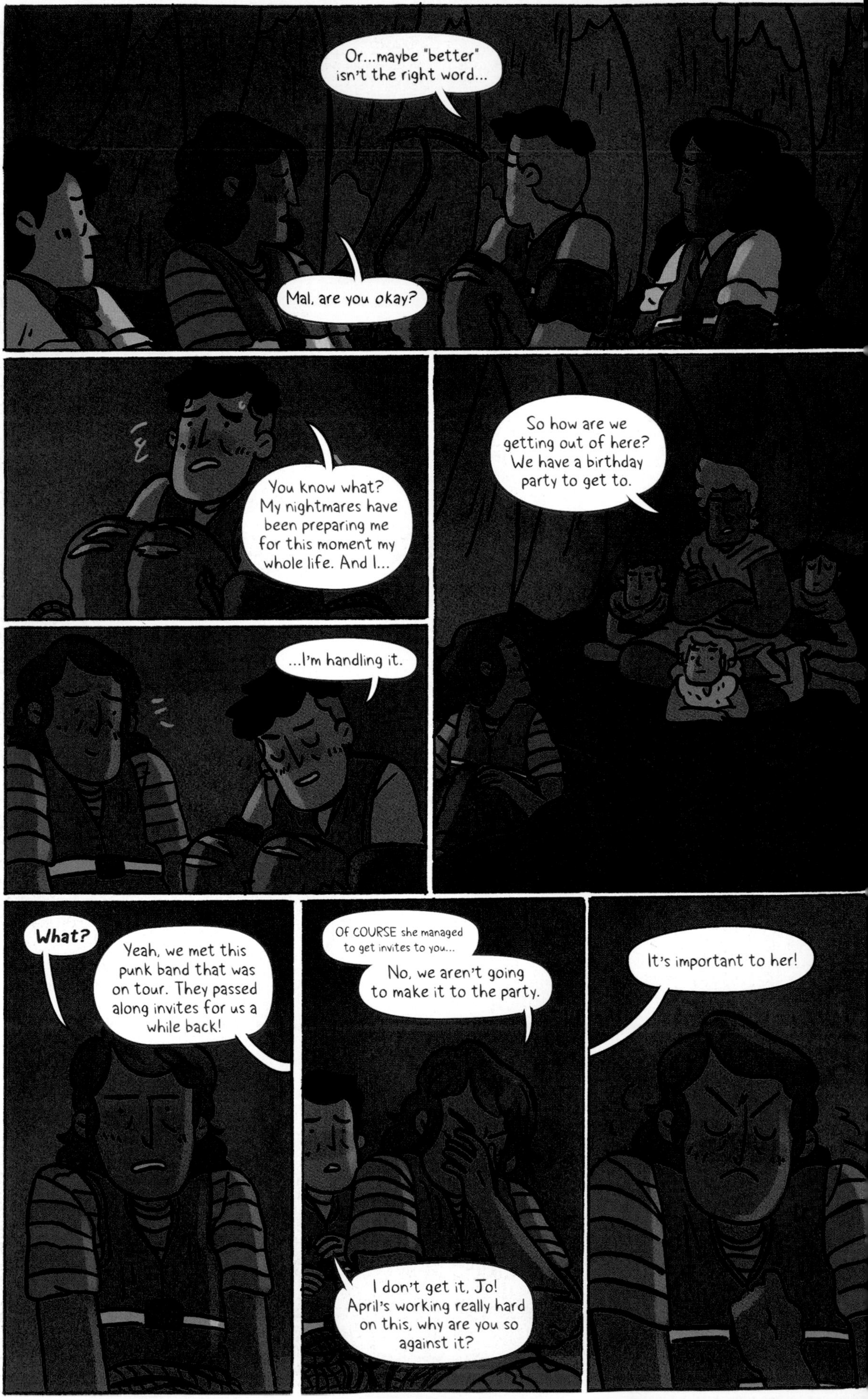
Or...maybe "better" isn't the right word...
Mal, are you okay?
You know what? My nightmares have been preparing me for this moment my whole life. And I...
...I'm handling it.
So how are we getting out of here? We have a birthday party to get to.
What?
Yeah, we met this punk band that was on tour. They passed along invites for us a while back!
OF COURSE she managed to get invites to you...
No, we aren't going to make it to the party.
I don't get it, Jo! April's working really hard on this, why are you so against it?
It's important to her!

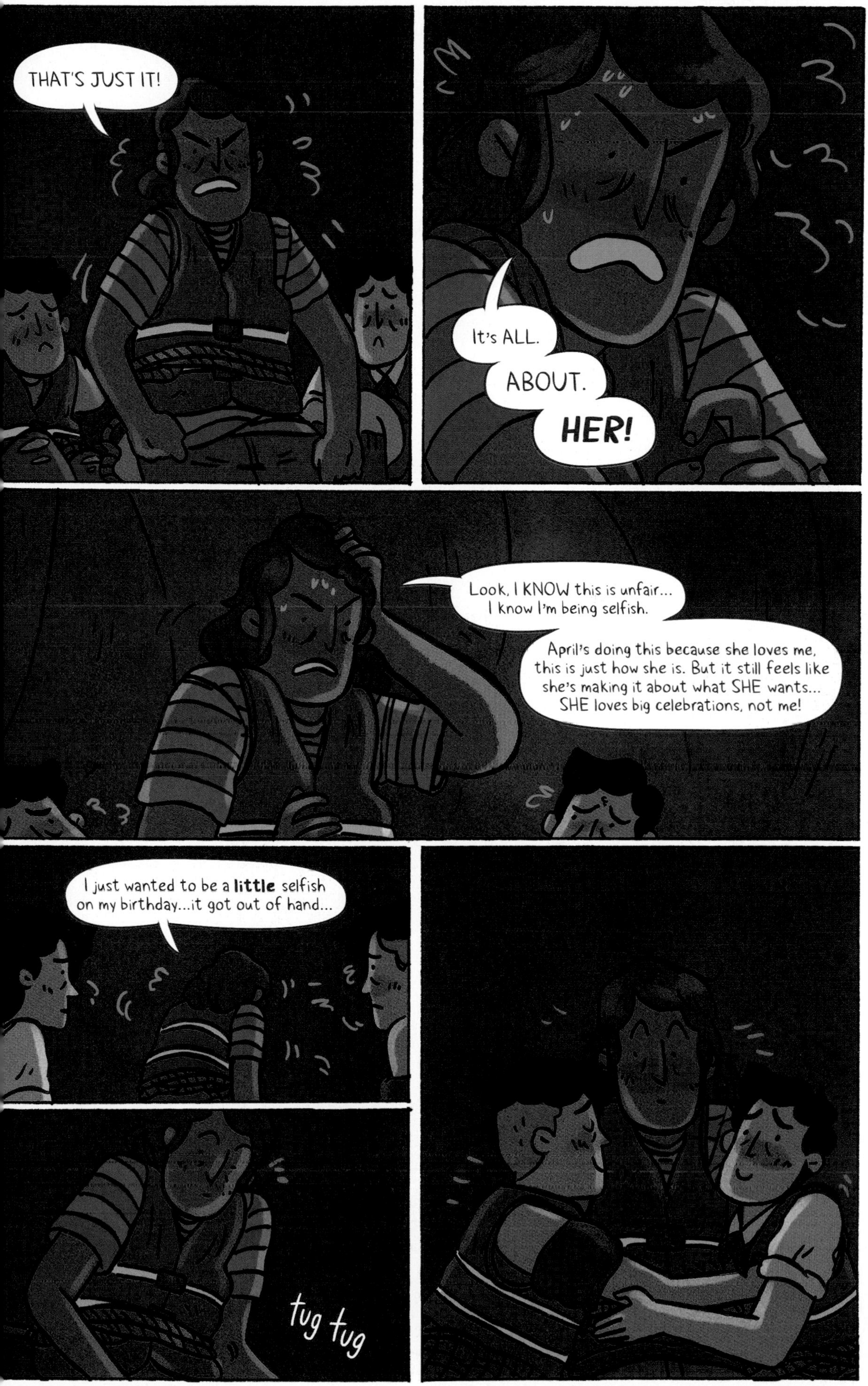
THAT'S JUST IT!
It's ALL.
ABOUT.
HER!
Look, I KNOW this is unfair...
I know I'm being selfish.
April's doing this because she loves me, this is just how she is. But it still feels like she's making it about what SHE wants... SHE loves big celebrations, not me!
I just wanted to be a **little** selfish on my birthday...it got out of hand...
tug tug

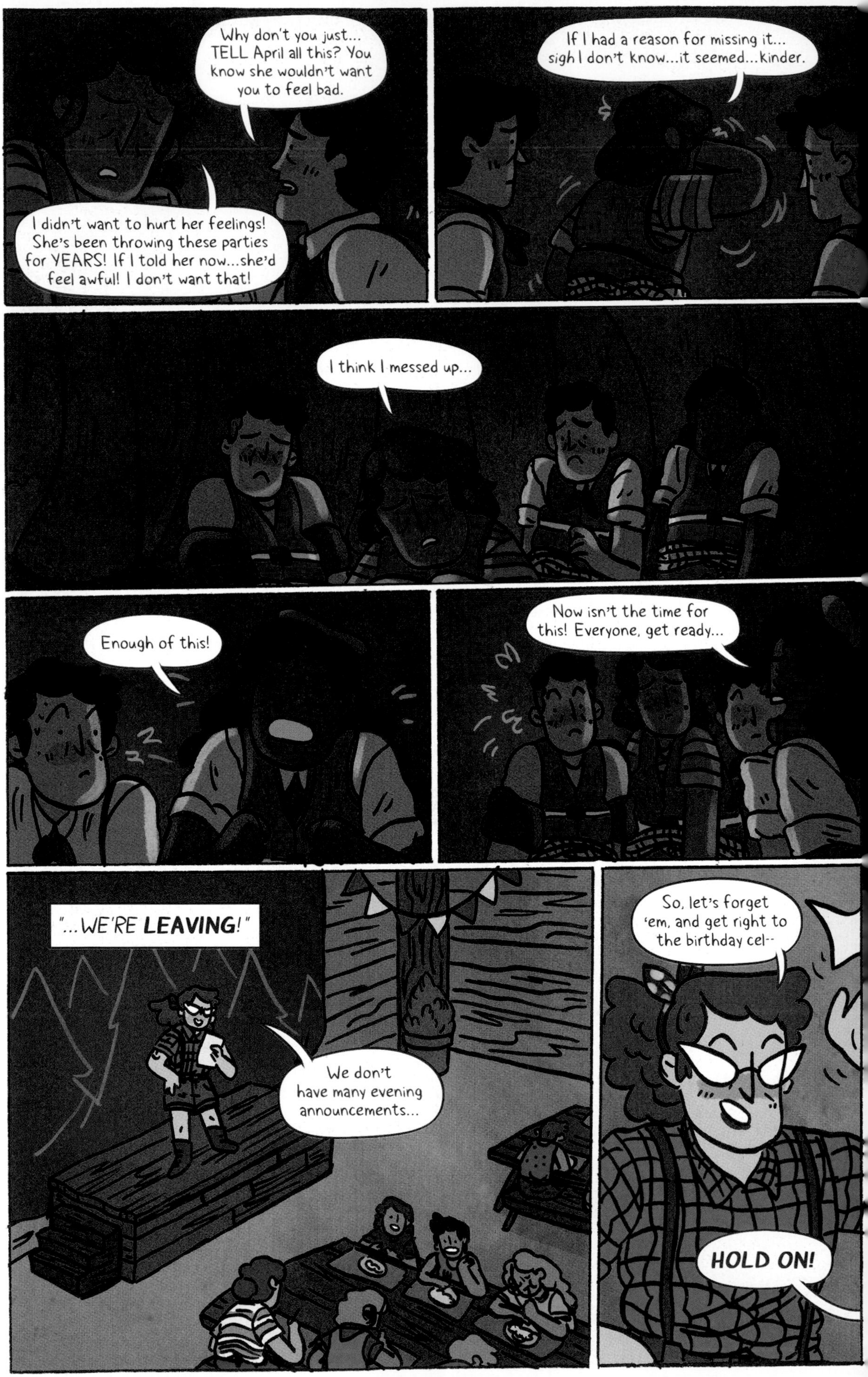
Why don't you just... TELL April all this? You know she wouldn't want you to feel bad.
I didn't want to hurt her feelings! She's been throwing these parties for YEARS! If I told her now...she'd feel awful! I don't want that!
If I had a reason for missing it... sigh I don't know...it seemed...kinder.
I think I messed up...
Enough of this!
Now isn't the time for this! Everyone, get ready...
"...WE'RE **LEAVING**!"
We don't have many evening announcements...
So, let's forget 'em, and get right to the birthday cel--
HOLD ON!

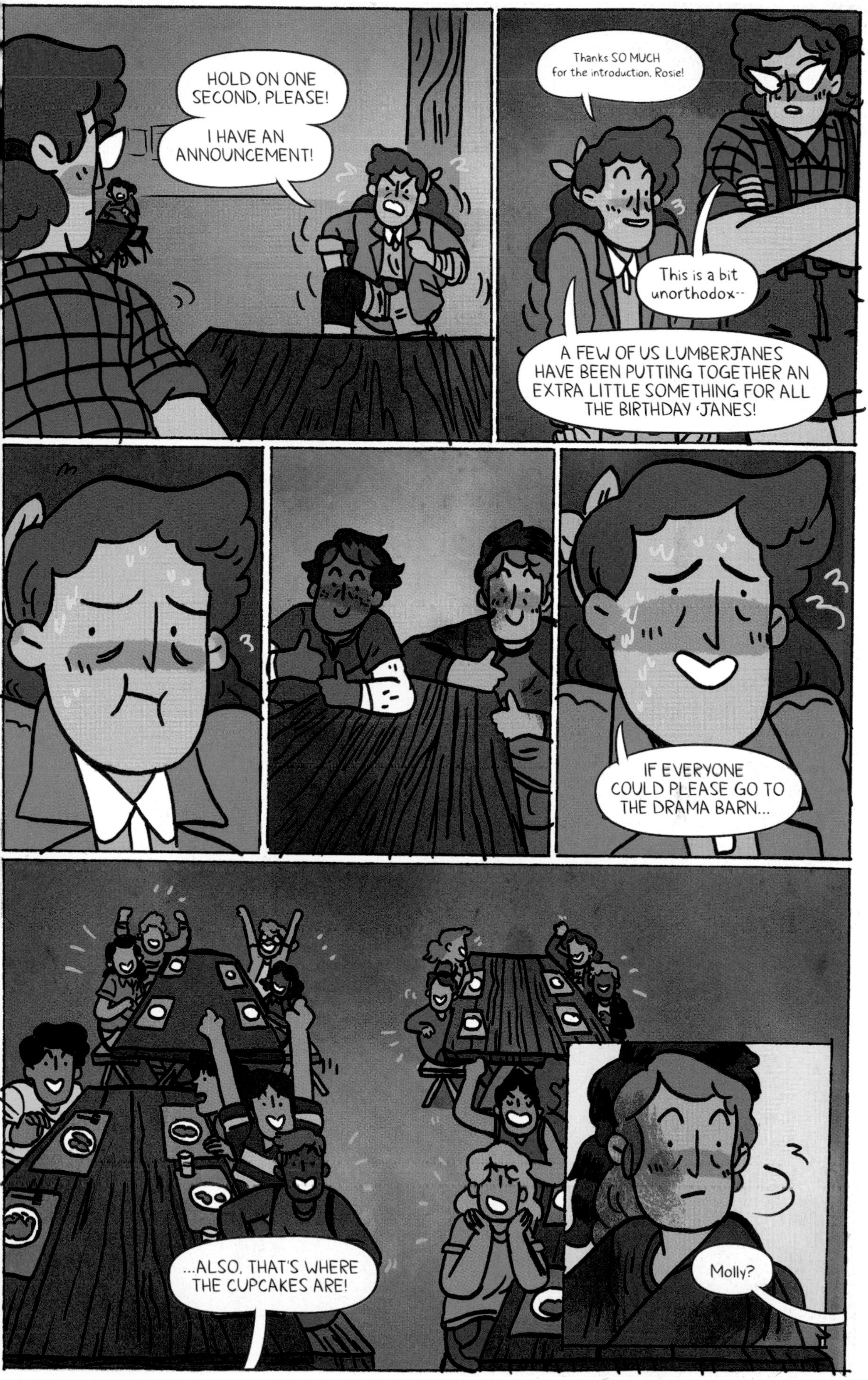
HOLD ON ONE SECOND, PLEASE!
I HAVE AN ANNOUNCEMENT!
Thanks SO MUCH for the introduction, Rosie!
This is a bit unorthodox--
A FEW OF US LUMBERJANES HAVE BEEN PUTTING TOGETHER AN EXTRA LITTLE SOMETHING FOR ALL THE BIRTHDAY 'JANES!
IF EVERYONE COULD PLEASE GO TO THE DRAMA BARN...
...ALSO, THAT'S WHERE THE CUPCAKES ARE!
Molly?

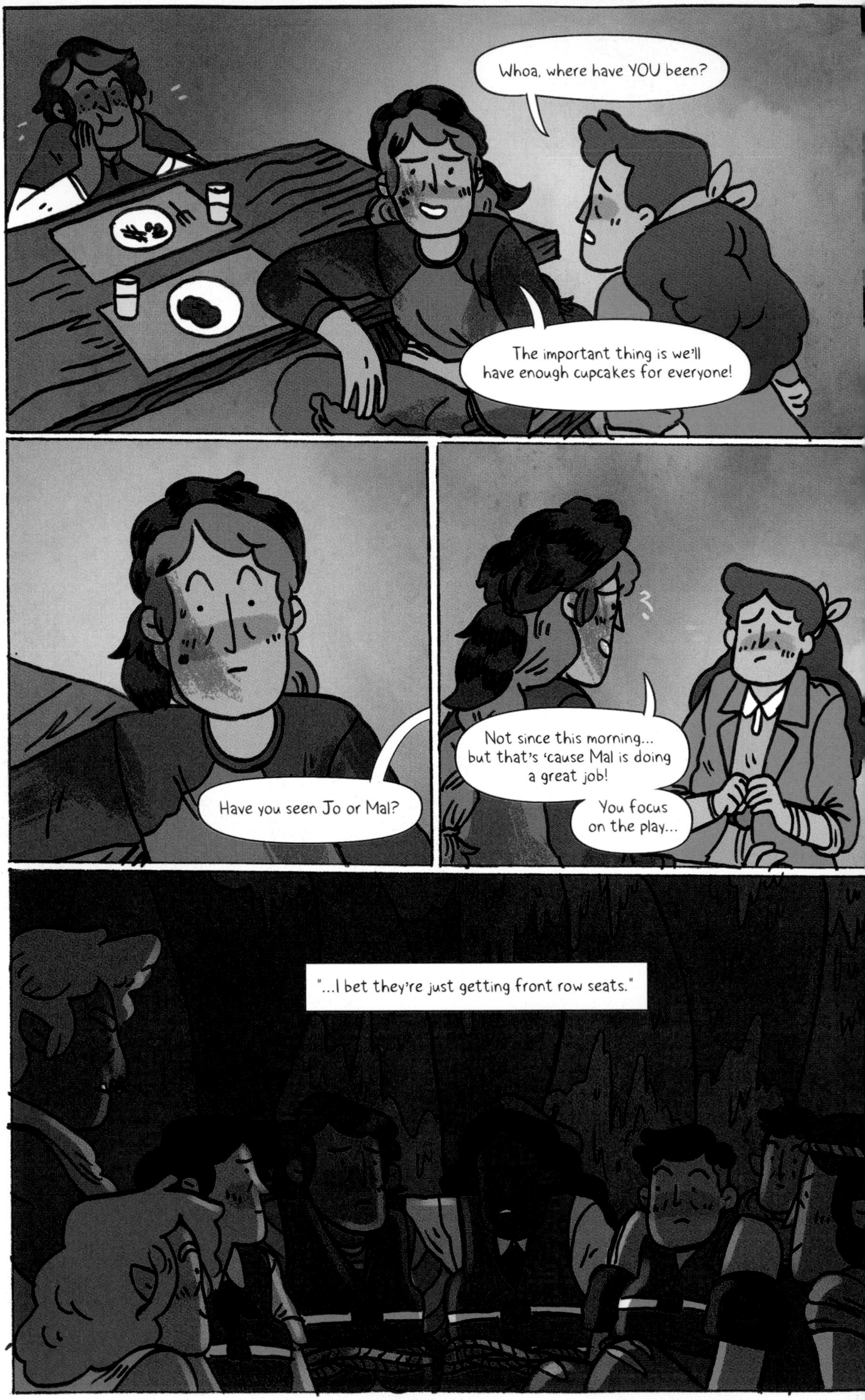
Whoa, where have YOU been?
The important thing is we'll have enough cupcakes for everyone!
Have you seen Jo or Mal?
Not since this morning... but that's 'cause Mal is doing a great job!
You focus on the play...
"...I bet they're just getting front row seats."

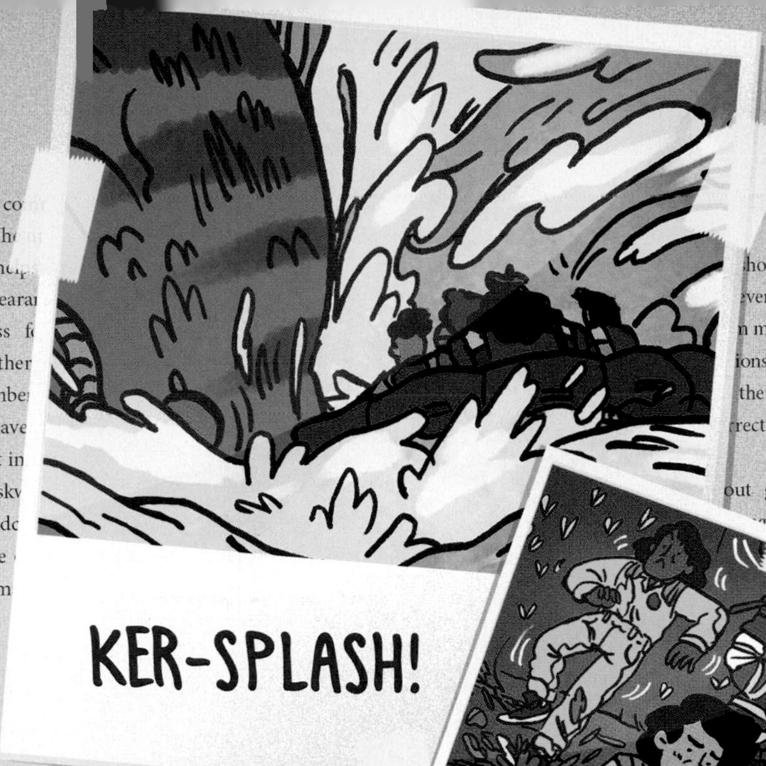
KER-SPLASH!

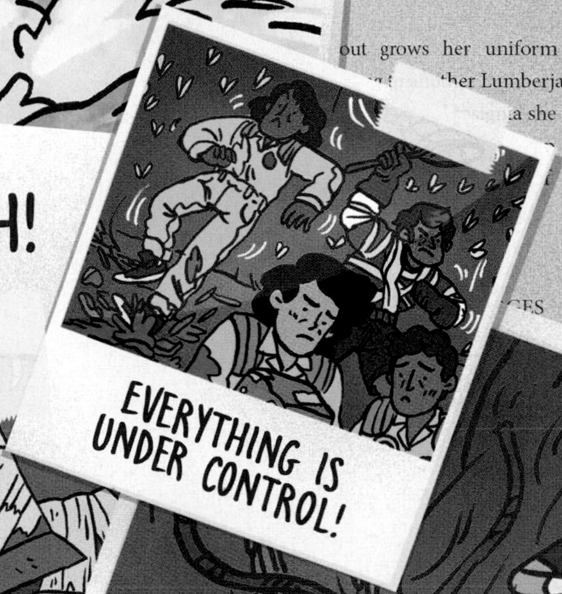
EVERYTHING IS UNDER CONTROL!

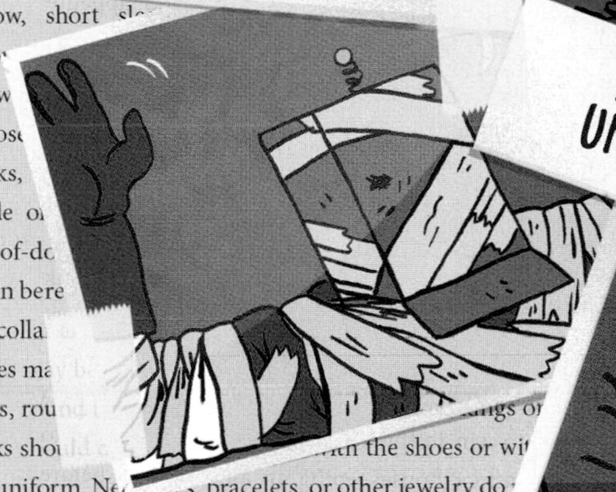

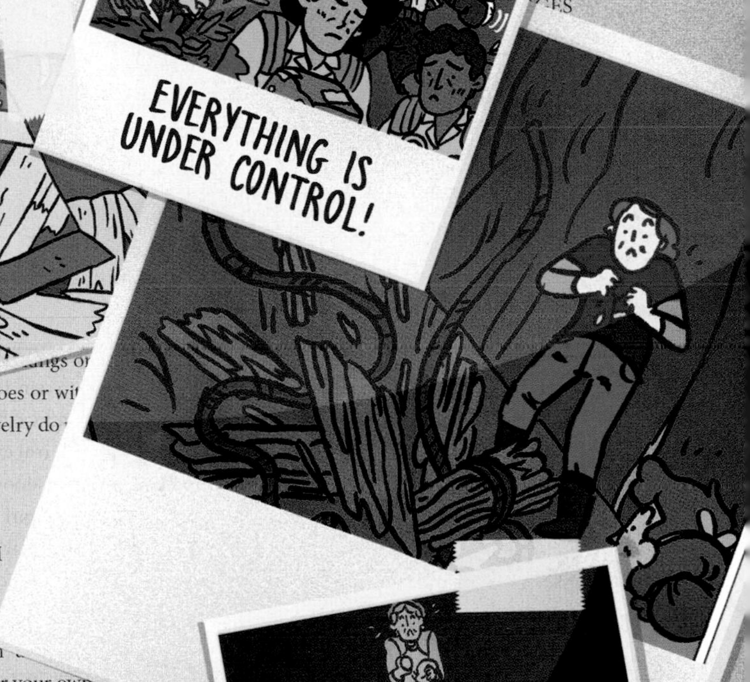

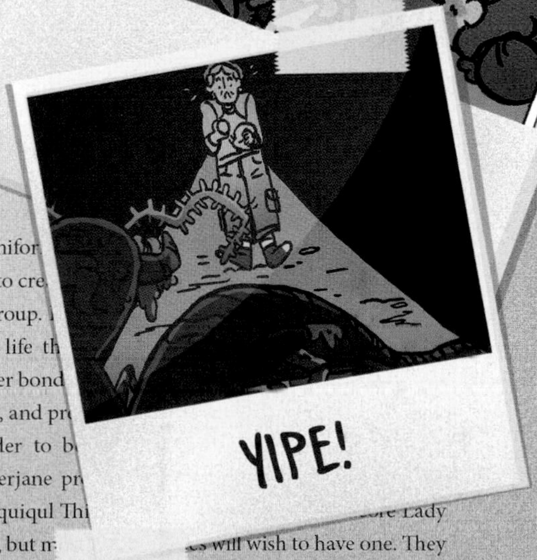
YIPE!

will co

The
It h
appearan
dress f
Further
Lumbe
to have
part in
Thiskv
Hardc
have
them

The
yellow, short sl
emb
the w
choose
slacks,
made o
out-of-dc
green bere
the colla
Shoes ma
heels, rou … ngs or
socks shou … with the shoes or wit
the uniform. Ne… bracelets, or other jewelry do
belong with a Lumberjane uniform.

…HE UNIFORM

…should be worn at camp …events when Lumberjanes …n may also be worn at other …ions. It should be worn as a … the uniform dress with …rrect shoes, and stocking or

… out grows her uniform or … her Lumberjane. … a she has … her … her

…CES

HOW TO WEAR THE UNIFORM

To look well in a uniform demands first of … uniform be kept in good condition—clean … pressed. See that the skirt is the right length for your own height and build, that the belt is adjusted to your waist, that your shoes and stockings are in keeping with the uniform, that you watch your posture and carry yourself with dignity and grace. If the beret is removed indoors, be sure that your hair is neat and kept in place with an inconspicuous clip or ribbon. When you wear a Lumberjane uniform you are identified as a member of this organization and you should be doubly careful to conduct yourself in a way that will show everyone that courtesy and thoughtfulness are part of being a Lumberjane. People are likely to judge a whole nation by the selfishness of a few individuals, to criticize a whole family because of the misconduct of one member, and to feel unkindly toward an organization because of the

The unifor
helps to cre
in a group.
active life th
another bond
future, and pr
in order to b
Lumberjane pr
Penniquiqul Thi… ore Lady
Types, but m… es will wish to have one. They
can either b… the uniform, or make it themselves from
materials available at the trading post.

LUMBERJANES FIELD MANUAL

CHAPTER
SIXTY

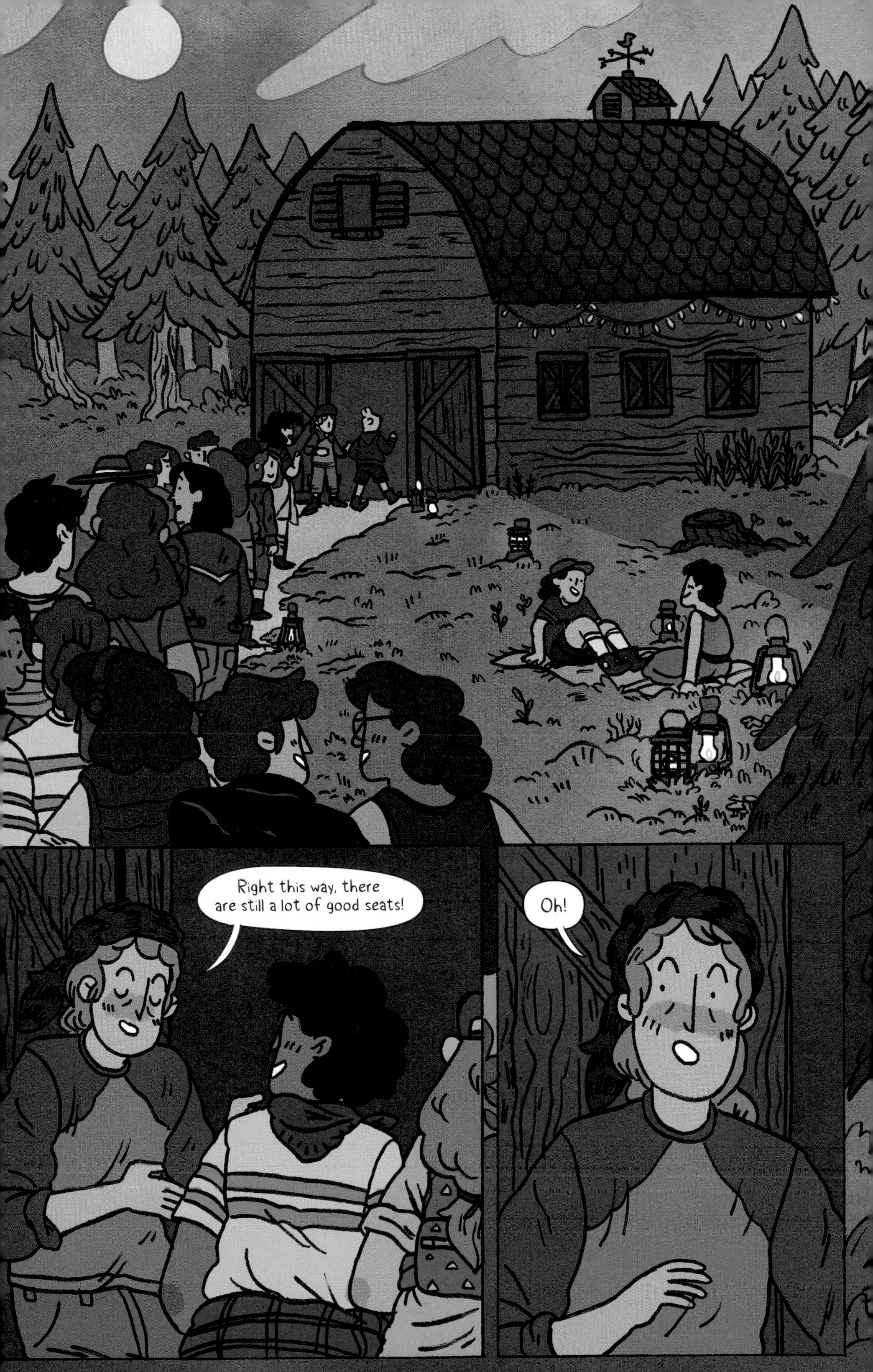
Right this way, there are still a lot of good seats!
Oh!

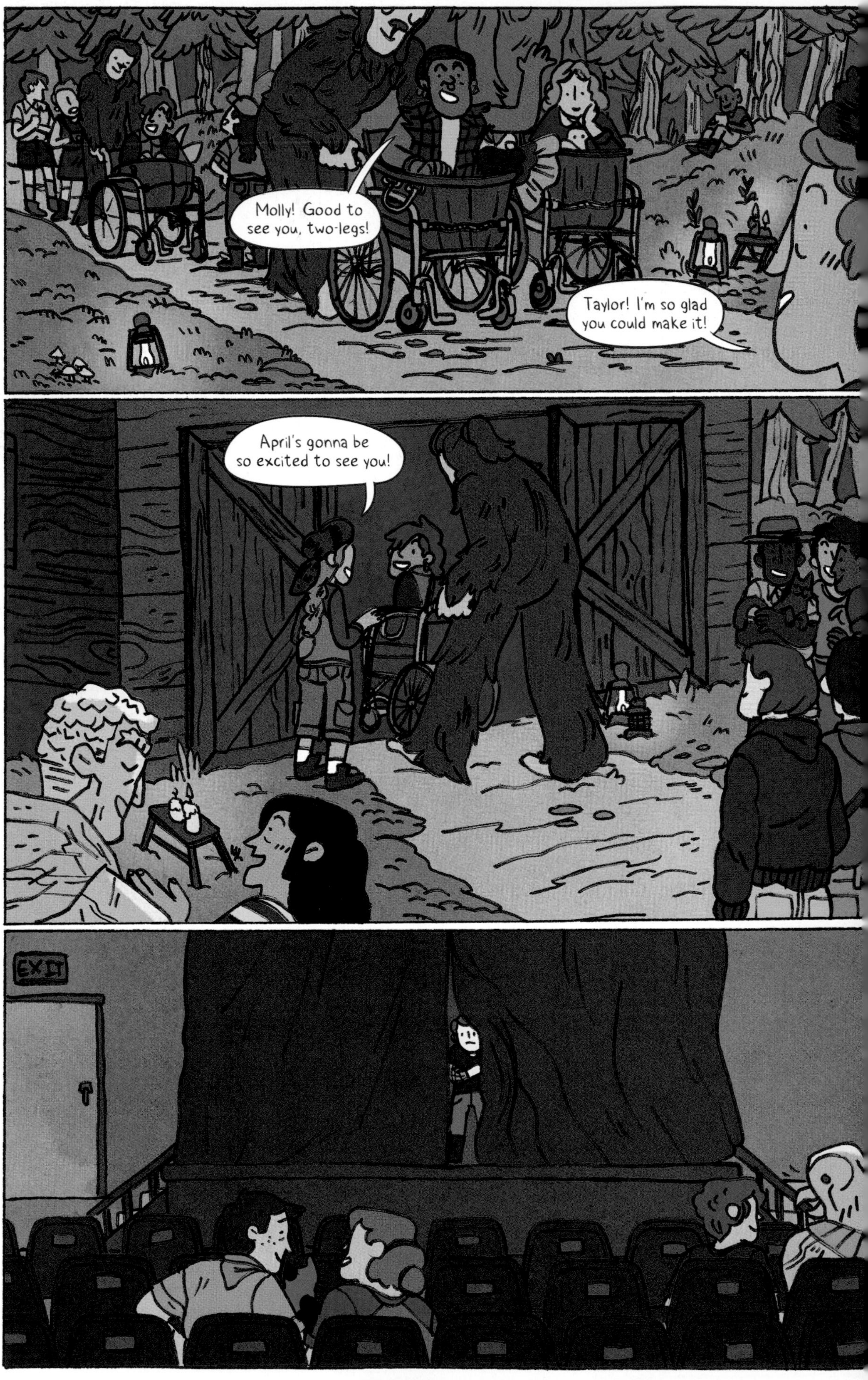
Molly! Good to see you, two-legs!
Taylor! I'm so glad you could make it!
April's gonna be so excited to see you!
EXIT

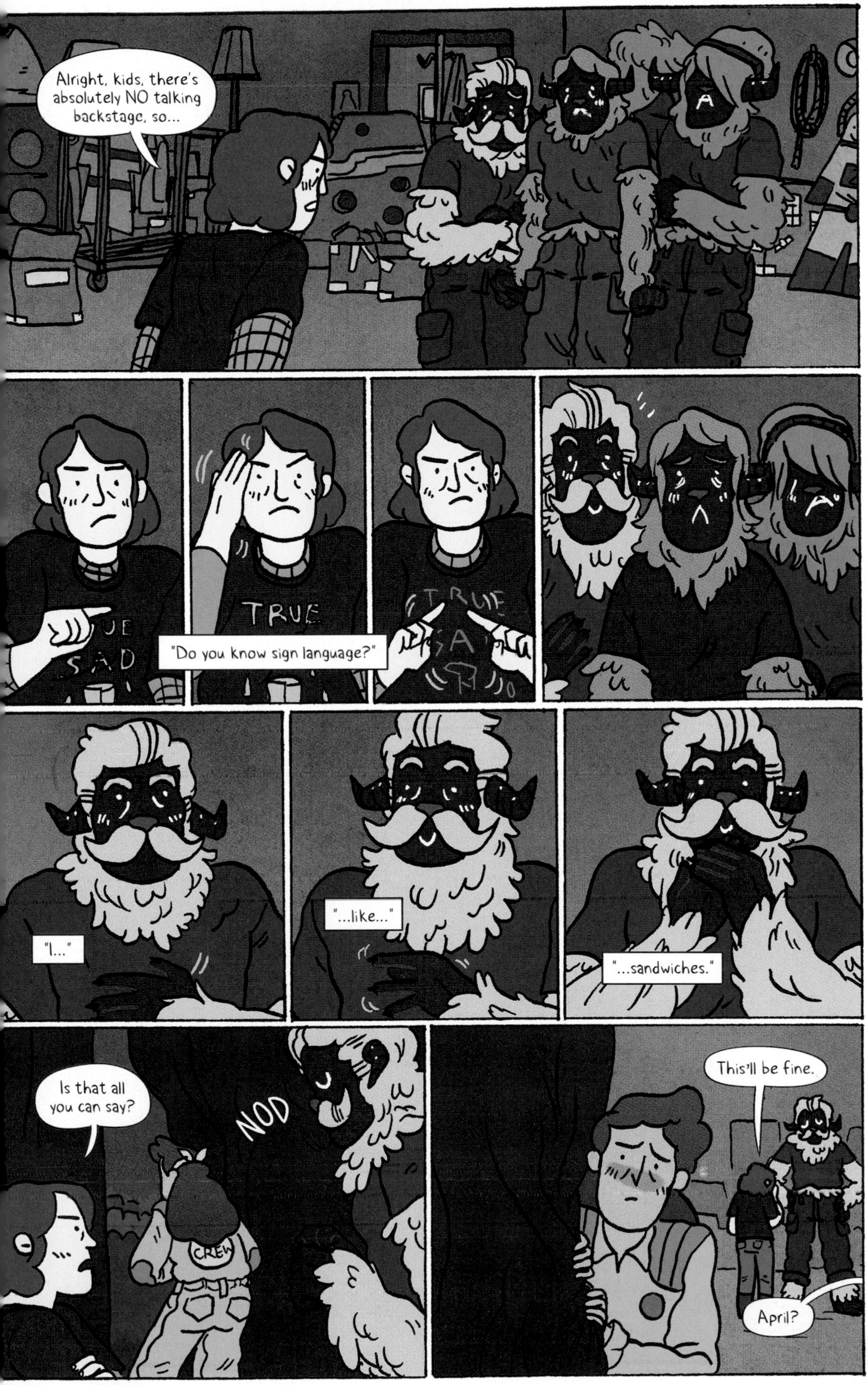

Alright, kids, there's absolutely NO talking backstage, so...
TRUE SAD
TRUE
"Do you know sign language?"
TRUE
"I..."
"...like..."
"...sandwiches."
Is that all you can say?
NOD
CREW
This'll be fine.
April?

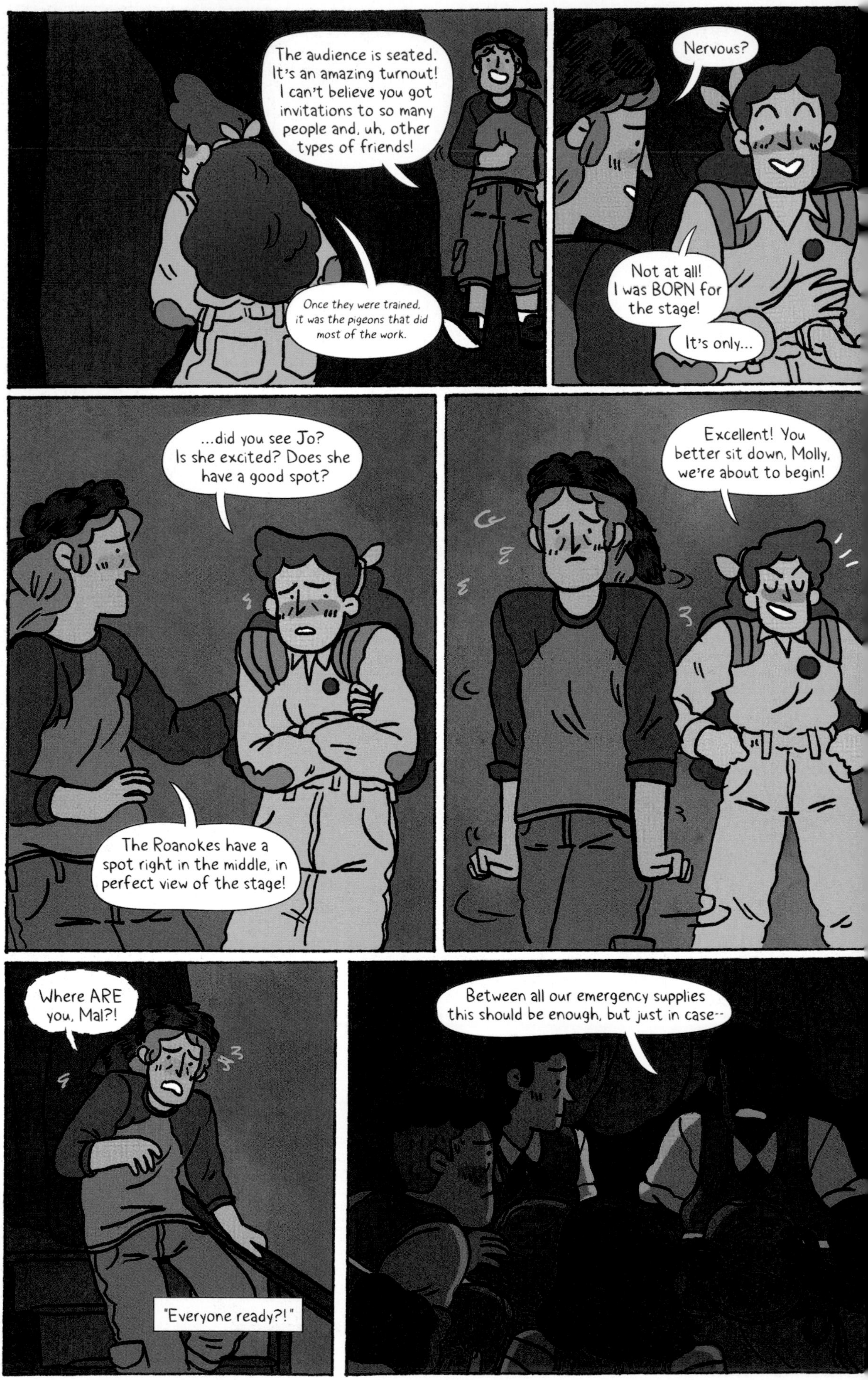
The audience is seated. It's an amazing turnout! I can't believe you got invitations to so many people and, uh, other types of friends!
Once they were trained, it was the pigeons that did most of the work.
Nervous?
Not at all! I was BORN for the stage!
It's only...
...did you see Jo? Is she excited? Does she have a good spot?
The Roanokes have a spot right in the middle, in perfect view of the stage!
Excellent! You better sit down, Molly, we're about to begin!
Where ARE you, Mal?!
"Everyone ready?!"
Between all our emergency supplies this should be enough, but just in case--

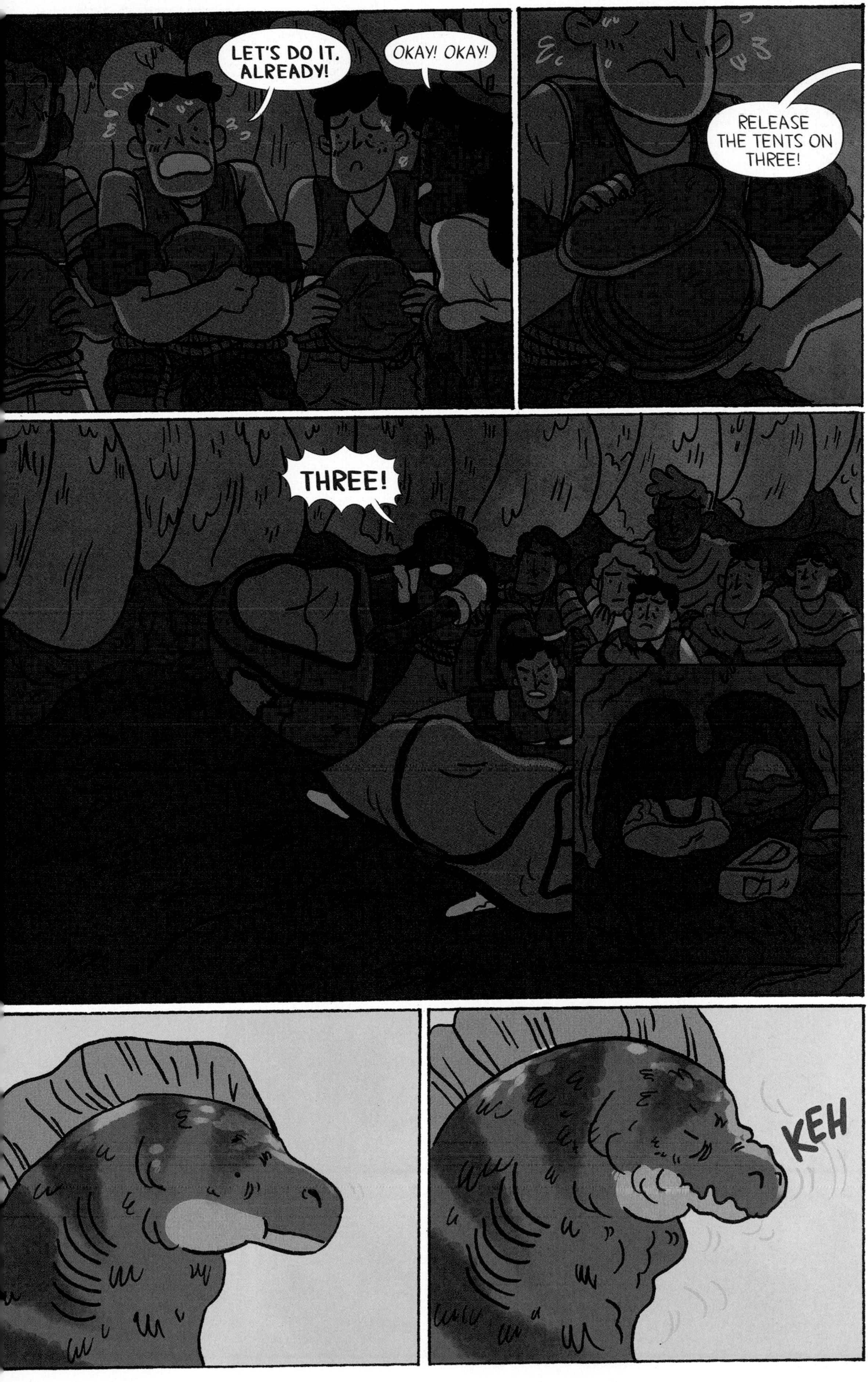
LET'S DO IT, ALREADY!
OKAY! OKAY!
RELEASE THE TENTS ON THREE!
THREE!
KEH

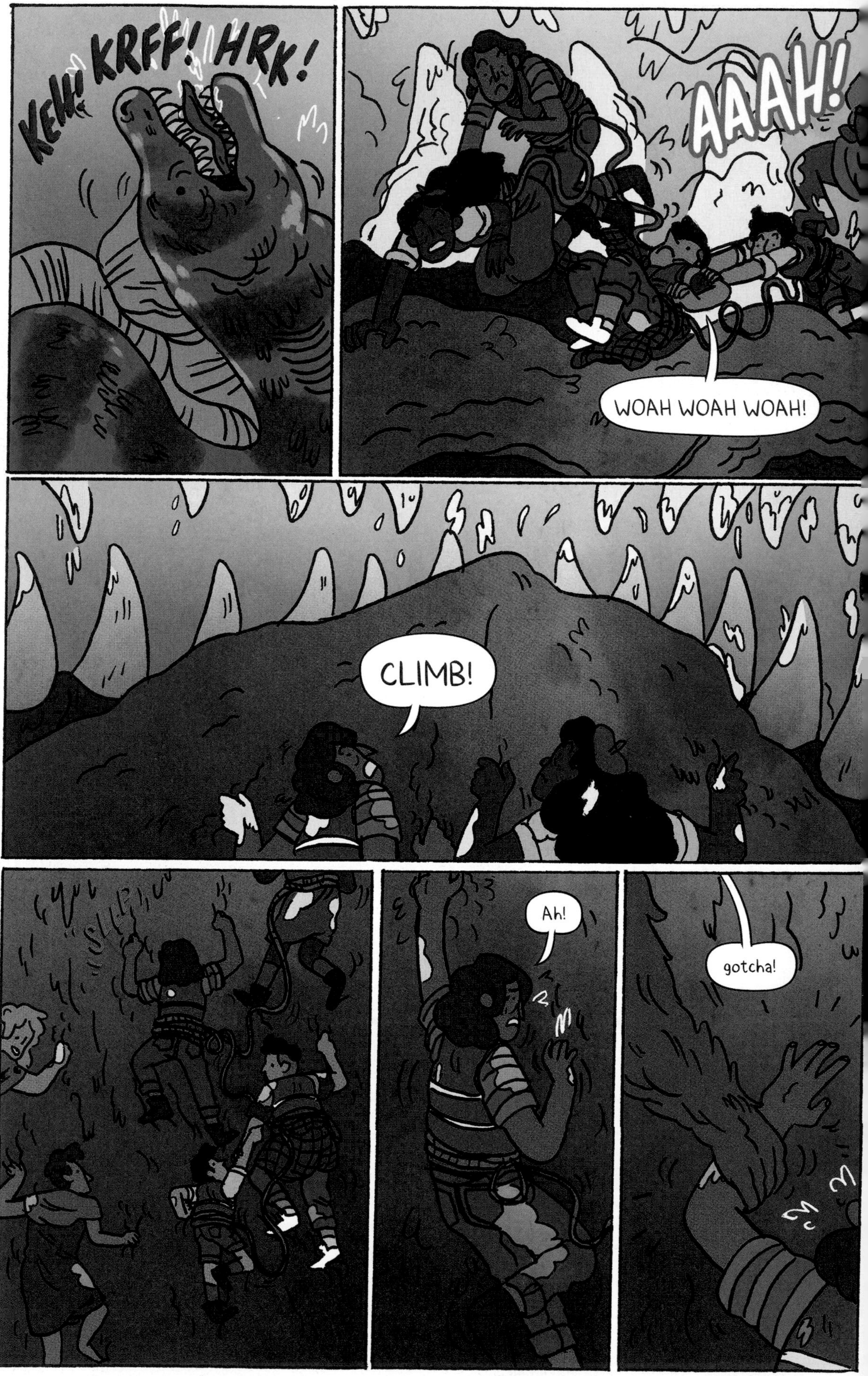
KEH! KRFF! HRK!
AAAH!
WOAH WOAH WOAH!
CLIMB!
SLIP
Ah!
gotcha!

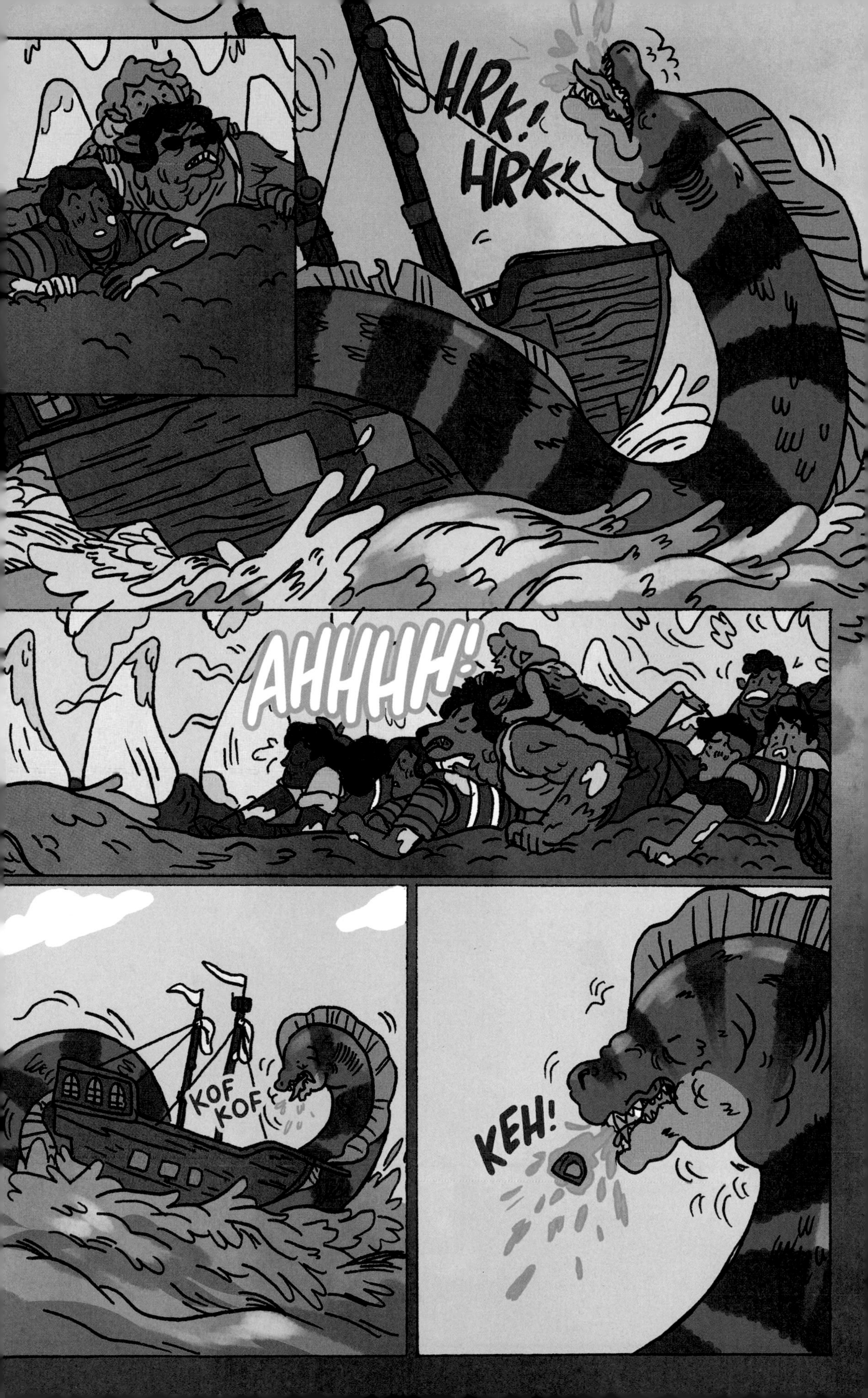
HRK! HRK!
AHHHH!
KOF KOF
KEH!

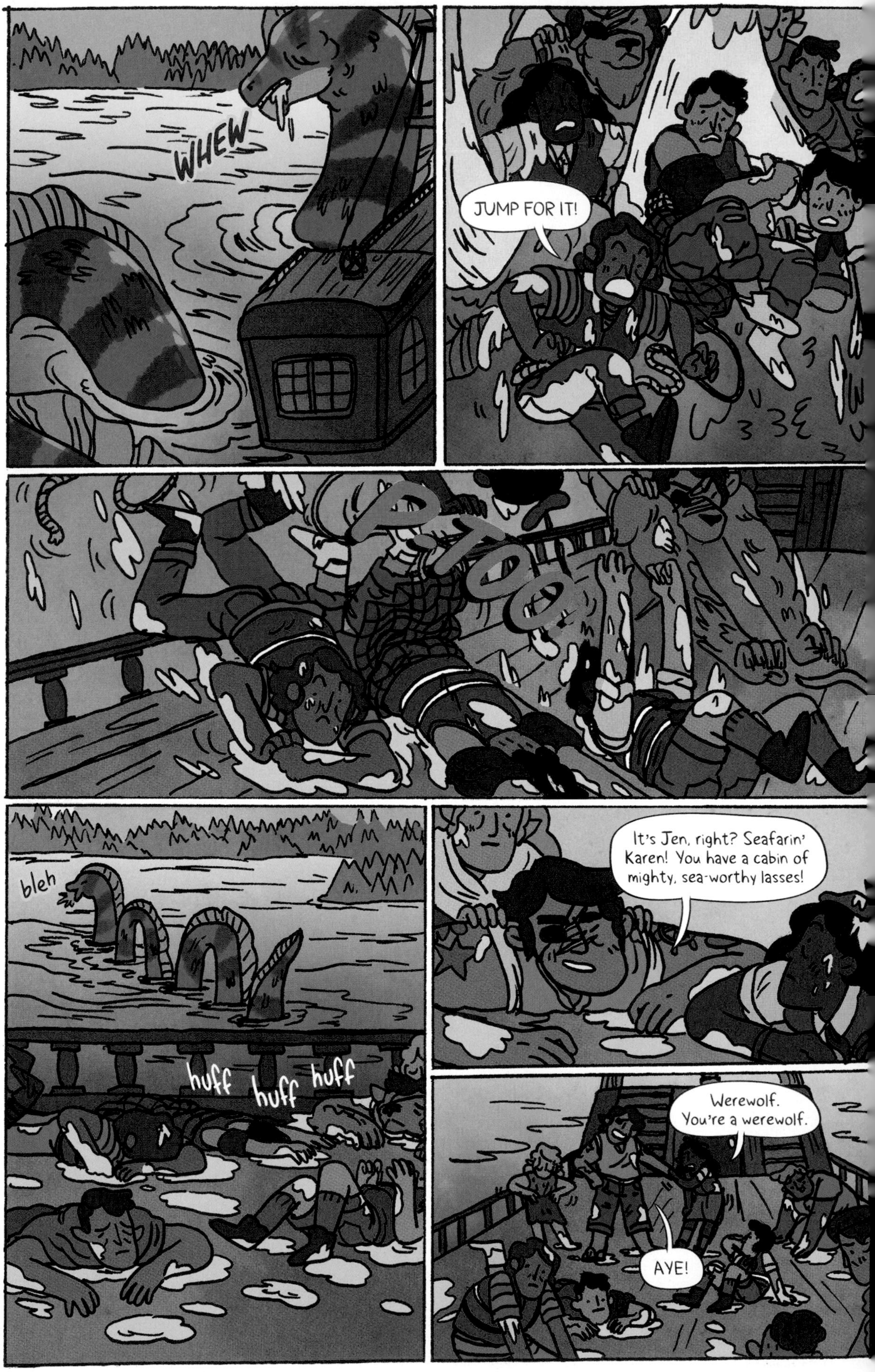
WHEW
JUMP FOR IT!
PTOOO
bleh
huff huff huff
It's Jen, right? Seafarin' Karen! You have a cabin of mighty, sea-worthy lasses!
Werewolf. You're a werewolf.
AYE!

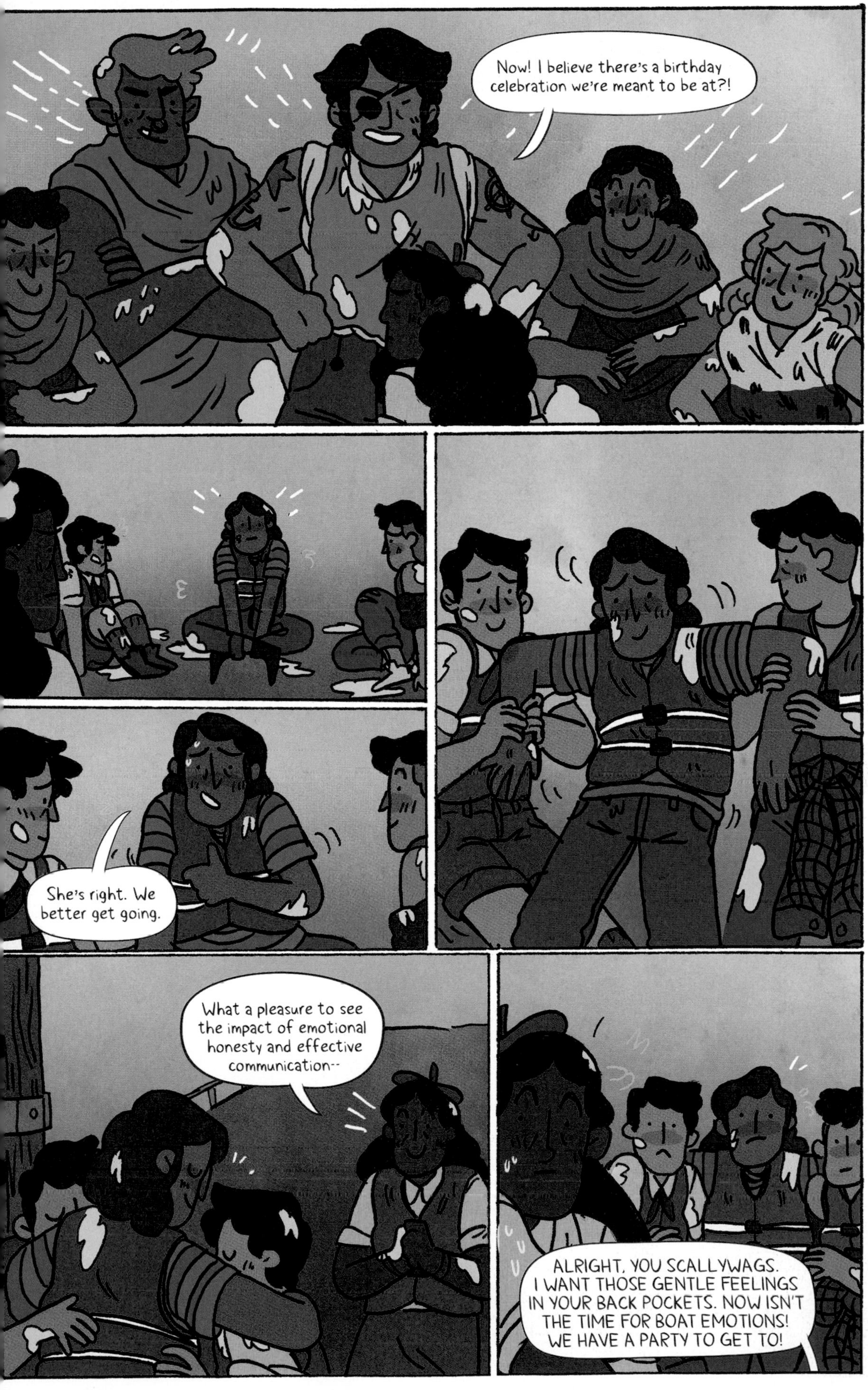
Now! I believe there's a birthday celebration we're meant to be at?!
She's right. We better get going.
What a pleasure to see the impact of emotional honesty and effective communication--
ALRIGHT, YOU SCALLYWAGS. I WANT THOSE GENTLE FEELINGS IN YOUR BACK POCKETS. NOW ISN'T THE TIME FOR BOAT EMOTIONS! WE HAVE A PARTY TO GET TO!

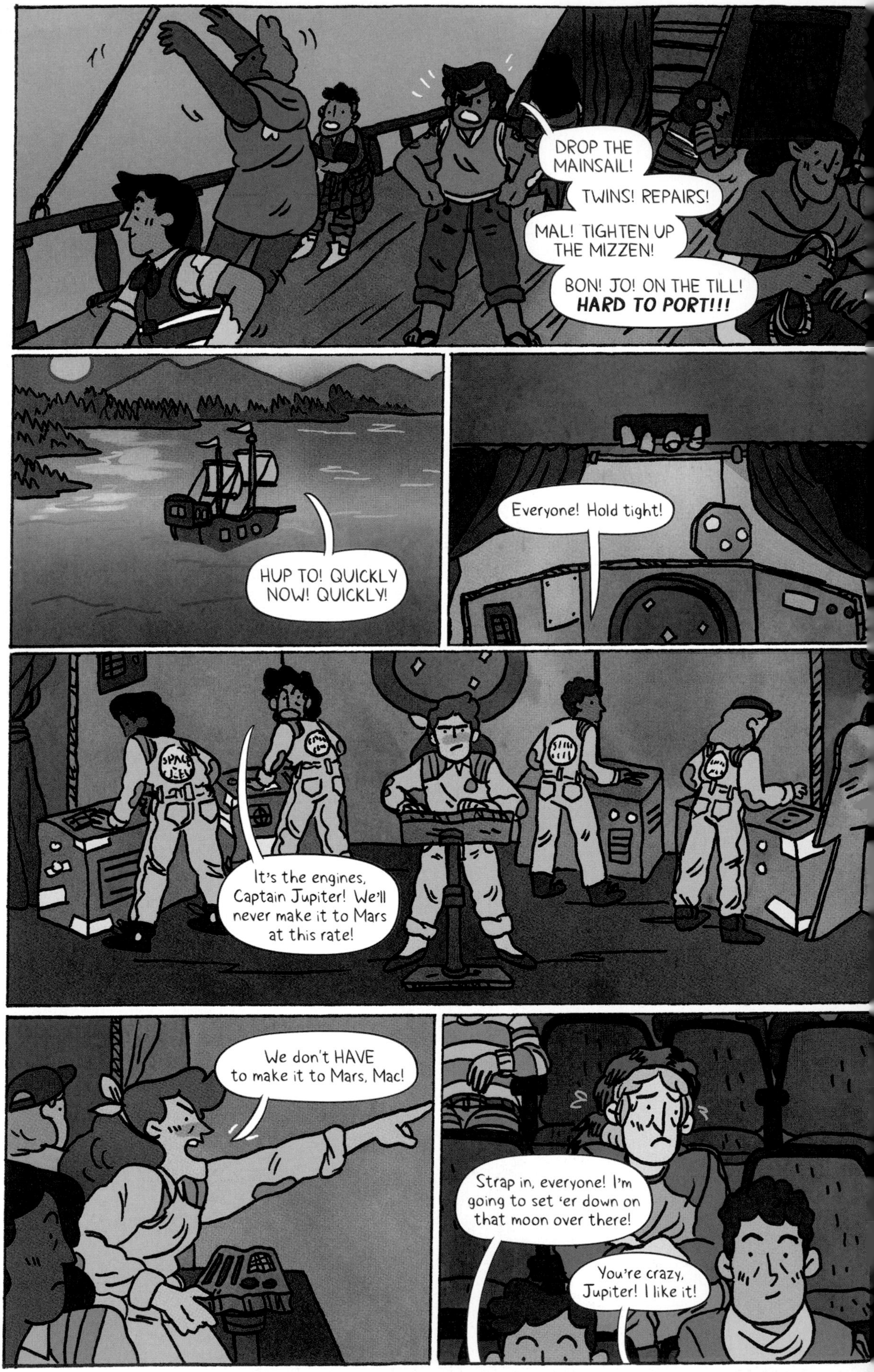
DROP THE MAINSAIL!
TWINS! REPAIRS!
MAL! TIGHTEN UP THE MIZZEN!
BON! JO! ON THE TILL! **HARD TO PORT!!!**
HUP TO! QUICKLY NOW! QUICKLY!
Everyone! Hold tight!
It's the engines, Captain Jupiter! We'll never make it to Mars at this rate!
We don't HAVE to make it to Mars, Mac!
Strap in, everyone! I'm going to set 'er down on that moon over there!
You're crazy, Jupiter! I like it!

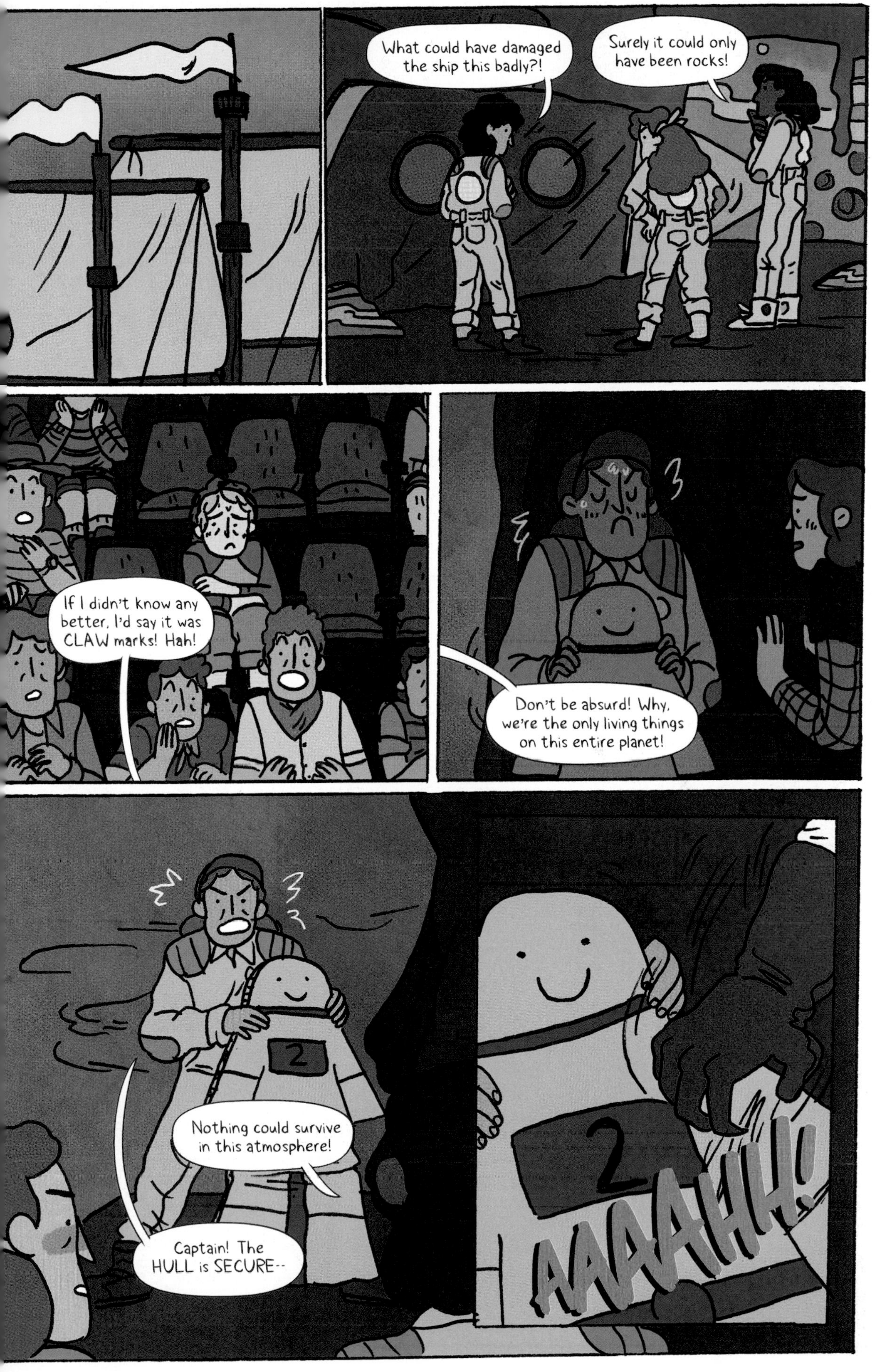
What could have damaged the ship this badly?!
Surely it could only have been rocks!
If I didn't know any better, I'd say it was CLAW marks! Hah!
Don't be absurd! Why, we're the only living things on this entire planet!
Nothing could survive in this atmosphere!
Captain! The HULL is SECURE--
AAAAHH!

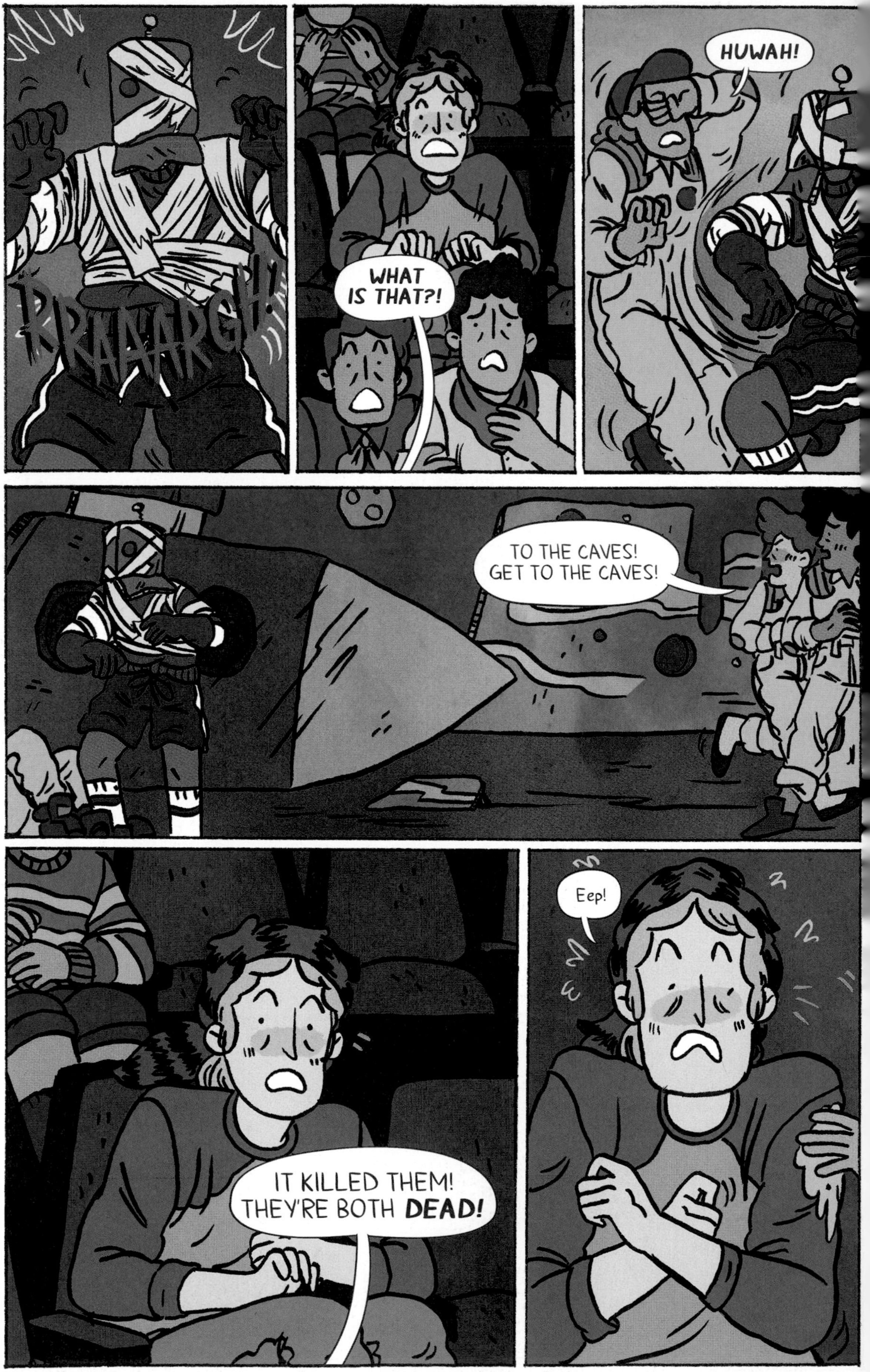
RRAAARGH!
WHAT IS THAT?!
HUWAH!
TO THE CAVES! GET TO THE CAVES!
IT KILLED THEM! THEY'RE BOTH **DEAD!**
Eep!

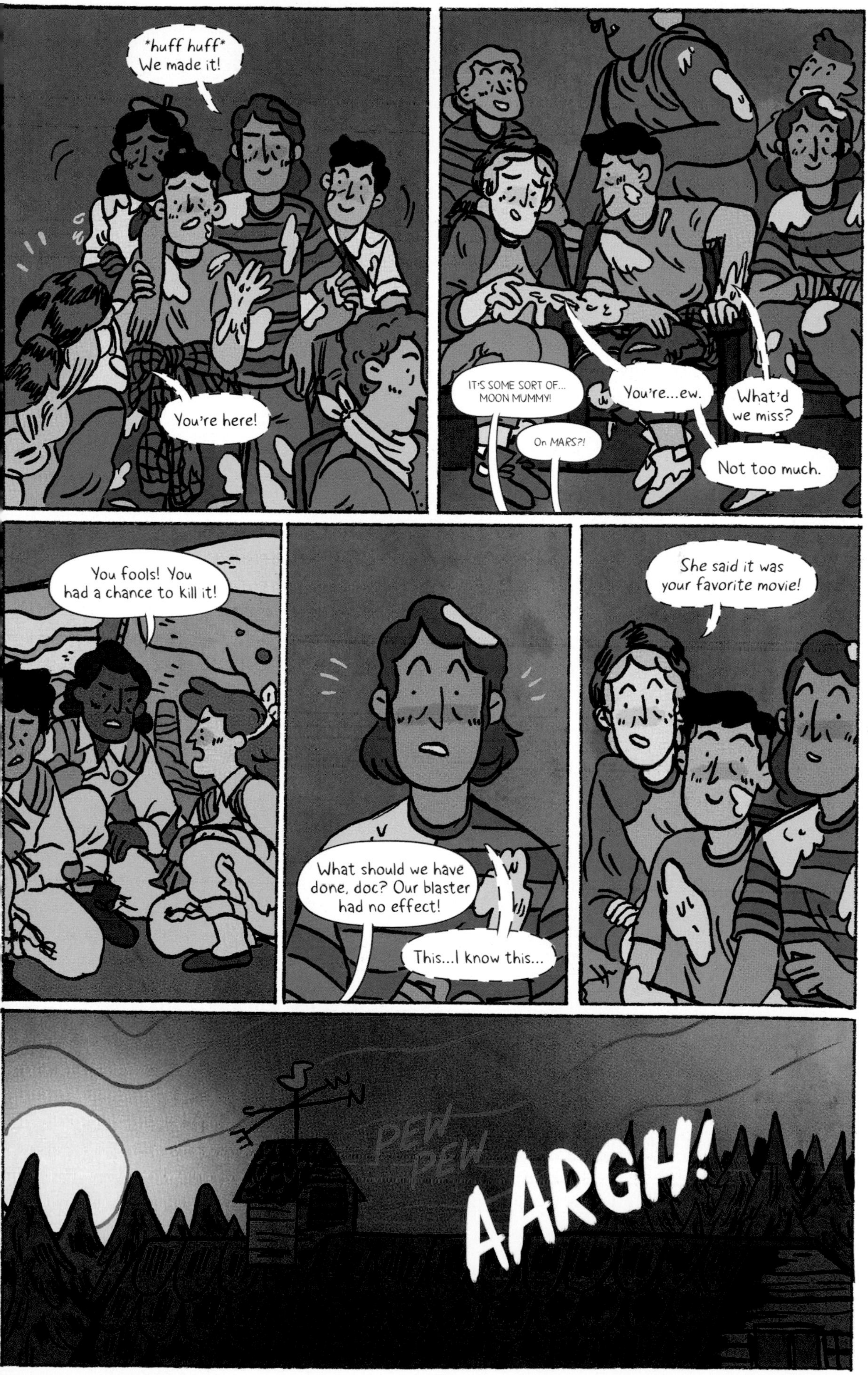
huff huff We made it!
You're here!
IT'S SOME SORT OF... MOON MUMMY!
On MARS?!
You're...ew.
What'd we miss?
Not too much.
You fools! You had a chance to kill it!
What should we have done, doc? Our blaster had no effect!
This...I know this...
She said it was your favorite movie!
PEW PEW
AARGH!

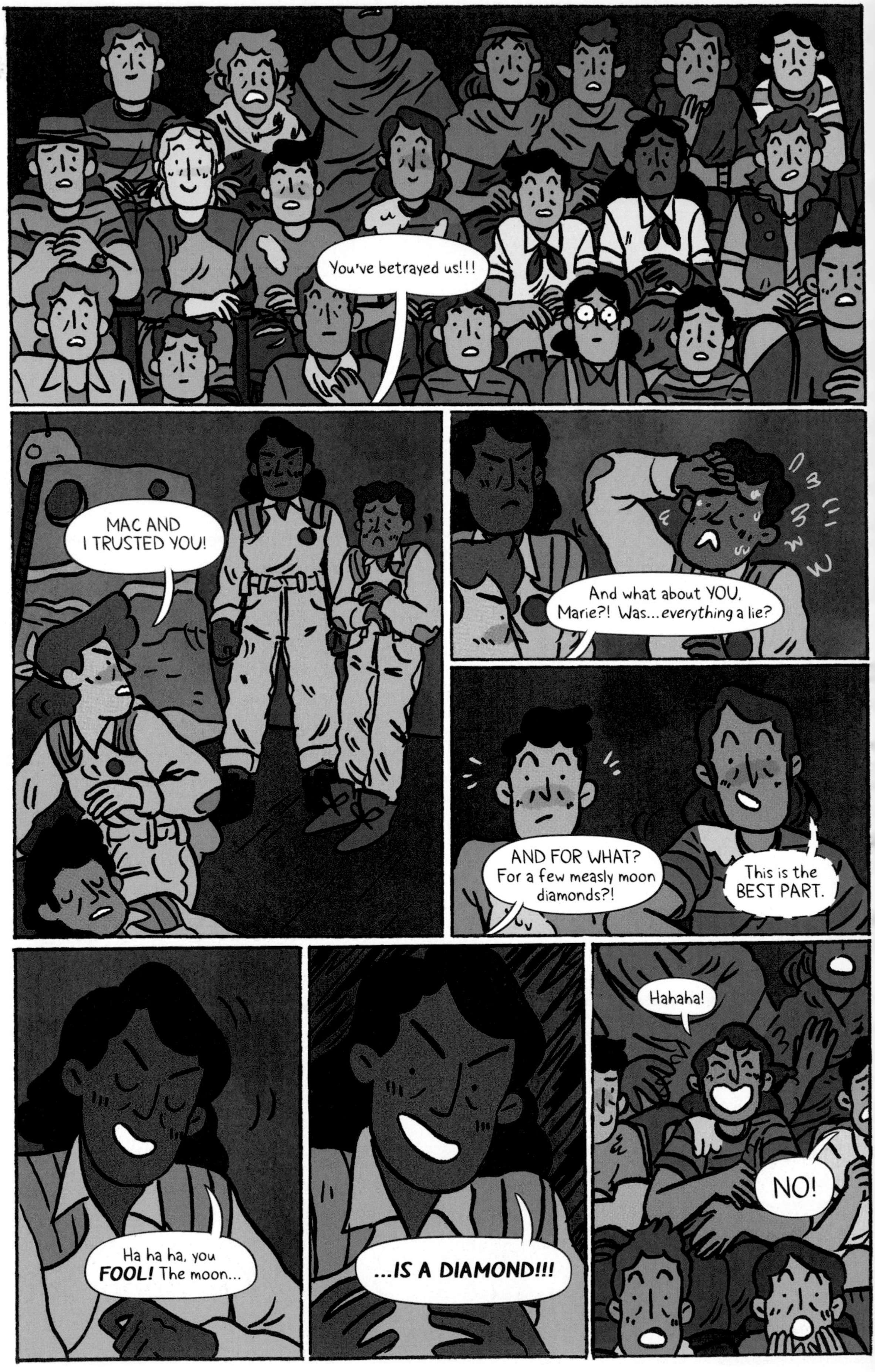
You've betrayed us!!!
MAC AND I TRUSTED YOU!
And what about YOU, Marie?! Was... everything a lie?
AND FOR WHAT? For a few measly moon diamonds?!
This is the BEST PART.
Ha ha ha, you **FOOL!** The moon...
...IS A DIAMOND!!!
Hahaha!
NO!

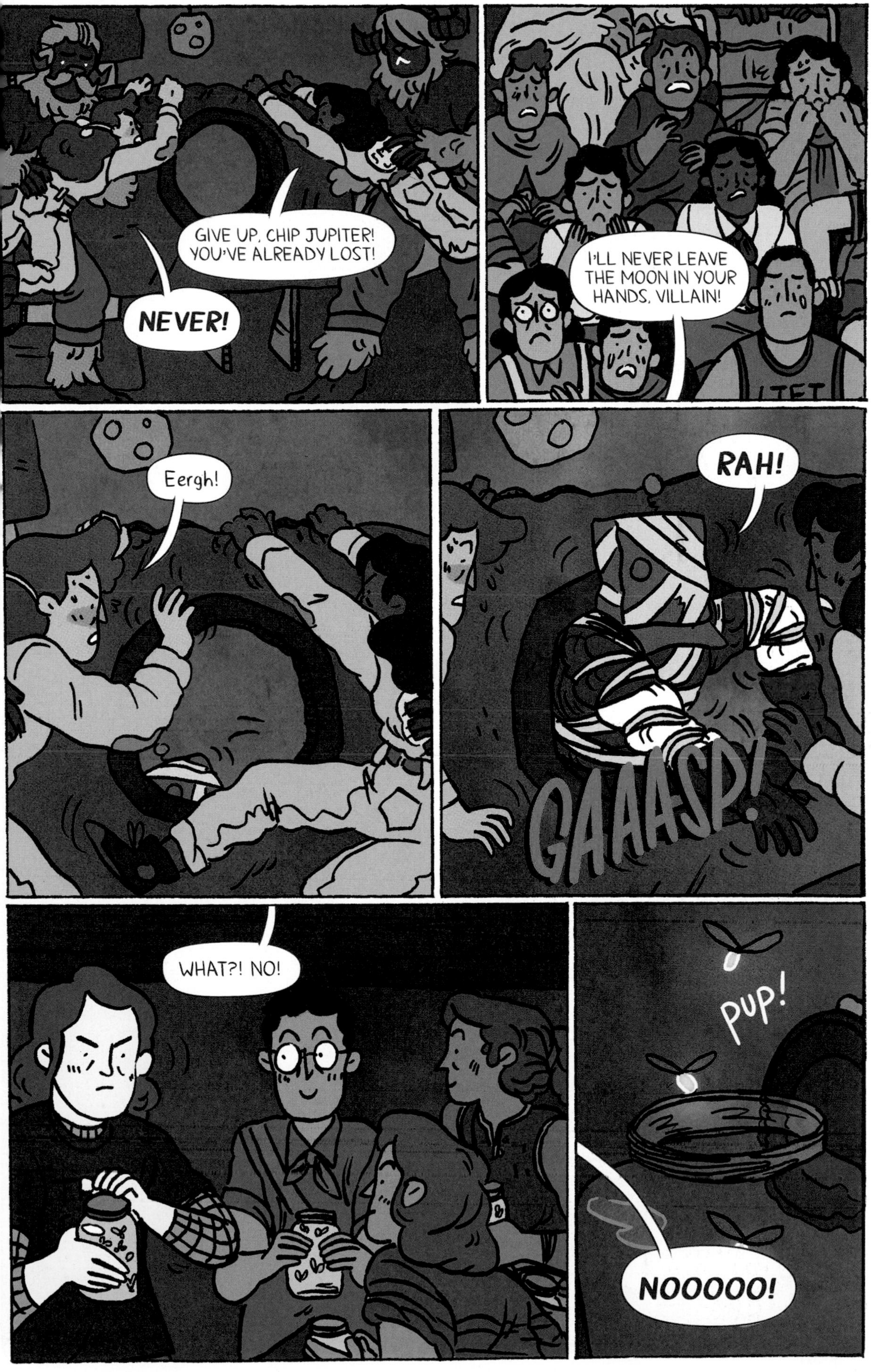
GIVE UP, CHIP JUPITER! YOU'VE ALREADY LOST!
NEVER!
I'LL NEVER LEAVE THE MOON IN YOUR HANDS, VILLAIN!
Eergh!
RAH!
GAAASP!
WHAT?! NO!
PUP!
NOOOOO!

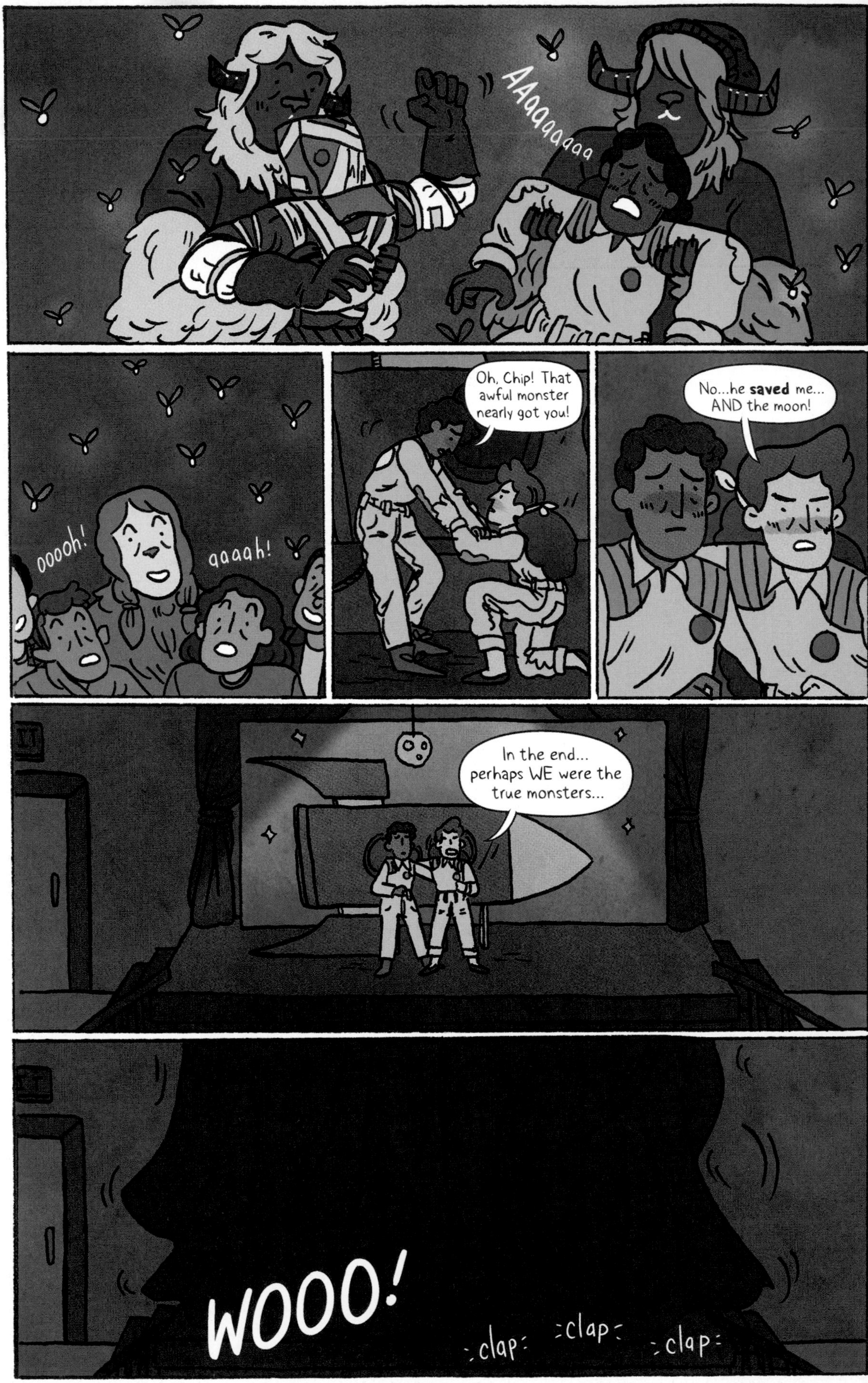
AAqqqaaaa
ooooh!
aaaah!
Oh, Chip! That awful monster nearly got you!
No...he **saved** me... AND the moon!
In the end... perhaps WE were the true monsters...
WOOO!
clap
clap
clap

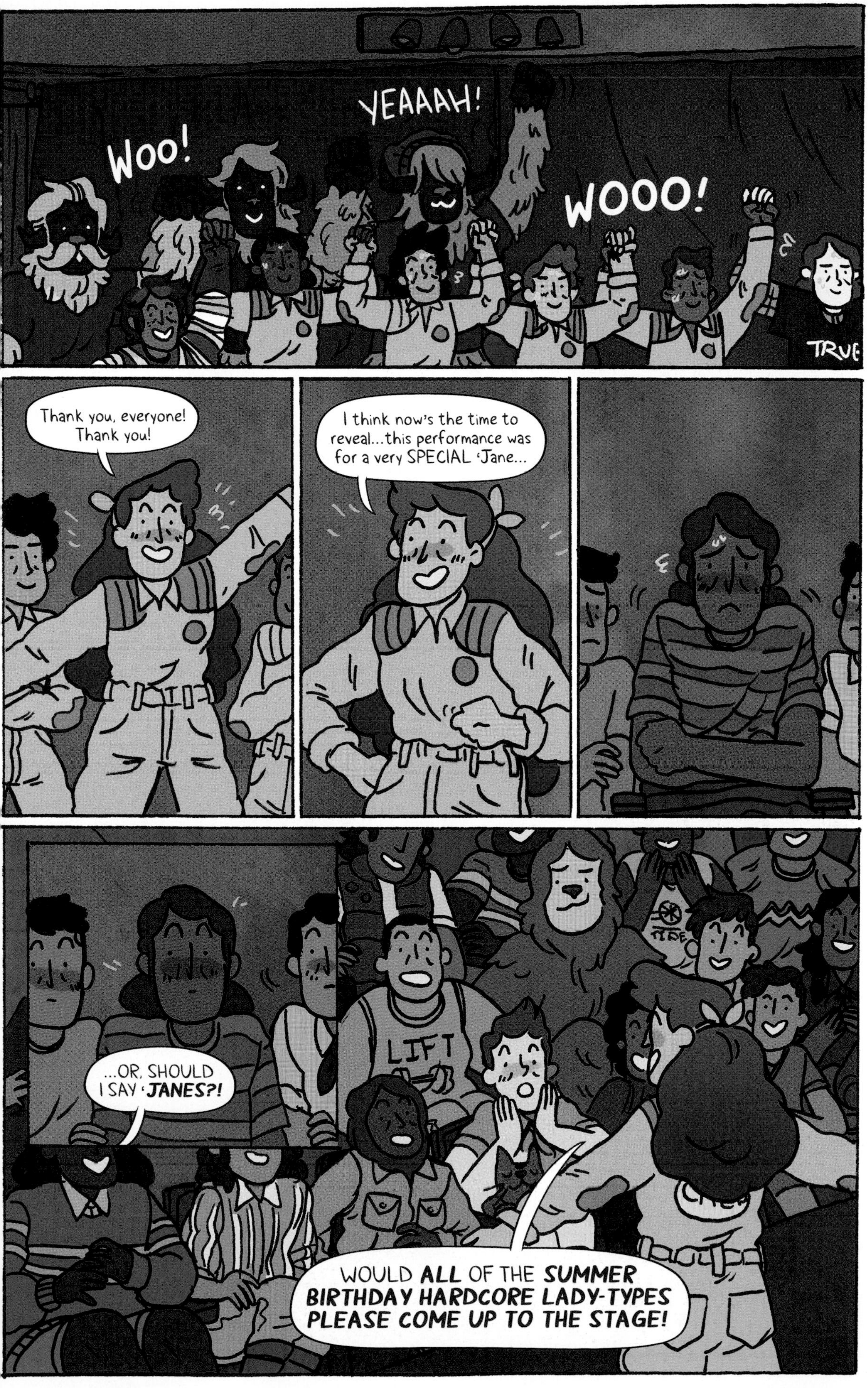
YEAAAH!
Woo!
WOOO!
TRUE
Thank you, everyone! Thank you!
I think now's the time to reveal...this performance was for a very SPECIAL 'Jane...
...OR, SHOULD I SAY 'JANES?!
WOULD ALL OF THE SUMMER BIRTHDAY HARDCORE LADY-TYPES PLEASE COME UP TO THE STAGE!
LIFT

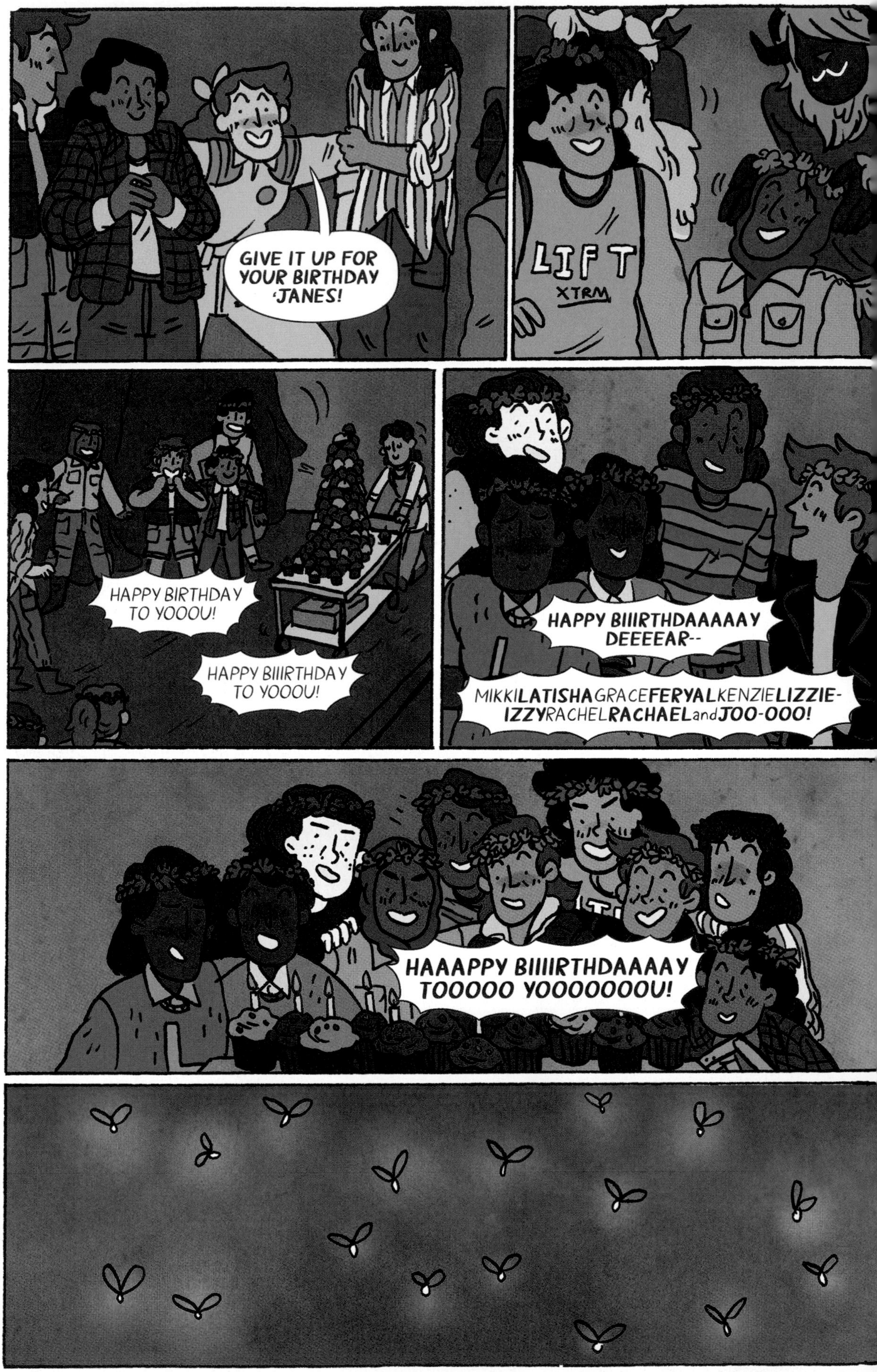
GIVE IT UP FOR YOUR BIRTHDAY 'JANES!
LIFT XTRM
HAPPY BIRTHDAY TO YOOOU!
HAPPY BIIIRTHDAY TO YOOOU!
HAPPY BIIIRTHDAAAAAY DEEEEAR--
MIKKILATISHAGRACEFERYALKENZIELIZZIE-IZZYRACHELRACHAELandJOO-OOO!
HAAAPPY BIIIIRTHDAAAAY TOOOOO YOOOOOOOU!

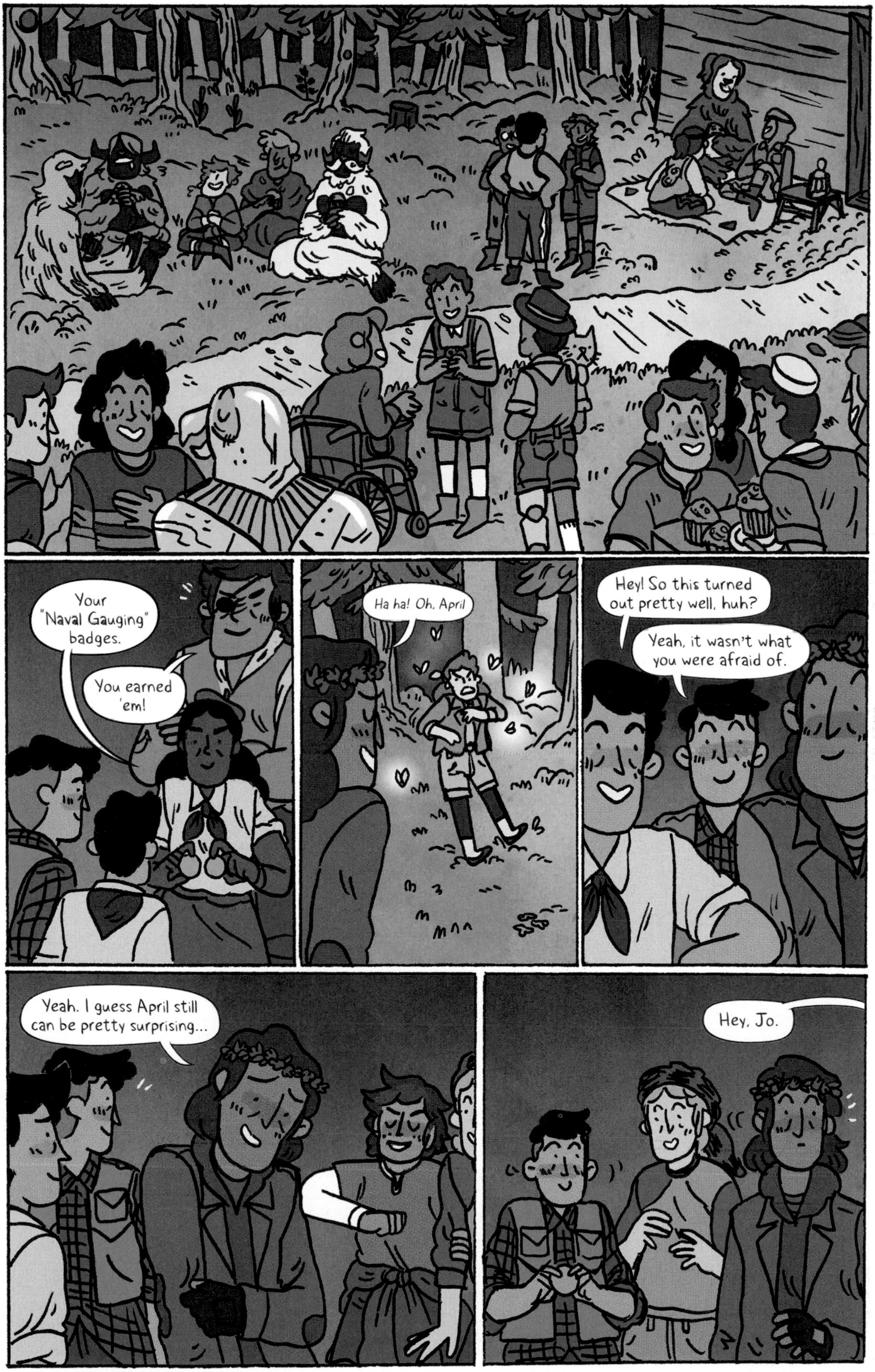
Your "Naval Gauging" badges.
You earned 'em!
Ha ha! Oh, April
Hey! So this turned out pretty well, huh?
Yeah, it wasn't what you were afraid of.
Yeah. I guess April still can be pretty surprising...
Hey, Jo.

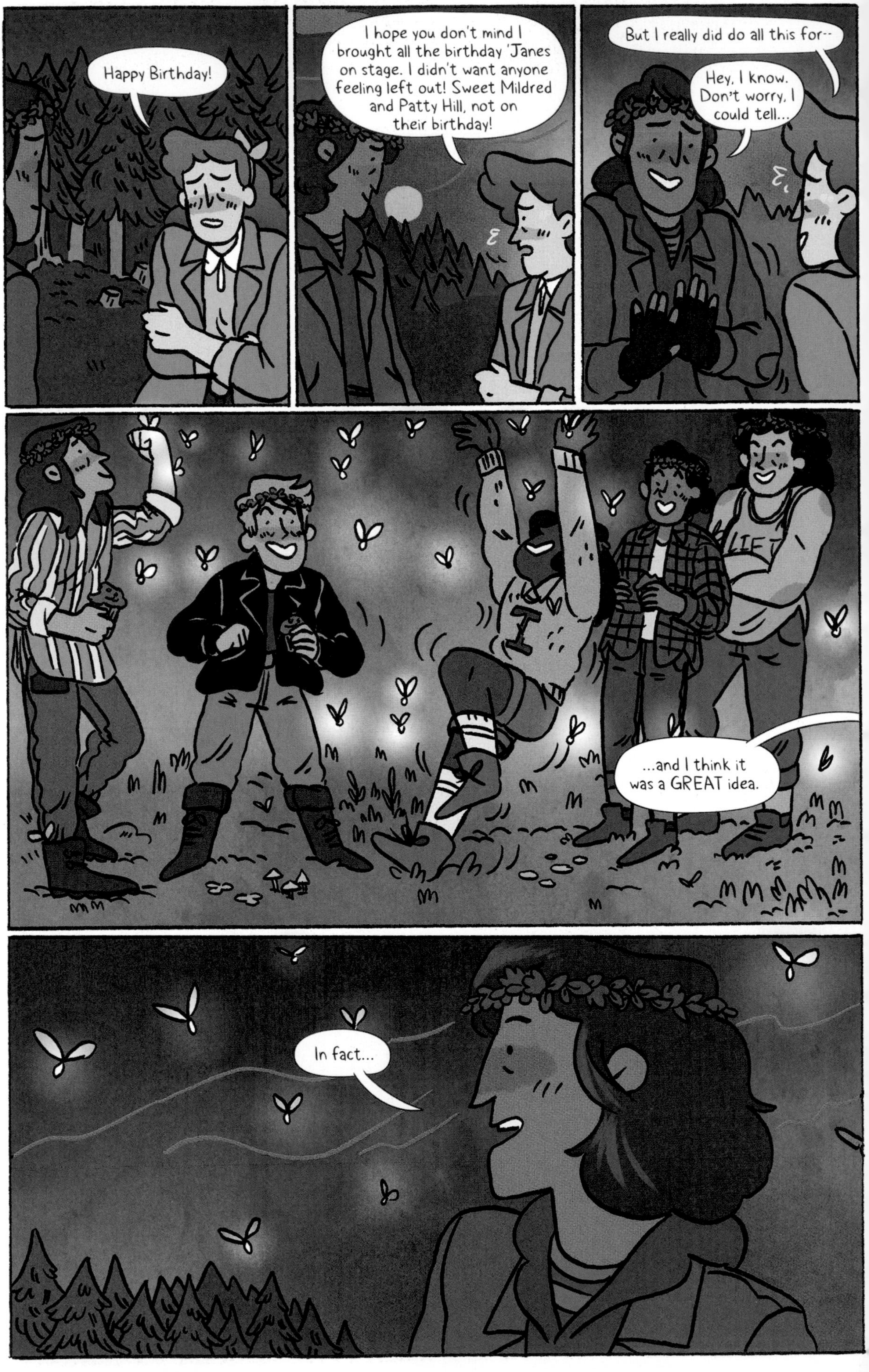
Happy Birthday!
I hope you don't mind I brought all the birthday 'Janes on stage. I didn't want anyone feeling left out! Sweet Mildred and Patty Hill, not on their birthday!
But I really did do all this for--
Hey, I know. Don't worry, I could tell...
...and I think it was a GREAT idea.
In fact...

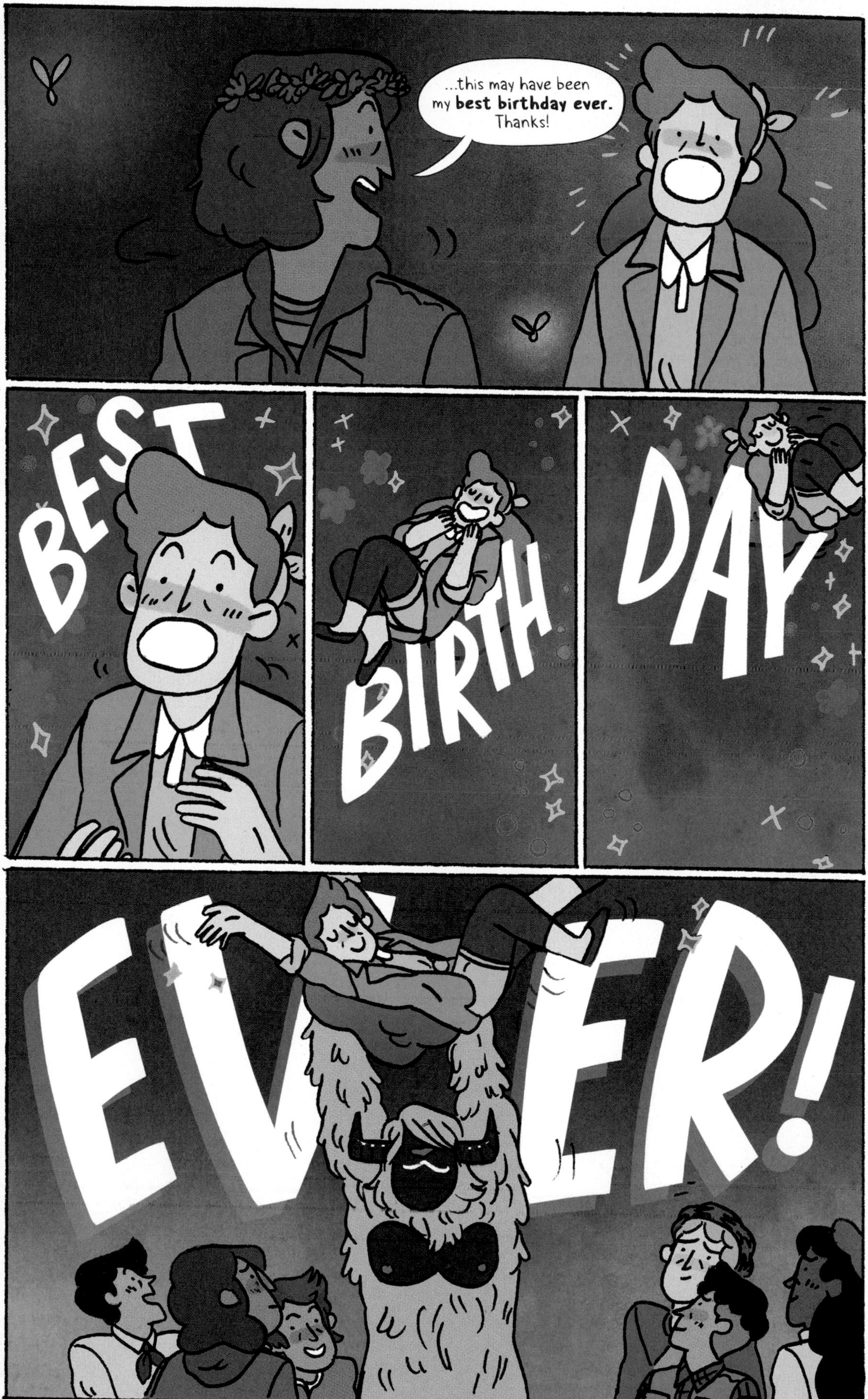

...this may have been my **best birthday ever.** Thanks!
BEST
BIRTH
DAY
EVER!

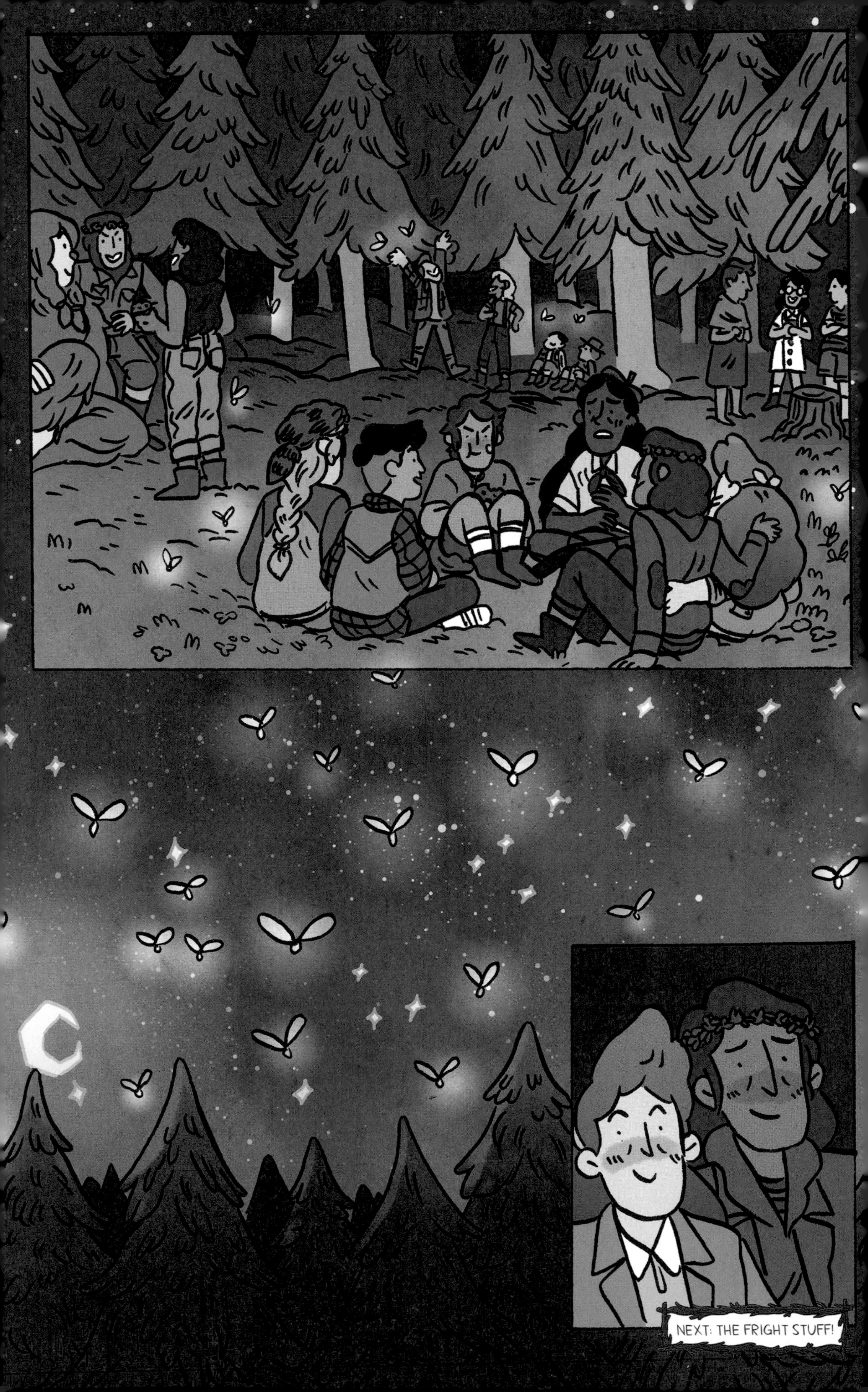
NEXT: THE FRIGHT STUFF!

will co

The

It he

appearan

dress f

Further

Lumber

to have

part in

Thiskw

Hardc

have

them

BACKSTAGE YETIS, REPORTING FOR DUTY!

The

yellow, short sl

emb

the w

choose

slacks,

made o

out-of-do

green bere

the colla

Shoes may b

heels, round

socks should

the uniform. Ne

belong with a Lumberjane uniform.

THE SHOW MUST GO ON!

HOW TO WEAR THE UNIFORM

To look well in a uniform demands first of
uniform be kept in good condition—clean
pressed. See that the skirt is the right length for your own
height and build, that the belt is adjusted to your waist,
that your shoes and stockings are in keeping with the
uniform, that you watch your posture and carry yourself
with dignity and grace. If the beret is removed indoors,
be sure that your hair is neat and kept in place with an
inconspicuous clip or ribbon. When you wear a
Lumberjane uniform you are identified as a member of
this organization and you should be doubly careful to
conduct yourself in a way that will show everyone that
courtesy and thoughtfulness are part of being a
Lumberjane. People are likely to judge a whole nation by
the selfishness of a few individuals, to criticize a whole
family because of the misconduct of one member, and to
feel unkindly toward an organization because of the

The unifor
helps to cre
in a group.
active life th
another bond
future, and pr
in order to b
Lumberjane pr
Penniquiqul Thi
Types, but m
can either bu
materials available at the trading post.

WHERE ARE THEY??

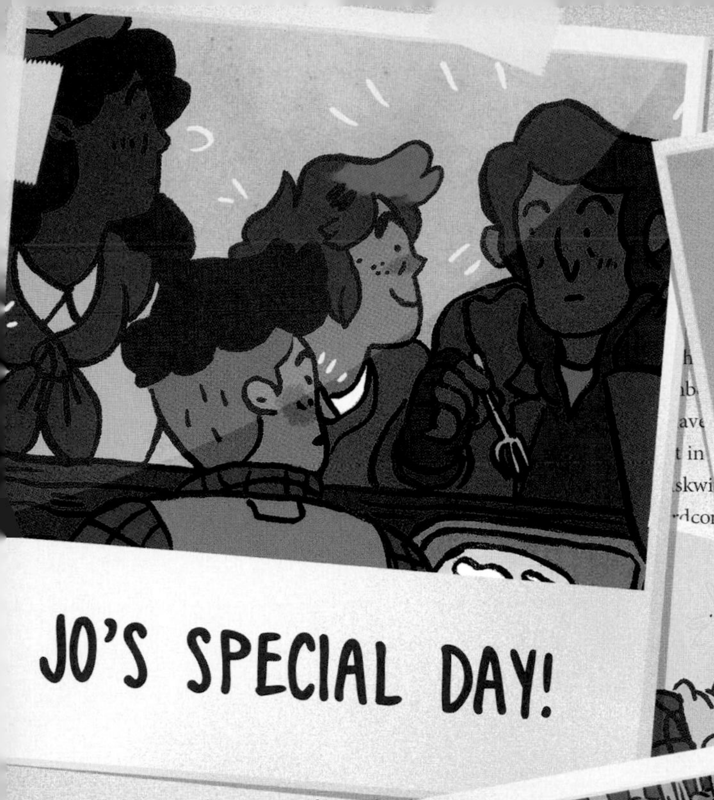
JO'S SPECIAL DAY!

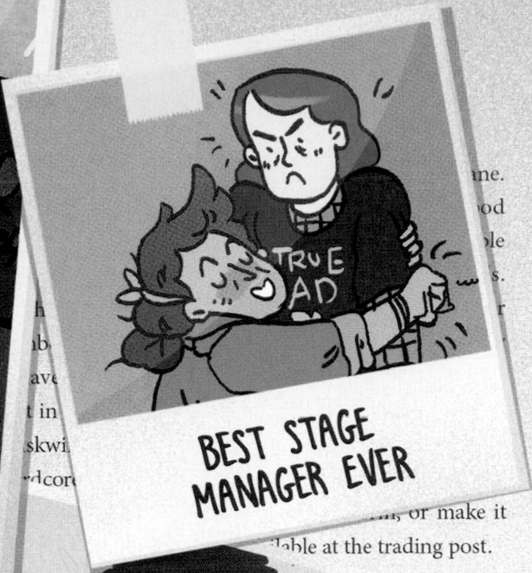
TRUE
AD
BEST STAGE MANAGER EVER

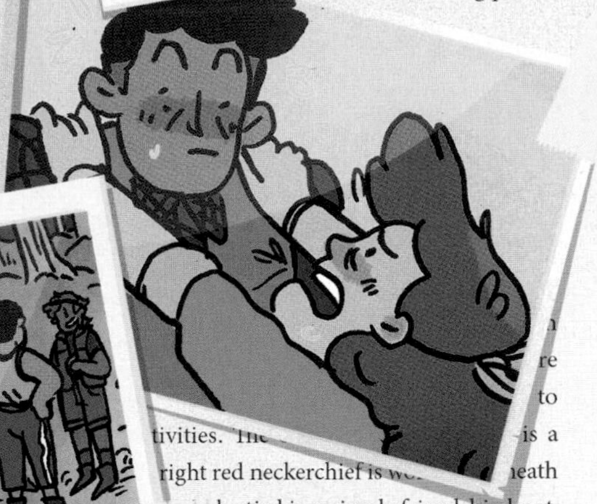

...m, or make it
...lable at the trading post.

The Lumberjane uniform sh...
meeting...

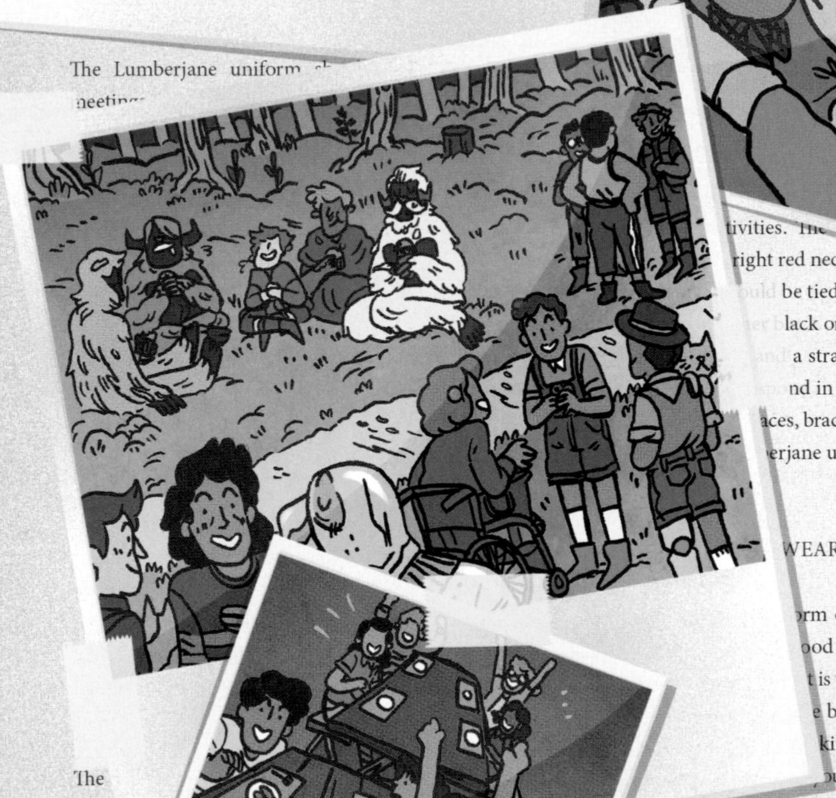

...tivities. The ... is a
...right red neckerchief is w... ...heath
...uld be tied in a simple friendship knot.
...lack or brown and should have flat
... a straight inner line. Stockings or
...nd in color with the shoes or with
...aces, bracelets, or other jewelry do not
...erjane uniform.

...WEAR THE UNIFORM

...orm demands first of all that the
...ood condition—clean and well
...t is the right length for your own
...e belt is adjusted to your waist,
...kings are in keeping with the
...our posture and carry yourself
...dignity and grace. If the beret is removed indoors, ...e sure that your hair is neat and kept in place with an inconspicuous clip or ribbon. When you wear a Lumberjane uniform you are identified as a member of this organization and you should be doubly careful to conduct yourself in a way that will show everyone that courtesy and thoughtfulness are part of being a Lumberjane. People are likely to judge a whole nation by the selfishness of a few individuals, to criticize a whole family because of the misconduct of one member, and to feel unkindly toward an organization because of the

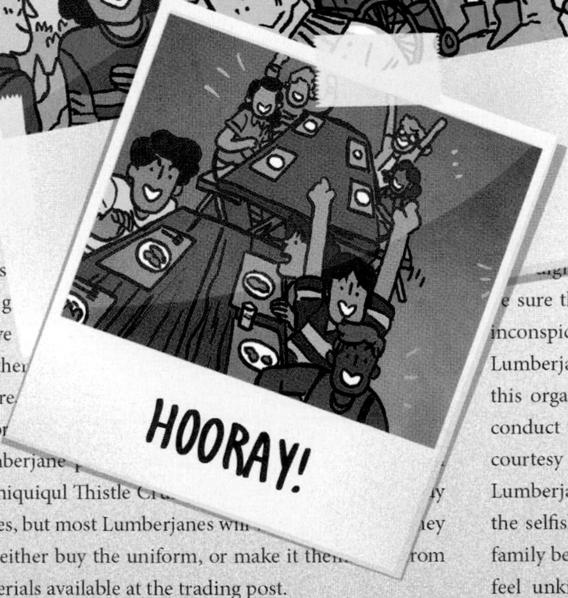
HOORAY!

The ...
helps ...
in a g...
active ...
another ...
future ...
in or ...
Lumberjane p...
Penniquiqul Thistle Cru... ...y
Types, but most Lumberjanes wi... ...ney
can either buy the uniform, or make it them... ...rom
materials available at the trading post.

COVER GALLERY

Lumberjanes "Out-of-Doors" Program Field

LIFE OF THE PARTY

"Making the Fiesta it!"

When it comes to festivities, Lumberjanes are always the life of the party! Whether you're marking a birthday, honoring a holiday, or just looking for an excuse to try out a new recipe, parties give us the perfect chance to gather with our closest friends and cherished family members!

Throwing a party is very different from attending one, though, and this badge is all about what it takes to pull off the perfect party. Playing host for a gathering, whether large or small, is one of the most loving, generous, and (sometimes) most stressful gifts you can give. There are more variables than you might expect, if you have never done it before! Of course, even as the host, you still get to eat the delicious food, and listen to your favorite music, but you are also responsible for choosing that music, and

for cooking, or purchasing that food. What's more, you are, in a sense, responsible for the party itself in addition to the parts that make up the whole. You are choosing to take on all of the many, many moving parts and disparate ideas that must come together, against all odds, to create one lovely evening.

Take the time to consider what would suit your friends' needs, and what would make them happiest, when you're planning a party for them. Think about how you might make the afternoon fun, while also bearing in mind what will be exciting for the whole group. Help guests when they need it and solve problems as they arise, but as you throw more parties, you will learn that there is also an art to letting go, and allowing an evening to develop as it wishes: a forest rather than a topiary!

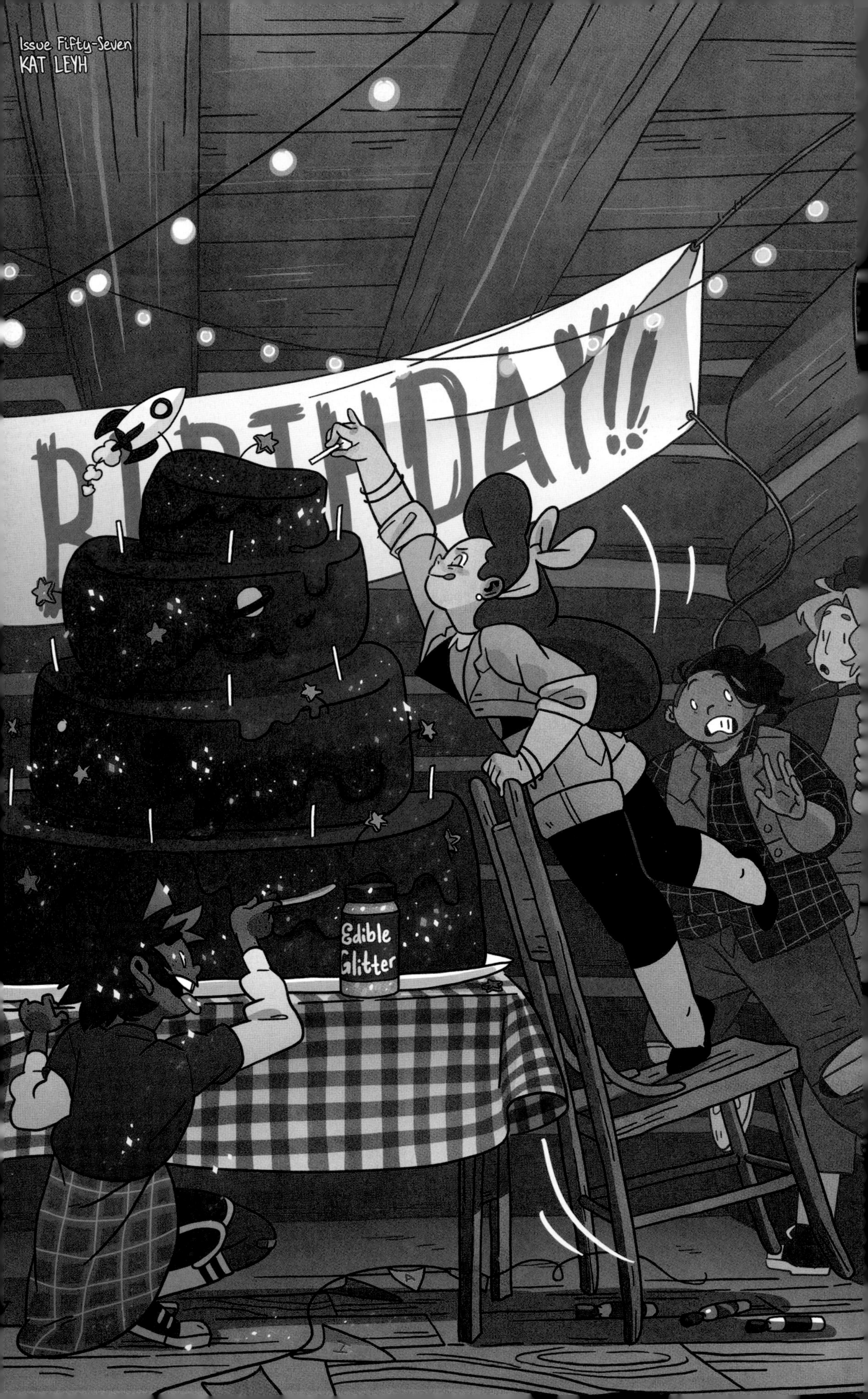
Issue Fifty-Seven
KAT LEYH
Edible Glitter

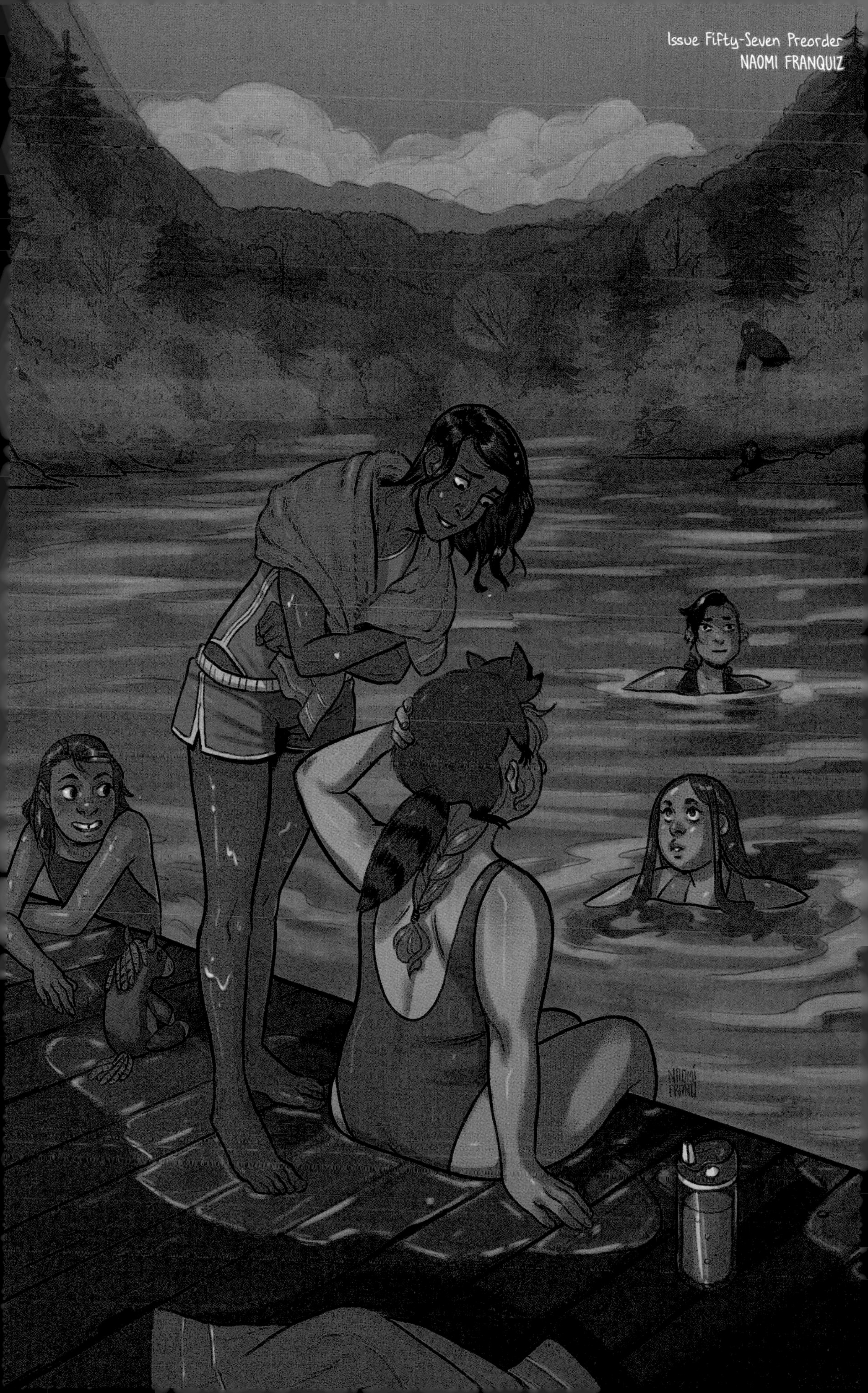

Issue Fifty-Seven Preorder
NAOMI FRANQUIZ

Issue Fifty-Eight
KAT LEYH

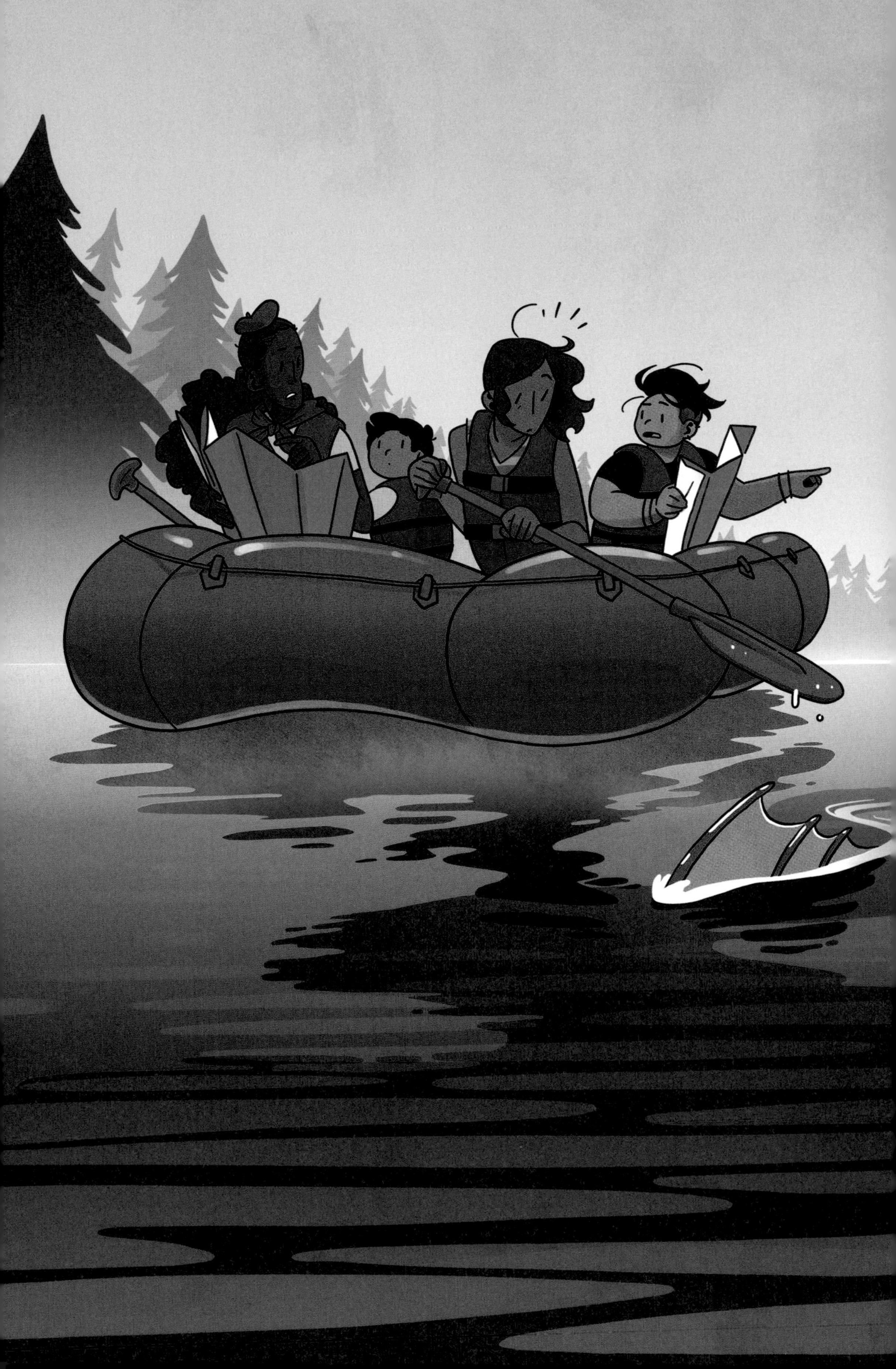

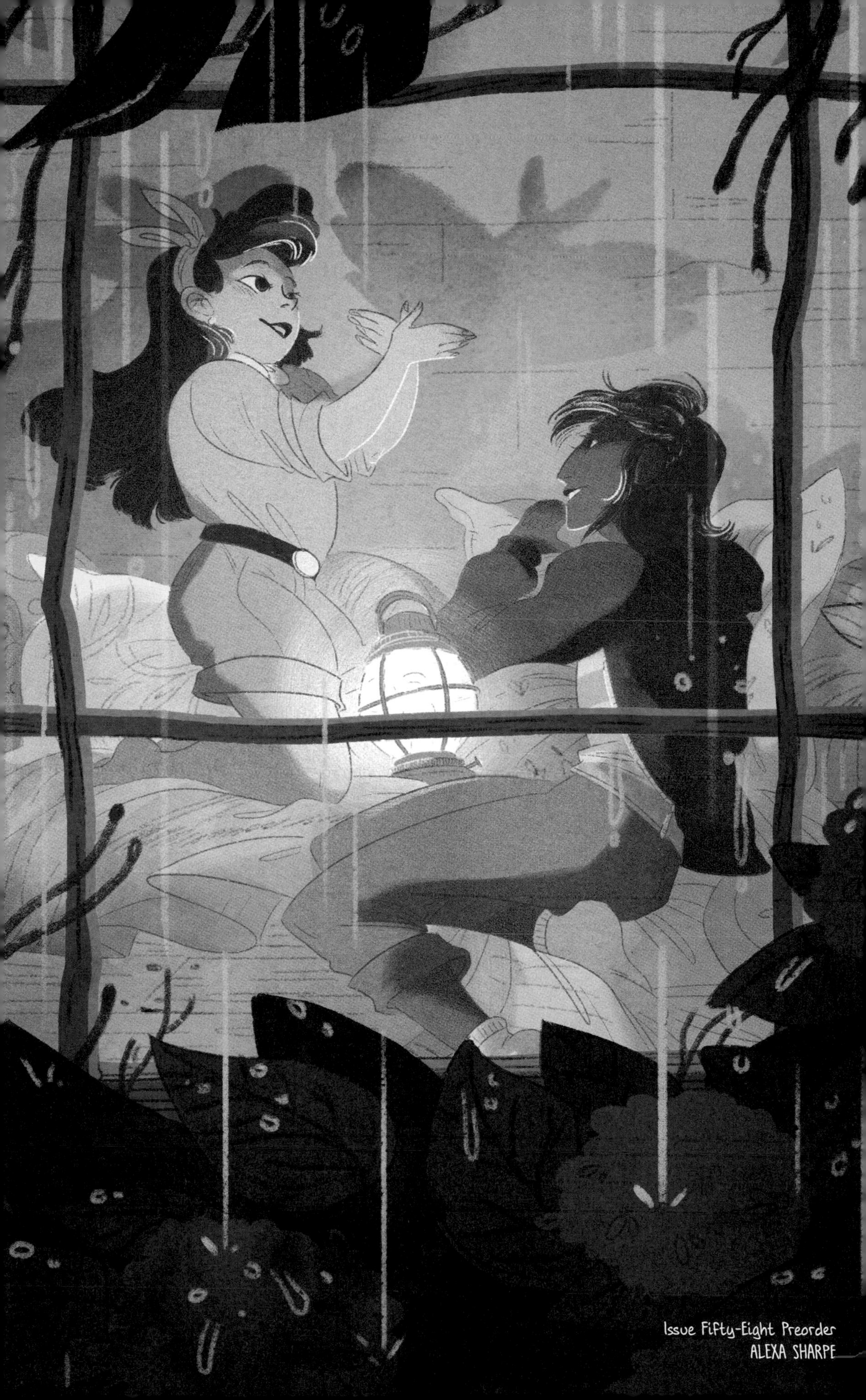

Issue Fifty-Eight Preorder
ALEXA SHARPE

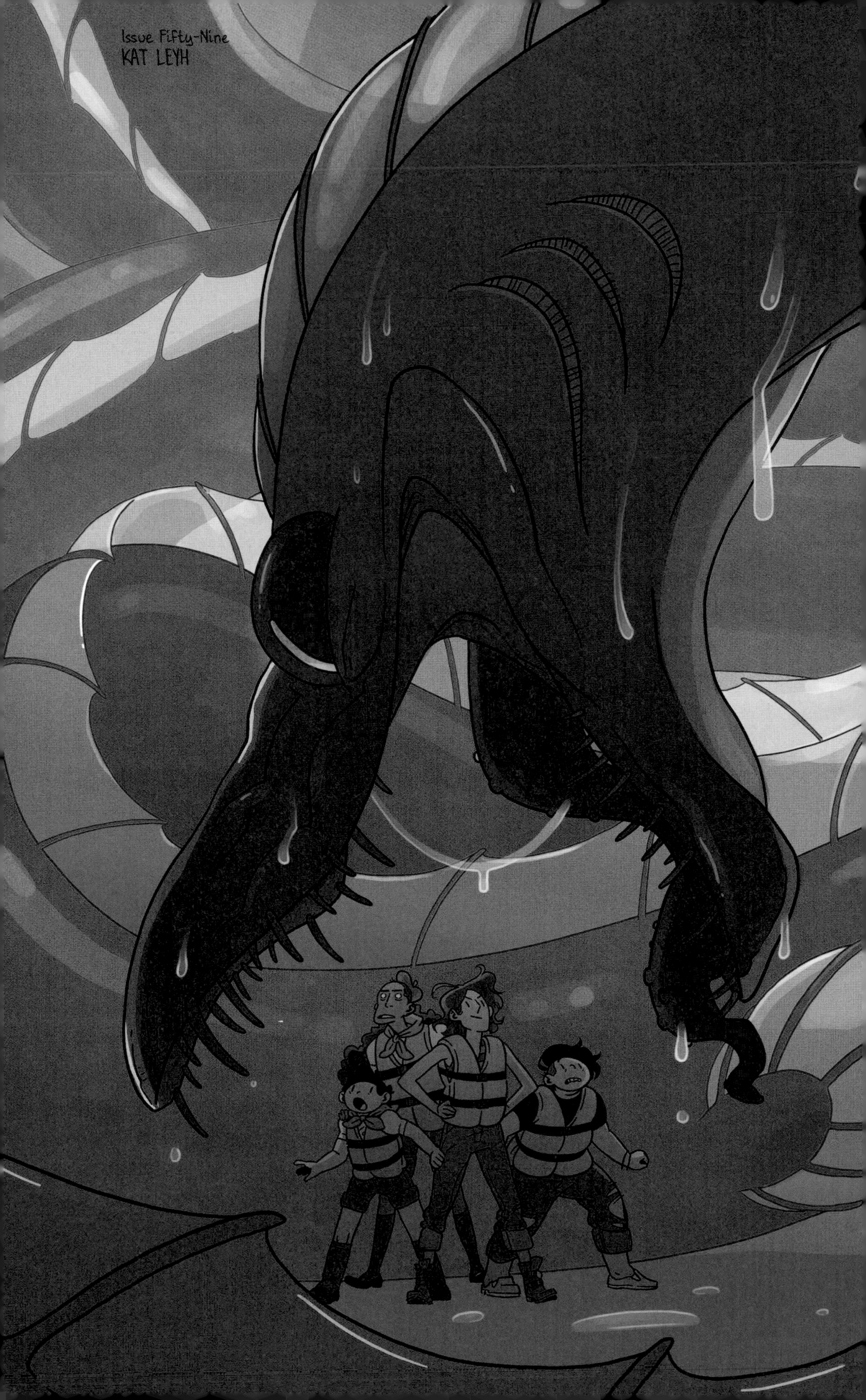

Issue Fifty-Nine
KAT LEYH

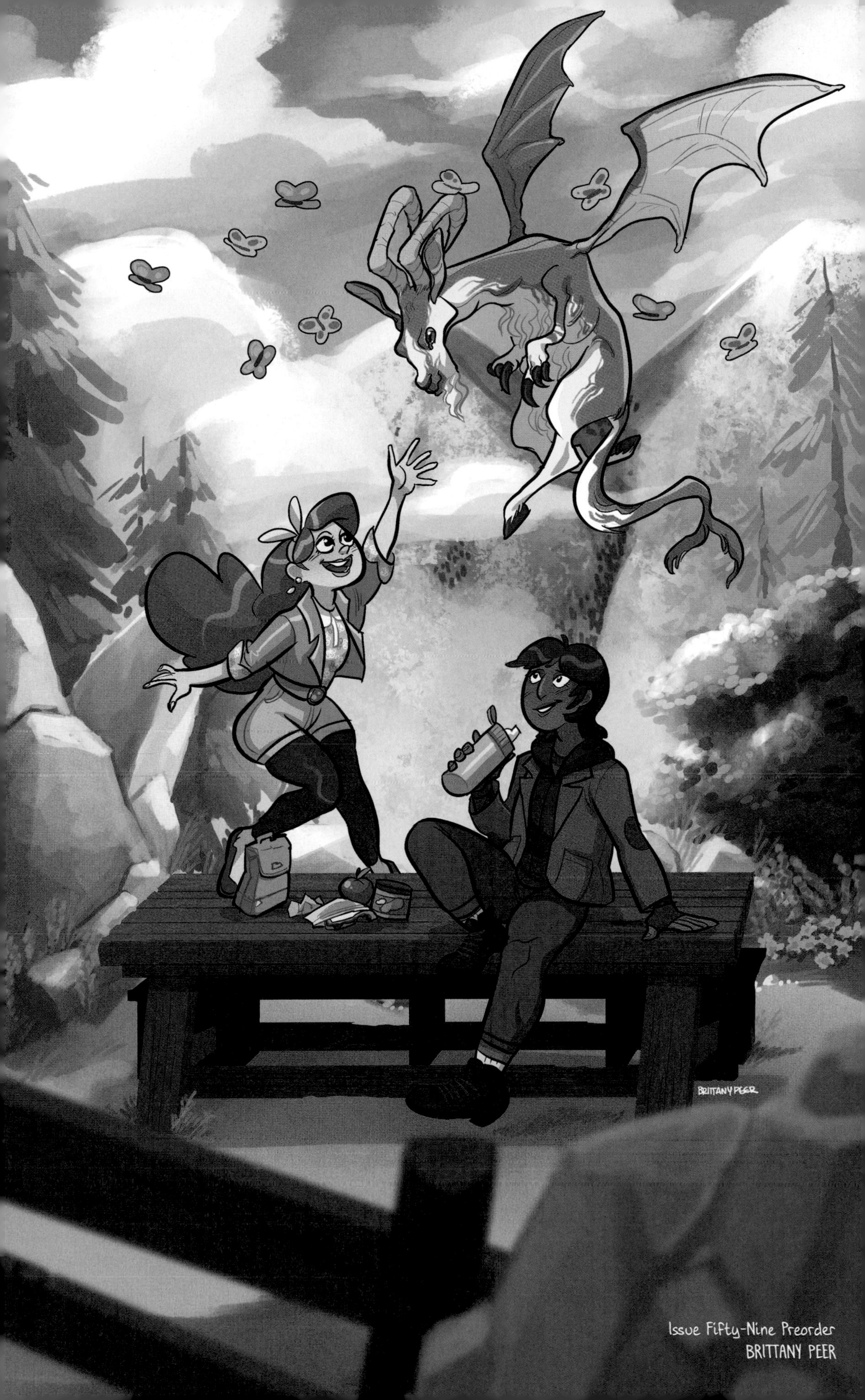
BRITTANYPEER

Issue Fifty-Nine Preorder
BRITTANY PEER

Issue Sixty
KAT LEYH

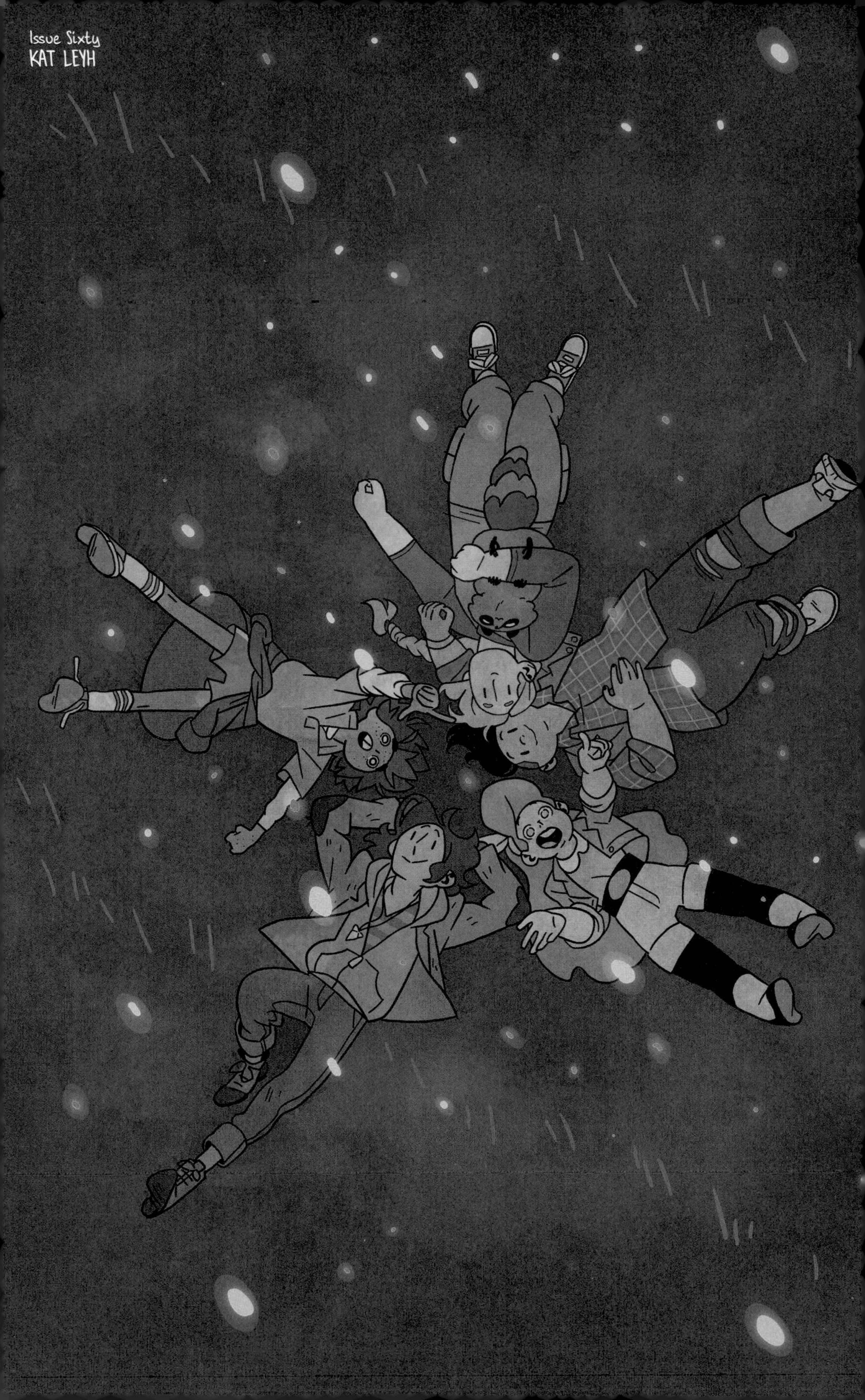

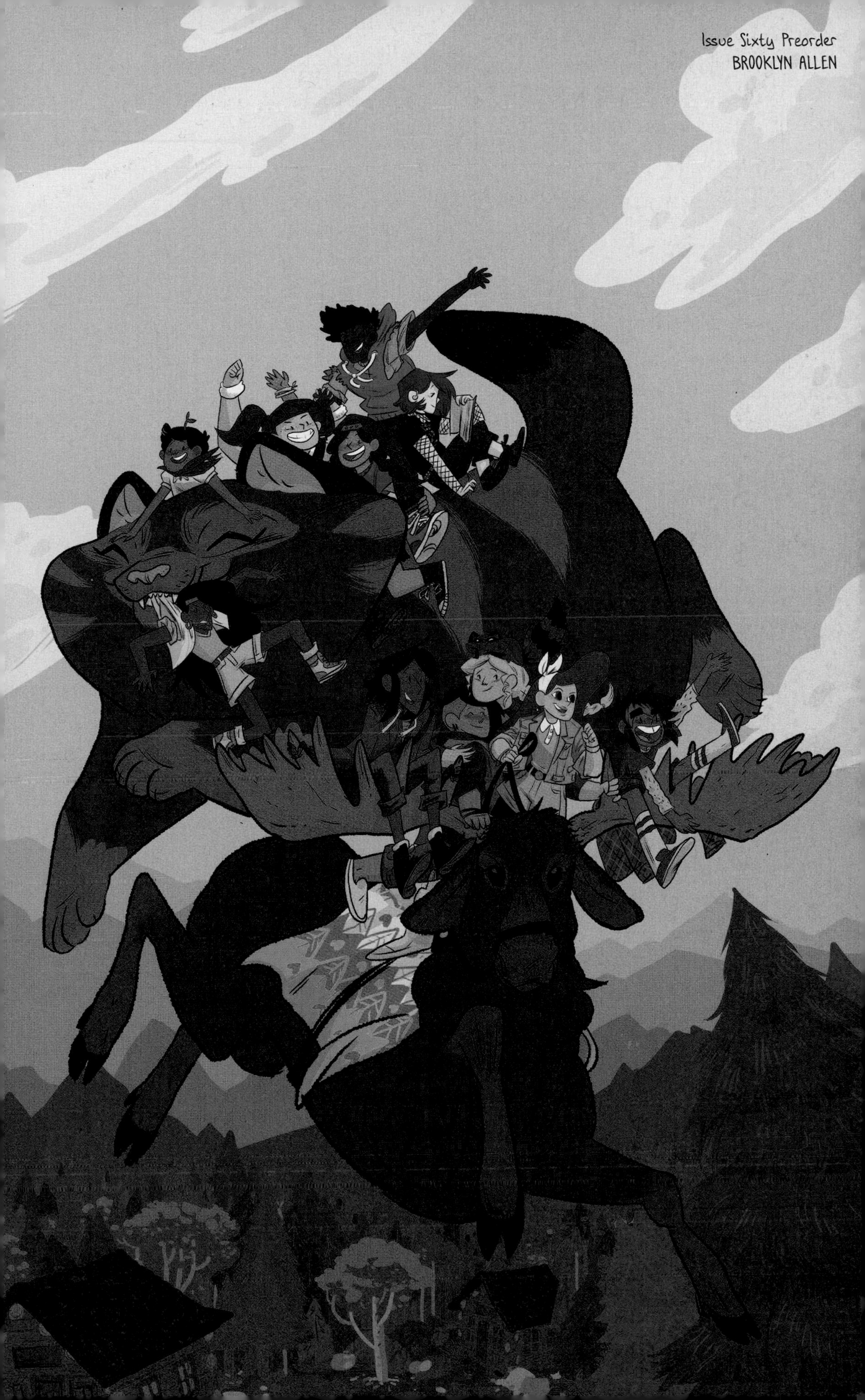

Issue Sixty Preorder
BROOKLYN ALLEN

DISCOVER
ALL THE HITS

STEVENSON · ELLIS · WATTERS · ALLEN
LUMBERJANES
NEW YORK TIMES BESTSELLING SERIES

GIANT DAYS

RIBON · FISH · PEER
SLAM!

Hope Larson · Brittney Williams · Sarah Stern
GOLDIE VANCE
"Scoot over Nancy Drew."
—Los Angeles Times
Volume One

JAMES TYNION IV · RIAN SYGH · WALTER BAIAMONTE
THE BACKSTAGERS

TYSON HESSE'S
DIESEL
IGNITION

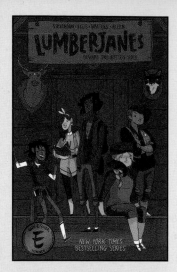

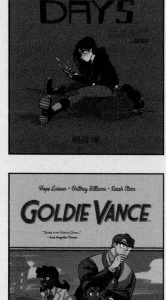

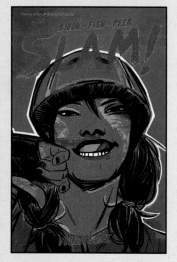

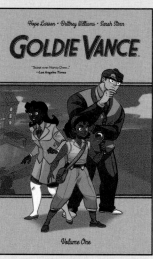

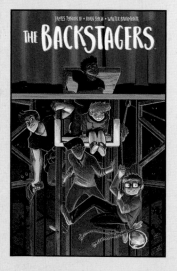

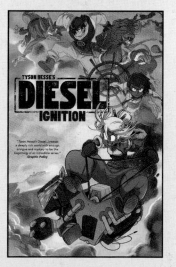

Lumberjanes
Noelle Stevenson, Shannon Watters, Grace Ellis, Brooklyn Allen, and Others
Volume 1: Beware the Kitten Holy
ISBN: 978-1-60886-687-8 | $14.99 US
Volume 2: Friendship to the Max
ISBN: 978-1-60886-737-0 | $14.99 US
Volume 3: A Terrible Plan
ISBN: 978-1-60886-803-2 | $14.99 US
Volume 4: Out of Time
ISBN: 978-1-60886-860-5 | $14.99 US
Volume 5: Band Together
ISBN: 978-1-60886-919-0 | $14.99 US

Giant Days
John Allison, Lissa Treiman, Max Sarin
Volume 1
ISBN: 978-1-60886-789-9 | $9.99 US
Volume 2
ISBN: 978-1-60886-804-9 | $14.99 US
Volume 3
ISBN: 978-1-60886-851-3 | $14.99 US

Jonesy
Sam Humphries, Caitlin Rose Boyle
Volume 1
ISBN: 978-1-60886-883-4 | $9.99 US
Volume 2
ISBN: 978-1-60886-999-2 | $14.99 US

Slam!
Pamela Ribon, Veronica Fish, Brittany Peer
Volume 1
ISBN: 978-1-68415-004-5 | $14.99 US

Goldie Vance
Hope Larson, Brittney Williams
Volume 1
ISBN: 978-1-60886-898-8 | $9.99 US
Volume 2
ISBN: 978-1-60886-974-9 | $14.99 US

The Backstagers
James Tynion IV, Rian Sygh
Volume 1
ISBN: 978-1-60886-993-0 | $14.99 US

Tyson Hesse's Diesel: Ignition
Tyson Hesse
ISBN: 978-1-60886-907-7 | $14.99 US

Coady & The Creepies
Liz Prince, Amanda Kirk, Hannah Fisher
ISBN: 978-1-68415-029-8 | $14.99 US

BOOM! BOX

AVAILABLE AT YOUR LOCAL COMICS SHOP AND BOOKSTORE
To find a comics shop in your area, visit www.comicshoplocator.com
WWW.**BOOM-STUDIOS**.COM